SAVAGE RHYTHM

A Club Volare Rock Star Novel

Chloe Cox

Copyright © 2013 Chloe Cox

All rights reserved.

ISBN: 1492170348
ISBN-13: 978-1492170341

chapter 17	159
chapter 18	170
chapter 19	180
chapter 20	189
chapter 21	201
chapter 22	214
chapter 23	225
chapter 24	233
chapter 25	243
chapter 26	252
chapter 27	262
chapter 28	272
chapter 29	278
chapter 30	287
chapter 31	297
chapter 32	305
chapter 33	316

Just a Quick Note...

Dear Reader,

I don't know if I've ever wanted two characters to get their HEA this much.

I know that's weird to say, but any author will tell you that there comes a point where the characters kind of...start talking to you. They have their own opinions, their own reactions, their own pain—and it's your job to continue to put them through hell for a little while. And like many people I've known in real life, Declan and Molly have traumatic pasts that they cope with as best they can. It meant a lot to me to be able to help them find their way to each other—and then find the strength to face up to those pasts because of that.

But not before they discover that they can't keep their hands off of each other, of course. ;) And let me tell you, *everyone* should have a guy with Declan's particular, um, talents.

You'll see. :)

xoxo

Chloe

Those who fly...

chapter 1

Molly Ward was seriously reconsidering her choice of clothing.

She had wanted to look respectable. In control. Smart. A woman who was not to be messed with, a woman who could hold her own with Declan freaking Donovan, lead singer of Savage Heart. Instead she felt constrained and fake, the too-small conservative blouse pulling tight in all the wrong places, her skirt scratching at her, her shoes pinching, even while the heels kept getting stuck between the wooden slats of the dock. She was on a *dock*, for chrissakes, not at some corporate whatever. She'd just been so worried about meeting the man himself and losing the upper hand right away, so terrified that she'd blow this life-changing opportunity before it even got started, that she'd overcompensated. Even her hair was in a severe bun.

Someone like Declan would no doubt prefer that

she show up in no clothing at all.

Oh, that is a bad thought. Molly couldn't afford distracting thoughts like that if she wanted to nail this job. She had no idea how many people had applied for the ghostwriting job advertised out of Club Volare L.A., of all places, but Molly had gotten it, and she was determined not to screw it up. Adra Davis, one of the founding members of the L.A. club, had believed in her, even when Molly gasped a little when Adra told her the subject of the book would be Declan Donovan. It made sense, in retrospect—Declan's image needed a major overhaul after his fight in Philadelphia and his stint in rehab—but that didn't make it any less insane.

And that didn't make Donovan any less of an irresistible, womanizing force of nature. The man was legendary.

So, of course, she'd been having lots of bad thoughts about this job, starting right when she'd heard the name Declan Donovan. She'd had lots of excited thoughts, too, and lots of scared thoughts, and, most of all, lots of sexy thoughts, because not only was she touring with Declan and the remaining members of Savage Heart with the express purpose of getting to the bottom of Declan's fight with Soren, the lead guitarist, and the original band's break up—yeah, only the question everyone and their mother wanted answered—but, and this is what had obsessed her since she'd put two and two together, she had been hired for the job through Club Volare L.A.. Which meant that Declan Donovan was into BDSM.

Which, if Molly was any judge, meant that Declan Donovan, confirmed rock star sex god, was also a Dom.

Holy. Shit.

Molly had always fantasized about dominant men. She'd been drawn to the Club Volare posting because she wanted to learn more about their world. About the sorts of things a Dom might do with her. But never, not once, in her wildest dreams, had she imagined that Declan Donovan might be one of them.

Fuck. She could *not* afford to get carried away thinking about Declan in a sexual way, and not just because of the job, either. No way was Molly setting herself up to get fucked over by a guy like that again, even if Declan was the real deal, where Robbie had been a cheap facsimile.

No freaking way was she going to lose control. It cost too much.

But apparently she'd have to allow herself the occasional randy thought, because there seemed to be no stopping them. Also the occasional terrified thought, because, well, holy crap.

Molly took a deep breath, set her eyes on the clubhouse at the end of the dock, and walked forward. What kind of a privacy-obsessed sex club would throw a party on a dock? Maybe she didn't have the right to question, considering she was crashing said party, but it seemed incongruous. No matter. She was crashing this party, specifically, to get the upper hand with Declan Donovan, rock god Dom or no. She was here to let him know that she *would* get to the bottom of his fight with Soren Andersson, no matter how much he didn't want to talk about it. She was here to announce that Declan Donovan would *not* be dominating their interviews.

Right.

He can't sense weakness. If he senses weakness, he'll never open up, and the book will be a failure and everything will be ruined.

Molly put on her game face. She was almost there. She could see all the out-to-the-public members of Volare and their friends, laughing, flirting. She was sure they could see her, out of place in her cheap business casual attire, but there wasn't anything to be done about that now.

Unfortunately, the Volare people weren't the only ones who could see her.

"Hey, sexy librarian! C'mere!"

Molly jerked her head around. "Sexy librarian" was definitely new—new enough that it actually penetrated her invisible catcall shield.

The guys doing the catcalling, though—nothing new about that. Drunk. College-aged frat boy douchebags. Their clothing was more expensive than anything she'd ever owned, and they were doing their drinking while tying up an impressively large boat, but otherwise it was the same sort of harassment she'd gotten used to a long time ago.

But she hadn't expected to have to deal with it here. Volare had an impeccable reputation. These guys were definitely *not* Volare.

Not now, she thought grimly. But she'd made the mistake of letting them know she'd heard them.

"Hey, I'm talking to you," one of them said. She didn't turn this time. "C'mon, you're making me all hot for teacher."

The others laughed. Assholes. How was it

possible that otherwise normal adult males so frequently didn't know the line between flirtation and harassment? Like the fact that she was walking away, visibly uncomfortable, wasn't a clue?

Unless making her uncomfortable was the point. Gross.

Molly sucked in another breath and kept walking. Almost there. No big deal. She wouldn't let it throw her off her game. She'd dealt with far, far worse.

She could hear the party now, the clinking of glasses, laughter, mixing with the sounds of the waterfront, waves crashing into pilings, sea birds overhead, and she focused on that. Otherwise maybe she would have heard the douchebag come up behind her.

Instead she just felt his hand on her arm before she knew what was happening, and then his breath on her neck, hot and smelling of whiskey, such a distinct, terrible smell, a smell that brought back way too many memories.

She jumped and tried to pull away, violently. His hand was like a vise.

"Hey, relax," the frat boy said. He had sandy blond hair, same as Molly, blue eyes, a tan, and an annoyed expression. Like he was pissed at *her* for having the temerity to be scared.

"Get your hands off of me," Molly said, pulling again. She was starting to freak out a little bit. Starting to feel like she was losing control. What was it about this guy?

"You don't have to be such a bitch," he said. "We were just trying to talk to you."

He'd called her a bitch. A *bitch*. And the worst

part was that he wasn't letting her go. Molly was trapped talking to this asshole because he was stronger than her and he wouldn't let her go, and he freaking knew it. What did he want, an apology?

"Get. Your. Hands. Off of me." She seethed.

Molly felt herself start to blush with anger, and that only made it worse. This entitled jerk was humiliating her, was making her look weak, was making her *feel* weak, in front of the very people she needed to impress. She could feel the attention of the Volare party on her now; this was officially a scene. And she was already fucking up her one golden opportunity. Her one chance to get out of that goddamn trailer park full of people who thought she was trash, her one chance to get away from all the things that had happened there, from the person she had almost turned out to be. Her one chance to make sure her sister Lydia didn't have to go through the same things.

"Or what?" the frat boy said. Then he smiled. Like he knew, he smiled.

Like he fucking *knew* what she was, like he saw right through her. Like he knew he could do this because she was just what she'd always been, the trailer park slut, just like her mother, just like Robbie and his friends had said she was after what had happened.

Be strong. Molly wasn't going to let this jerk steal her future from her just because he felt like showing off for his jerk friends, and she wasn't going to let anyone tell her she was a slut, ever again. She gritted her teeth and prepared to get medieval on his ass.

But she never got the chance. The voice came rumbling from behind her, a voice she would have recognized anywhere, deep and resonant, the kind of voice that could have gotten rocks to get up and move out of its way.

"You really want to find out?" it growled.

And if she hadn't been a fan of Savage Heart back in the day, the look on the frat boy's face would have confirmed it. Declan Donovan was standing right behind her.

Declan Donovan was threatening the frat boy. For her.

"Dude, you're Declan Donovan!" the frat boy shouted. He looked back at his friends like he was going to share the incredible news when a giant hand encircled his wrist. A giant hand attached to an equally giant forearm. Molly stared at the tattoos swirling around the cords of muscle and watched them all flex as Declan squeezed. Hard.

"Get your hands off of her," he said.

The frat boy winced and dropped her arm like it was on fire.

"Hey, it wasn't like that," the frat boy said, all eager to be buddies. "Just a mis—"

"Get the fuck off my dock."

The frat boy blinked. Molly couldn't help it: she turned to look up at the man who was coming to her rescue, and only then did she realize that she'd been avoiding looking directly at him.

For good reason.

Her mind went blank, confronted with that chest. Donovan was huge in real life, his tight black tank top clinging to muscles she could see even through the fabric, his arms knotted up in hard ridges of muscle, his skin covered in mesmerizing ink. He'd cut his black hair short in rehab, and it showed off his square jaw and angular cheekbones, while his black eyes glowed with anger at the cowering frat boy. She remembered that Donovan had never been one of those wilting, skinny rock guys; he'd always been the physical embodiment of the powerful music he made. But now? Had he actually gotten bigger in rehab? Or was that just the sheer fucking magnetism of the man?

It was impossible not to stare at him once you got sucked in. Molly was already gone.

"Oh, shit," she whispered.

Then she felt his hand on her arm, burning hot, and he gently pulled her toward him, away from the frat boy. "I said *leave*," Declan snarled, his eyes boring holes in the smaller man.

The frat boy left.

Molly felt a thrill, watching the asshole leave with his tail between his legs, and that thrill embarrassed her thoroughly. How had she already lost her head just being this close to Declan Donovan? The more she thought about it, the more annoyed she was. She could have taken that guy. She *wanted* to be able to take that guy. To be the one to stand up for herself, to prove that she wasn't helpless, that she wasn't anything like Robbie or anyone else had said she was. To take back control. Molly felt like she constantly had to prove herself, and no one was quite as harsh a critic as Molly Ward herself.

But worst of all, now Declan Donovan thought she was weak, too. The one guy she needed to take her seriously. The one guy who...

Oh God. He was looking at her. They were so close she could practically feel the heat coming off of him, and she knew it was crazy, but she would have sworn, *sworn*, that she could feel those eyes leaving a hot trail up and down her body.

"Are you ok?" he asked her.

That voice. God.

If she thought she'd felt weak before, she had no idea what weak was.

Suddenly she was furious. Not really with anyone in particular, but with the world, the universe, whoever. This was so manifestly unfair — she had worked so hard, had struggled so much, and now she was just another damsel in distress? Bullshit.

"Is this *your* dock?" she asked him.

"What?"

"You told him to get the fuck off your dock. It's yours?"

Declan's hand had migrated from her arm to her lower back while he scared off the frat boy and he hadn't moved it, not even as she turned to him so that it rested on her hip. Now his eyes met hers and it became very, very clear to her that he wasn't going to move it, unless maybe she asked. Molly considered herself a strong woman, but not quite strong enough to do that. Not just yet. In a minute, maybe.

"It's mine while I'm on it," Declan said.

Molly licked her lips and rallied. This was stupid. Silly. "Like a territorial thing?" she asked, one incredulous eyebrow raised.

A hint of a smile flickered at the corner of his full lips, the softness there offset by the scruff on his jaw.

"Yes," he said.

He didn't seem to think he needed to say anything else.

Molly swallowed. She hadn't expected that. Hadn't thought he would just straight up own the caveman thing. Did this mean she was in his territory? Part of his territory?

The idea both turned her on and infuriated her.

Declan studied her face and smiled. He was amused. "You're mad I took care of that guy," he said. A statement, not a question.

"No," she said, maybe too quickly. "Maybe. It's just that I could have taken care of him myself. I'm not helpless."

"No one said you were."

"No, you only acted like it."

What the hell was she *doing*? Picking a fight with Declan Donovan? It was like the childish, try-hard version of trying to impress him. She knew she had a valid point, but that wasn't all she was reacting to. She was reacting to Declan himself. To how overwhelmed she felt just standing next to him. Like she had to fight for every breath, every thought that was not about him.

What would happen when she was stuck on a tour bus with him twenty four hours a day?

Oh God.

He was still looking at her. Calm. His hand hot and heavy on her hip. Jesus. She had to draw a line, here and now, before she lost control of the whole project.

"Your hand—" she started.

His voice cut through the air, sharp and strong.

"Tell me your name."

Without even thinking, she told him. "Molly Ward."

She blinked. She'd just...obeyed. The look on his face said he'd noticed. His thumb pressed into her hip bone a little bit more.

"The writer," he said, almost to himself, his voice a low, satisfied hum. "Ain't that lucky."

Whoa. Danger, Will Robinson. Molly shook her head and stepped back to get free of his molten touch, and immediately felt more in control. Jesus, but the man was lethal.

She forced herself to look him in the eye and said, "You need to keep your hands off of me."

chapter 2

Declan removed his hand, but he couldn't keep his eyes off of Molly Ward. He missed contact with her already. He hadn't even thought about it, just put his hand on her, like it was normal. It took both of them too long to realize it wasn't.

This was something.

"As you wish," he said.

Molly looked at him sideways and then rewarded him with a sly smile. "Don't *Princess Bride* me, Declan Donovan," she said. "I have a feeling you only obey orders when it amuses you."

And where had this woman come from?

"You would be correct," he said, grinning. "What clued you in?"

"This *is* a Club Volare event, right?"

Declan let his eyes drift south momentarily to the straining buttons on the front of Molly's shirt. No button should be put through that. Come to think of it, no man should be put in close proximity to a woman like this if she was going to be off limits. Especially not on a tour bus. For eight weeks. His balls ached just thinking about it. She was dressed up in a way he could tell wasn't natural for her, just by the way she held herself, and yet *damn*. Those curves. Those brown eyes. That dirty blonde hair, starting to wisp out of that bun and play around her face.

Fuck me.

He said, "You should know, that won't be the last time I touch you."

Declan believed in honesty. There was no shortage of women willing to throw themselves on his dick, but this one seemed determined to avoid his touch like the plague, even though it visibly turned her on. Nipples didn't lie, not when they were tight and poking through her cheap shirt, and neither did her dilated pupils or her flushed skin, and if she cared to look down she'd have seen how freaking hard he was already. There was just no explaining physical chemistry, and between the two of them it was potent. All the physical indicators he'd trained himself to recognize as a Dom screamed, "Do me now!"

And yet she was telling him no.

He'd always liked a challenge.

Molly stiffened. "Excuse me?"

"That won't be the last time I touch you," he said again. "Only next time, you'll beg me to."

Her eyes hardened.

"Are you going to pee on me next?" she said. "Mark your territory a little more?"

She could cut a lesser man down with that tone, that wit. Declan only grinned.

"I'm not into that, so no," he said.

"I meant I'm not your damn property," she said, a flush starting on her cheeks again. "I'm not some fucking groupie who will do whatever you want."

Declan tensed. That word hit him hard: *groupie*. There was no way this little writer knew about it. He'd only told Adra, outside of the band, and he knew Adra wouldn't screw him like that, even if she did think that Declan should come clean about what had happened in Philadelphia. No way in hell that was happening. He wasn't going to do that to Bethany, "groupie" or no. Let the world think he was a violent drunk; it didn't fucking matter. Especially not to Soren.

Damn it. That whole situation was still… He'd rather think about the woman in front of him.

"Good," he said eventually. "Groupies write bad books."

Molly Ward paused. She seemed conflicted. She looked like she wanted to fight him, but she also couldn't stop biting on her lower lip. It was distracting as fuck. He loved that she was giving him shit, that it seemed her natural state was to be a ball buster, even while she'd automatically given him her name when he'd demanded it. The combination was damn sexy. And damn suggestive.

He wondered how well she'd respond to other commands.

"What are you doing here?" he asked suddenly. He'd thought they weren't due to meet until the tour. He'd also thought the writer would be someone boring, not someone so evidently fuckable. "Did Adra tell you to come here?"

"No," she said.

Then she lowered her eyes. There was something she wasn't telling. It tweaked his Dom sense.

"Answer the question," he demanded. "What are you doing here?"

"Don't order me around."

Declan crossed his arms, though he was hiding a smile. This woman. Already, this woman. He couldn't trust any of the women in his life to tell him to go to hell if he deserved it, except the women at Volare—and now this one. He hadn't had a submissive in a fucking age because his fame tended to warp a woman's perception of what she was actually comfortable with, and that made BDSM dangerous. He was aching to dominate a worthy sub. Felt it throb in every freaking nerve, every last capillary, every waking thought.

And now Molly Ward had showed up, beautifully responsive when he gave her an order, even if she didn't want to admit it. A woman with natural submissive tendencies who vied for control. Fun.

She was trouble, no doubt, but fuck it.

"You'd love it," he said softly.

Molly Ward blushed right up to the tips of her adorable little ears. Declan laughed.

"I'm here because I thought it would be a good idea to meet you before the tour," she said hotly. "Get acquainted? Since we have this book to write."

"You wanted to ambush me," he countered. "You want me off balance for your interviews."

Her mouth dropped open.

What he could do with that. Jesus.

"How did you…" Molly seemed to forget herself for a minute, just a minute, and the hint of her vulnerability pulled him in even further.

"I'm good with people," he said. "And you're not the first writer to get clever. So don't bother lying to me, it'll just piss both of us off. You feel like you have something to prove, coming here dressed like that, trying to surprise me at a private, personal event?"

"That's awfully presumptuous of you," she whispered.

Things seemed to have gotten quieter between them, more still. The party was still going on behind him, and Declan knew it was loud as hell on the dock, but somehow he wasn't focused on anything but Molly Ward. Focused so much that he could hear her whisper into the freaking wind.

"But I'm right," he said.

She was staring right back at him. Goddamn.

"So what if you are?" she said finally. "You're obviously kind of blunt, right? You like it when people are direct?"

Fuck me. Direct. Yeah. He resisted the urge to hook his fingers into the front of her tight little skirt, pull her close, and kiss her hard.

"What do you think?" he said.

"Ok, well, here it is direct," Molly said, standing a little straighter, refusing to let her eyes waver. "You don't get to have me, Declan Donovan. That's not what's going to happen. What's going to happen is that I'm going to get to the bottom of what happened between you and Soren Andersson in Philadelphia, and you're going to let me, because you're going to trust me. Because you're going to respect me. And then I'm going to write the best goddamn book you've ever read. And at the end of it—"

"You're going to let me fuck you senseless," he said.

Molly's eyes went wide. He'd shocked the words right out of her mouth. Christ, if that was all it took, he couldn't imagine...

"You're going to thank me," she said. She was a little breathless, still looking at him with those big, open eyes. "I don't know where you get off—"

"Quiet," he said.

She shut up.

She almost seemed surprised by her own reaction. But Declan felt his cock twitch, like the damn thing knew a sub was nearby. He was sure of it. Well, then he'd give her what she needed. Clear, concise commands.

"Give me your phone," he said.

Molly only hesitated a moment. She was staring at him like she couldn't quite figure out what was going on, but she very much wanted to. Then she narrowed her eyes and wordlessly dug into her oversized purse by feel, never taking those challenging, inquisitive eyes off of him, and came up with her phone.

Declan took it from her without explanation and dialed his own personal cell phone number, since he'd left his phone in his jacket. He waited until it went to voicemail, then saved the number under "Declan."

"What are you doing?" she asked.

He gave her the phone back, and winked.

"Making sure you know when to pick up."

Declan was all ready to parry another outraged barb from Molly Ward—was looking forward to it, in fact—when real life got in the way. If Savage Heart could be considered real life, anyway.

"Declan!"

It was Adra's voice, getting closer. But Declan just did not want to stop looking at Molly. That combination of confusion and curiosity was almost as attractive as the defiance and submission combo she had going on earlier.

Almost.

"What's up, Adra?" he said without turning around. Let Molly know what he was looking at. He could tell she liked it. In fact, the woman was looking right back.

"Eric's called you so many times he started calling me," Adra said, catching up. He felt Volare's resident agent look at him, then look at Molly, and back to him. "There's obviously something you need to deal with. I think he's freaking out."

Damn. Eric was an old friend, an amazing guitarist who'd given up on the rock dream and had cut a decent living as a studio musician instead, and he had been perfectly happy with that up until Declan told him Savage Heart needed a new guitarist freaking yesterday. Eric had saddled up and saved the tour, which had been a godsend. He knew all of Savage Heart's songs, and had known the band forever, but now the pressure was getting to him. Savage Heart had their first show since Philadelphia that night—a surprise appearance at the brand new public part of the

Volare club in Venice Beach, just to test some stuff out before they hit the road. No one knew how the fans were going to react, but they were probably going to give Eric some shit just because he wasn't Soren.

So Eric was panicking.

"Yeah, I'm on it," Declan said. He gave Molly one long, last, lingering look. "See you soon, Molly Ward."

Just his luck the one woman who'd set off his Dom sense in months without being weird about his fame was the one woman determined to keep it professional. And the one person who seemed to think she could get him to talk about Philadelphia. Declan wasn't worried about getting her into bed—fighting attraction like that was like fighting a force of nature. She'd lose, and he'd teach her the things she craved. It was inevitable.

So why did he get the feeling Molly Ward thought it was just as inevitable that she'd get him to talk?

chapter 3

Molly had triple checked everything around the house, making sure it was ready for her friend Shauna, who would be housesitting. Molly hadn't felt comfortable leaving it empty for eight weeks, and she couldn't stop worrying. She told herself that it was because Robbie and his boys still loved to fuck with her on occasion, and an empty, unguarded trailer would probably be too tempting, but really it was her own tendency to stress. Shauna had been too willing to step in, needing a break from her own situation. Besides, Molly needed someone to deliver the rent for her, in cash.

Yeah, not sketchy at all. She couldn't wait to get out of Pleasant Valley Park. There was just nothing pleasant about it.

Good thing she didn't have much stuff, and neither had her mother. After her mom died, Molly had wondered if eventually the trailer would start to feel like it was really hers, and she'd hated the thought. Feared it. She just wanted out of that place, and now she was gratified, in some small way, that she'd managed to stay emotionally detached, if still a little bit obsessed with making sure everything went the way she had planned. It made leaving easier. She'd packed up for eight weeks in no time.

The only thing she was really attached to was far, far away, anyway.

Molly stared into the eerie blue glow of her laptop and hit refresh. Really, this was kind of pathetic. Facebook stalking your own sister? Yes, that was definitely somewhere on the sadness scale, with possibly a creepy factor thrown in. But this was the only contact she had with Lydia, at least until Molly could make enough money to offer her a decent place to live, away from this horrible trailer park where the Ward girls would always be fair game. And away from their father, who Lydia lived with now.

But Lydia would be eighteen soon. The only thing she needed was somewhere to go.

Molly tried to pretend it didn't worry her that Lydia hadn't answered her last message. Or that she hadn't posted anything in...four days. Socially active teenagers had things to do besides chat with their sisters, especially when they had to do it behind their dad's back. She shouldn't freak out.

It was probably nothing.

But of course Molly had spent all afternoon obsessing about that scene at the dock and why she'd let those frat bros get to her, so much so that she had started off her association with Declan Donovan by *fighting* with him—really, what the fuck?—and the answer, once she thought about it, was Lydia. Of course it was.

Molly hadn't been humiliated like that in front of someone who mattered to her since Robbie and his boys had detailed all the reasons that she was a slut for her baby sister. She hadn't felt that weak, or that powerless, or that out of control in a long time, possibly because she hadn't let many things matter to her in a long time. And because she knew she had to always be in control.

But this job? Getting this right? This mattered. Which meant that Declan mattered. And she felt like she had zero control with him. Molly'd given herself a year to make something of herself writing before she had to go get a real job, something that would provide a steady paycheck for her and Lydia, and the Savage Heart gig alone might cover her last credits at night school *and* provide enough cash to get a real apartment big enough for both her and Lydia.

Except, of course, that she'd just fucked it up.

Probably.

Honestly, she couldn't tell. Declan Donovan obviously wanted to do her, but that wasn't what she was going for. Or at least that wasn't what she was going for right now. And she'd been kind of a bitch. She couldn't get that old cliché Robbie used to say out of her mind: "You never get a second chance to make a first impression," blah blah blah. She hated that Robbie still had any real estate in her head, but she had to admit, as clichés went, that one had some truth to it.

Didn't help that Savage Heart had been one of Robbie's favorite bands and Declan Donovan one of his idols. Molly really needed to get some new mental associations. She couldn't afford to have flashbacks to her dickhead ex and traumatic past while interviewing Declan.

Somehow, though, she didn't think that would be much of a problem. She was much more worried about keeping enough blood in her brain to be able to form words.

That man…

She swore she could still feel his touch on her hip. Like he'd branded her. Every time she thought about it, about Declan standing tall over her, about Declan touching her, about Declan ordering her to be quiet, she got more turned on, until she felt practically incandescent. And now she was supposed to spend eight weeks on a cramped tour bus right next to him while keeping it together enough to write a book.

Molly shuddered.

She needed to *focus*.

Then her phone buzzed in her pocket with a new text message, and the likelihood that she'd be able to focus on anything other than Declan Donovan got vanishingly small.

DECL.A.N: "Volare in Venice. 10 pm."

What the shit?

Molly's leg bounced up and down uncontrollably while she stared at her phone. He was summoning her to *Club Volare?*

To do what?

Ok, well, no way was she waiting until ten. She needed to talk to Adra, *stat*.

~ * ~ * ~

Molly pulled her beat-up old LeBaron up to the Volare compound gates and gave the security guy a sheepish look. She fully expected to have to plead her case and make embarrassing phone calls in order to get in or to be told flat out that they didn't want her car anywhere where actual people could see it, but the big guy just said something into a headset and opened the gate for her.

Weirdly, this made Molly more nervous. Inside was the hottest place in L.A. Even the public area of Club Volare was difficult to get into, and the private area? No one knew what went on. The whole place was exclusive, but not necessarily in the normal way. Rumor was that the guy who ran it, Chance Dalton, had no patience for people he deemed "dicks." There were plenty on the A-list who couldn't get in, and it burned them all.

At least that's what the gossip rags said.

And here she was, driving her LeBaron wreck into the very limited private parking area, where Adra — oh, bless her — was already waiting for her.

And grinning ear to ear.

"What did you hear?" Molly asked warily, giving the car door the final hip bump it needed to close properly.

"Nothing. It's what I *know*," Adra said.

Molly smiled. Adra was infuriating, but amazing. They'd clicked immediately, had spent the entire four-hour job interview becoming fast friends, and had been in constant contact since. It had been such a relief to feel like there was someone who wanted to take her under their wing that it made Molly realize how much she missed that sense of being looked out for. She'd had to remind herself not to read too much into it, but she was grateful as all hell for Adra.

"And what do you know, oh sage?" she asked as Adra linked their arms.

"I know that you're here because Declan asked you to be here. So I know that you must have impressed the hell out of him, because tonight is invite only, and he has control of the guest list."

Molly could only imagine.

"You let him have control of a guest list?" she said in mock horror.

"Don't change the subject."

"Well, ok, I won't. But can you please tell me what is going on? Why am I here?"

Adra grabbed her by the arm and pulled her under a covered path, the canopy woven with tiny little lights, that led to a large, modern looking building. "Well, the bigger question of why, I can't answer. But tonight is the first surprise performance of the reconstituted Savage Heart."

Molly froze. "Are you serious?"

"Yup."

Molly immediately looked down, wishing she'd spent more time on her appearance. She'd stubbornly decided that she wouldn't do anything, really, besides pull on her favorite cut offs and tank top and run some sea spray through her hair. Anything more would be suggestive, and she was definitely not trying to suggest anything to Declan.

"You look great, Mol," Adra said. "Actually, you look so good it's kind of annoying. Do me a favor and *don't* tell me how long you spent getting that tousled surfer girl look down, ok? Declan's going to freak when he sees you."

That did it.

"Oh God, Adra, I don't know what to do," Molly said, collapsing into a pile on the bench. "I am so, so, so determined not to fuck this up, and I think I may already *have* fucked it up."

Adra stared at her. "How could you have done that in all of five minutes?"

"I yelled at him?" Molly said, running an anxious hand through her hair. "Which, whatever, but there's also just this…chemistry. I don't know, I can't explain it. He basically announced that we're going to have sex."

She could tell Adra was trying not to smile. To Adra's credit, she did a pretty good job.

"And what did you say?"

"I said that we were not, in fact, going to have sex. I said that, instead, he was going to tell me all his deepest, darkest secrets, and then I was going to write a book about it."

"So, an impasse."

"Adra, I'm just afraid that he's not going to take me seriously. I mean, I can't sleep with him, not just because I want to be professional, but…" She trailed off. Molly had decided that the only way to make sure her past didn't become her future was to refuse to relive it constantly. There was no reason to go into the whole thing.

"I just can't," she went on. "And now it's there. Between us. And you knew I was completely inexperienced when you hired me, and believe me, I am feeling that right now."

"Overwhelmed."

"Totally."

"You think you can't get a good interview out of him with all this sexual whatever floating in the air? Which, by the way, five minutes and there's already enough sexual tension to make you crazy? That's got to be a record."

"Tell me about it."

"So sleep with him."

Molly stopped short. "What?"

Laughing, Adra detoured over to a bench just at the edge of the light coming from the path they'd been following, the sort of thing you wouldn't be able to see if you didn't know it was there. Molly could hear the party now, a pulsing rhythm coming from inside the building, like a heartbeat. They were alone outside, except for a sense of vastness. Maybe it was the dark, maybe it was the privacy, but it felt...safe.

"I'm saying, Mol, that if you think the tension is going to mess up your professional performance, get it out of the way."

Molly was suddenly glad for the poor visibility. She could feel Adra studying her. And even though they'd only known each other for a short time, they had an instant rapport, the kind where Molly wouldn't be able to hide how disturbed she was. Not at the idea of sex with Declan—God, no, that had been practically all she'd thought about since she'd met him in the flesh—but the fact that Adra's argument made sense, in a way.

Which meant that it wasn't solely her professional concerns that made her so anxious.

If she were being truly honest with herself, she'd

have to admit she was a little intimidated by the idea of a sexual relationship with anyone, let alone Declan Donovan. Or not even a relationship; just sex. Granted, the last guy she'd had sex with was Robbie. And that had ended about as badly as a sexual relationship could.

But it had been four years. Four *years*.

"I think there's something wrong with me," Molly said quietly.

"Everyone has something wrong with them," Adra said. "You spend most of your adult life fixing stuff. Sometimes you get to find people to fix it with."

Molly looked at her sideways. "Was that...innuendo?"

"Maybe." Adra smiled. "Look, honest truth? Declan is not one of those guys who loses respect for the women he sleeps with. Those groupies he's famous for banging aren't, like, Nobel laureates, but he respects them as people..."

"Ugh."

"He's just not one of those guys. We wouldn't have anything to do with him if he was. And if you feel uncomfortable and genuinely don't want any of that, he'll know, and he'll back off. And if you *tell* him to back off, he'll back off. He's a good guy and is actually pretty paranoid about consent because of the whole fame thing. Only... Look, did I ever tell you about the cookie competition?"

For a moment Molly thought she must have misheard, but nope: cookies. She laughed. "The *what*?"

"Yeah. So Declan is like, super competitive and driven. If you took frigging Genghis Khan and then made him a rock god, you'd get Declan. Weirdest combination. So I decided to have some fun with him, right? I challenged him to a bake off."

"You didn't."

Adra cackled. "I *did*. And he lost. No, he didn't just lose—I destroyed him. Completely. Like, made him my little cookie bitch."

Molly clapped her hands with glee. Somehow the image of Declan wearing an apron and a frown, getting his baking ass handed to him, was delightful. And made him seem a whole lot less intimidating.

"What'd he do?" she asked.

Adra shook her head. "That's the thing. He *kept* baking cookies. Multiple times per day, every day. The Volare kitchen smelled terrible. It was like a cookie war crime in there for at least a week. And then...he got really, really good at it."

Molly thought about this for a second. She couldn't deny she was attracted to driven men, but she also knew exactly what happened if you got in the way of a driven man's plans: you got run the fuck over. She still had tire tracks on her back from Robbie's getaway. But that didn't seem to be the most pertinent part of the cookie story.

"So he's persistent," Molly mused. She imagined all the things he might be persistent about and squirmed a little.

"Yeeeeaaah," Adra said. "It's a big part of who he is. And so is his sexuality. If you want to get to know him, you could probably do worse than to give in to an attraction that's already driving you nuts. On the other hand, you know what's best for you. But you are probably gonna have to talk to him about it all."

Adra looked at Molly's face and laughed.

"C'mon, creampuff, toughen up. I hired you because you're a fantastic writer *and* a baby badass. Go in there and show him the badass part."

chapter 4

Declan sat in his makeshift dressing room and brooded over his phone. The rest of the world might as well not exist until he got this text. Same as every night, except this time he had a show. First time in six months. And this time, there was the image of Molly Ward, teasing at the edge of his thoughts.

He shook his head, not willing to compromise his vigil. He couldn't think about whether he would carry this guilt and worry on stage right now, and he damn well shouldn't be thinking about Molly Ward. Not until he got the nightly text.

There was a knock on the door just before it opened. Gage, Savage Heart's drummer, popped his head in.

"Dude, are you gonna make it?"

"It'll be fine."

"You heard yet?" Gage asked, his fingers toying

with the disks in his ears.

"Nope."

"Dec, man, you don't have to do this. None of it was your—"

"I know that, Gage, that's not the fucking point. I'll be ready. Just give me a minute."

That was a lie, though. Gage knew it, too, but shrugged and closed the door quietly behind him. Declan had never been this messed up before a show. Normally the idea of getting on stage zenned him out, gave him clarity, let him *feel*—the same way dominating a sub in a good scene would. He hadn't gotten to do either of those things in months and he was about ready to explode.

And now he was waiting on a goddamn text.

He knew it wasn't his fault, but it didn't change anything. He still needed to know that Bethany was ok. And, just in case he wasn't torturing himself enough already, he'd texted Soren, too: "Just let me know you're ok, man."

Nothing.

So.

He stood up and stretched his body out, running a hand over his newly shorn hair. Took some getting used to, just like everything else. But then his mind drifted back to Molly Ward and he smiled; he wouldn't have to get used to her, ballbuster or no. That was one bright spot, at least. He was definitely looking forward to being around that woman for the next two months.

In fact, the closest he'd come to feeling like his old self was arguing with Molly. Threatening that asshat on the dock, for Molly.

That was some batshit insane chemistry right

there, like nothing else he'd ever seen, like she just fit. Some kind of animal, pheromone-type science behind that, no other explanation. And Declan hoped to God that Molly was sane, because she could be a black widow and that probably wouldn't stop him from trying to get her into bed.

He grinned. Actually it might make him more determined to dominate her. Wasn't that some twisted shit?

His phone buzzed, and Declan immediately felt guilty for not feeling *more* guilty—he'd let himself drift off, thinking about Molly Ward, when he should have been worrying about Bethany. He was thinking with his dick.

BETHANY: "Just checking in. I'm doing ok. They're saying I might be ready to leave in a few weeks!"

Declan smiled and ignored the little bit of worry he felt. If the doctors thought she was almost ready, then she was almost ready. It was a good thing.

DECL.A.N: "Congratulations. :) I'll check in tomorrow. Have a good night."
BETHANY: "You, too. :)"

Declan collapsed back onto the couch with relief. He knew he shouldn't get this tense; Bethany hadn't missed a single check-in since she'd been away. But he couldn't help it. He couldn't help feeling responsible for what happened six months ago, just like he couldn't help feeling responsible for what had happened sixteen years ago.

Didn't matter that none of it made any sense.

Fuck, you have a show, Declan. Get it together.

The closest he'd been to getting his pre-show headspace back was thinking about Molly. Specifically, the things he wanted to do to Molly. The way he felt around her, when he thought about her? Hungry and strong and fucking *dominant*. Ready to fucking roar.

Once he got going, he couldn't stop thinking about what she'd be like in bed. What it would be like to watch her discover how much she liked to submit—he could tell already, with the way she flushed when he used the voice, the way she responded to an order. Damn. He could make her fantasies come true. He'd find out how big those brown eyes got when she came.

He fucking *knew* she was out there, right now, knew she'd come for the show when he'd texted her. Didn't know how he knew. Maybe he had lost his mind already, but who cared? He could feel it.

He laughed. He was about to go on stage for the first time in six months in front of a crowd that wanted to kill him, and all he could think about was what a girl he'd just met tasted like.

And it felt *good*. Fuck it. It was good to feel like that, all juiced up, after being down for so long. Declan didn't care if it was nuts. He thought about her. About Molly Ward. About how she'd come. About how she was so fucking afraid of what she felt, that what it must be like when she'd finally, finally let it all go…

Sing for Molly fucking Ward; forget the rest.

He threw open the door and yelled, "Let's go kick some ass."

~ * ~ * ~

Molly felt like a proper badass, as Adra had instructed, for all of about five minutes. Then she realized she was surrounded by the handpicked crowd of die-hard Savage Heart fans and L.A. celebs and she started to remember how incredibly out of place she was.

Volare L.A. itself was incredible. At least the public part of the club was—the first floor was one huge room, a giant performance space with beams crisscrossing the ceiling several stories overhead, freaking chandeliers all over the place, private boxes, several bars…

It felt like a dream world. And Molly found herself wondering what the more private areas of the club were like.

Everywhere there were little clues about what might go on at the more private events—little metal loops bolted into the walls, padded posts, odd-looking furniture. Or maybe she was just imagining it. That wouldn't surprise her in the least. She had imagined plenty of things, thinking about Declan and his big hands.

Not helpful.

Molly picked up a drink and tried to find a quiet corner where she could observe the show in true writer form. She was there to do a job, after all. Unfortunately, everything she observed reminded her of Declan. The whole place was dizzy with the anticipation of seeing Declan Donovan and Savage Heart—or "Half a Heart," as she heard some fans mutter. They were all pissed about Soren. Not knowing what had happened, at least half of them blamed Declan, and now, to make things worse, Soren was basically missing. The rumors online and floating through the crowd were all various shades of crazy: Soren fucked Declan's girl, Soren stopped Declan from doing something twisted (Molly found this one unbelievable, if intriguing—she knew at least some of the things Declan might be into), it was all a mess over some groupie...

No one really knew what had happened in Philadelphia. It was gonna be an interesting show.

But some of the female fans, at least, didn't seem to care about the past. Or the show. Or the band. They were all over the place, to the point where Molly couldn't ignore them anymore, and they were practically feverish.

"Oh God, I don't even care, I'll climb on stage and suck him in front of everyone."

It was a six-foot blonde woman, announcing that to the entire world at the top of her lungs. Like she was calling dibs? Molly couldn't place her—maybe she wasn't famous, just a model? *Right, "just" a model.*

Also? Suck him *on stage?* Molly had an inexplicable urge to smack the woman, even though she'd probably just cut her hand on one of those cheekbones.

Eat something, Molly thought bitterly.

Her friend laughed it off. "You are such a slut."

"A selective slut. Don't tell me you wouldn't do the exact same thing."

"Hell no, hooker. I'm going to do it backstage."

Molly moved away from the sounds of their laughter, gritting her teeth. It wasn't news to anyone that Declan was one of the hottest men on the planet, but she didn't need what she couldn't have — wouldn't have — thrown in her face.

Suck him on stage...

Molly suppressed a shiver.

Then the lights went out.

The crowd roared, stomped their feet. It was deafening. Even over all that, Molly could hear hecklers, actual hecklers, people chanting, "Soren, Soren, Soren." *What the fuck?* Who would come to the show to do that, like the guitarist might magically appear if they just said his name a few times? Just as many were screaming for Declan, competing to be heard, until it got unbearably loud in the small space, frighteningly hot and close in the claustrophobic dark.

Molly was jittery, on the verge of panic, when she heard him, and everything changed.

When everybody heard him.

A wild, animal scream tore from Declan's throat as the light hit him and only him, as he seized the mic with his whole, muscled body, and owned the damn room. The place went silent but for Declan, tearing apart the opening lines to "My Sometime Girl."

"Sometime you gotta know;
Sometime you gotta learn..."

The guitar and drums crashed in and everything stopped. Molly's heart stopped, the whole world stopped, she would have sworn time fucking stopped while she watched that man look around, looking for something, singing that song.

*"You dance with a man like me;
I'll show you what it is you need."*

She couldn't breathe, couldn't move. She could barely hear the women around her, screaming, jumping up and down, sounding like they were about to come just from the sound of his voice. All Molly could see was Declan on that stage, sweat gathering on his chest, eyes looking hungry, mean, predatory. Still looking for something. The first drops of sweat trickled down his chest to his ridged abs and Molly shuddered.

*"You'll burn, baby;
You'll burn;
For me."*

She couldn't take her eyes off him.
And then *his* eyes found *her*.
His eyes pinned her in place while he sang that song. While she heard what he would do to her if she let him. *When* she let him. He'd said he would make her beg. He'd said he would touch her again. And now Molly felt him on her skin, her breasts, her thighs. She was wet. She was shaking. He was fucking her right there, and there was nothing she could do about it.
There was nothing she wanted to do about it.
I am in such deep shit.
That was the last thing that went through her mind before the security guard pulled her away.

chapter 5

The guy was big, beefy, professional security, which was a good thing, because he had to practically carry Molly with one hand. She felt seriously lightheaded, weak, unsteady on her feet. She couldn't have gotten back to the main room by the same path if she'd tried; she could only hear Declan now, and the crowd, losing its collective mind.

The security guard led her to an upstairs lounge, a place full of roadies and groupies and people with black jeans and tattoos who looked like they belonged. Molly looked around in a daze.

"Wait here," the security guy said.

And then he was gone.

What had he even looked like? Had he given her his name?

Molly could still feel the beat through the floor, the pulsing, driving beat, and it matched the throbbing between her legs. She laughed softly to herself, because the whole thing was ridiculous, and collapsed onto a couch in the corner.

She covered her mouth with her hand, trying to pretend she wasn't smiling, and looked out the window.

What was that?
What am I waiting here for?
Oh God, what was that?

She was drenched. She had sweat pooling between her breasts, and she was sure she was soaking through her panties, and the tension in her core coiled a little tighter with every beat of those drums.

Two months of this. She'd maybe known, in the abstract, how primal he was, how male, but nothing compared to seeing him perform in the flesh. To having him look her in the eyes as he sang. This was what it was like to be near him, to be the one he sang to, to know what every woman wanted from him. This was why he was who he was. It was a fucking revelation. She just had to try to remember not to take it personally.

Lock it down, Molly.

She got out her phone and started writing.

She had paragraphs on Declan already by the time she noticed the music had stopped. She checked her phone; it couldn't be over already, could it? The bass started up again below her, something she could feel through the floor, but it wasn't a Savage Heart song.

Molly started to breathe a little faster. If he wasn't on stage, where was he? What was he doing?

Why had she been brought up here?

The air in the lounge had changed. The energy. The high buzz of the groupies chattering and gossiping had stopped, and the roadies looked serious, prepared for work. Everything tense.

The door burst open, and it was like a freaking dam broke: the women, wearing practically nothing at all, rushed ahead and pressed in on Declan Donovan. The rest of the band melted off to the sides, found their regulars, their own fans, but the pack stayed with Declan. He was huge, bigger even then he'd looked on stage, steaming with sweat and breathing hard.

But it was something else, something animal: those eyes again, roving, hungry. All those women, calling his name, *touching* him—he ignored them. Cut a path through them. A force of nature, a goddamn tornado.

Molly watched, mesmerized, again. She tried not to respond as a woman, but holy hell, she could see the adrenaline surge in him left over from the show, could see the pure physical need in him, the *power*, and she answered with her own need. What would that feel like between her legs? On top of her. Inside her.

Oh God. Be a professional. It's just the magic of the show; it's not real. Get a hold of yourself.

He saw her.

She saw his chest heave and his nostrils flare, and then he was moving toward her, too fast for her to do anything but scramble to get up. Molly saw other women peel off him like shadows, unable to really focus on anything but him; he still wore whatever it was he had on stage that made him a genuine star. Magnetism. Charisma. Passion.

Whatever it was, she could feel it. She could feel herself getting drunk off of it.

The whole room was drunk off of it. The whole room wanted him.

It's NOT real, she told herself again. She remembered Robbie pulling this kind of thing, trying on that rock star swagger, and seeing Declan now just made it all the more clear what a cheap imitation Robbie had been when he'd tried to front his own band. But Declan was the real deal, the womanizing, drinking, destructive force of nature that Robbie had only pretended to be, and look at how much damage *Robbie* had done to her. Declan would destroy her utterly. Terrible things happened when Molly lost control. She *wouldn't* lose control now.

The whole room watched him stop in front of her. Stand over her. Loom over her.

He put out his hand.

"Come."

Molly put her hand in his before she even thought about. Nodded, before she even thought about it. And then before her brain could catch up with her body — her body, her traitorous body, that had just reflexively done what he wanted, no questions asked — he was pulling her away, up the stairs, into more darkness.

What the fuck am I doing?

She could smell him. Oh God, she wanted to be covered in him. Her heart pounded so loud she was sure he could hear it, and she knew he felt the sweat on her hands and the heat coming off her body, and before she knew it he'd pulled her into a private room.

His dressing room.

Alarm bells went off in Molly's head. All of them. Every single alarm bell she had, blaring. She wasn't afraid of him, or what he might do; she was afraid of herself.

Jesus Christ, get it together. For Lydia.

There was a couch, a desk. Someone's office. Molly moved to the other side of the couch, as far away from him as she could get.

"Why am I here?" she asked. Her voice was choked.

Declan stared at her. Not confused. Not thinking.

Wanting.

Finally, he said, "You're supposed to write a book."

A beat.

Then Molly laughed out loud, relief spilling over her as Declan gave her a big, wicked smile. She'd forgotten his reputation as a funny guy, the wild kind, the kind of guy who gets away with outrageous pranks because he's famous.

"I forgot you were supposed to be funny," she said, breathing hard.

Shit, she really felt drunk. What this man did to her hormones...

"That's fair. I forgot you were supposed to be writing a book," he said, and his look told her what he'd been thinking about instead. Just like that, she was whipped right back to the edge of self-control.

"Oh shit," she murmured. "No, really, why am I here tonight?"

"You didn't like the show?"

"I loved the show."

"I know you did."

He said it so simply. So knowingly. She blushed, hot and fast.

"It was a good show," she said, maybe a touch defensively.

Declan grinned again. "Yeah, I owe you."

Before she could ask what the hell *that* meant, he walked over to the desk and opened one of the drawers. Suddenly Molly was indescribably irritated with the man. She'd never been this turned on and confused and, frankly, intoxicated in her entire life, and all while she was trying to nail her first real writing job, and it was entirely his fault. And he was enjoying it.

And she would rather be irritated and angry than have to deal with the ache of wanting to feel him inside her. It would pass. Of course it would. It was just the fucking show.

"Why am I here?" she snapped.

He looked up. He was *amused*, damn him.

"So we can negotiate our terms," he said.

"What?" Molly was dumbfounded. "I already signed a contract."

"You signed a contract with Volare and with my holding company," Declan said calmly. There had been a shift. He sat behind the desk, and something about his demeanor was…different.

Still larger than life. Still with that burning fire in him, but contained now, burning tighter and brighter, like a laser. Controlled.

It didn't help. She wanted him just as badly, bare-chested and still slick with sweat. It might have even made it worse.

"You still need to sign a contract with me," he

said.

Molly shook herself out of her apparent trance. "What? What are you talking about? For what?"

"Right now, as a precaution. Later it might be something more. Then we'll renegotiate."

There was something about his level stare that was driving her nuts. The way he had all the information and wielded it, taking control of the conversation. The way she was completely lost, clinging to him for guidance. She knew it wasn't an accident. It was a demonstration. And it was turning her on while he watched.

Fuck.

Fight it. Be a badass.

She met his eye and said, "So are you going to tell me what it is, or are we going to play twenty questions?"

Declan just smiled again. Nothing she said could get to him. Infuriating.

"Are you on birth control?" he asked.

"Of *course* I'm on birth control!" she sputtered, before she realized that she had *actually answered that question*. She'd freaking *answered him*, again, like he had a right to that information. Well, she wasn't going to tell him the rest. She wasn't going to tell him the reasons why she'd never even consider risking it again.

Molly opened her mouth to speak, then stopped, taken completely by surprise. This was a pattern now, Declan Donovan getting her to do things automatically. Telling her to do things, and her doing them.

"What about you?" she asked, feeling desperate to claw something back. She crossed her arms, as if that could help, and then closed her eyes briefly when she realized she'd just asked a man if he was on birth control.

Then Declan surprised her.

"Me, too," he said, with that evil grin again. "Got 'em snipped, ages ago."

"So...nice to meet you, I guess?" she ventured. This was a weird conversation to be having. Not many men got vasectomies that young. "Is this how you get to know people?"

Declan laughed, a deep, musical sound that reminded her of what he'd been like on stage. *Don't think about it.*

"No, just you," he said.

"I told you I'm not sleeping with you," Molly said.

He ignored her, smiling, leaning back in his chair like some kind of lord of the manor. "This contract requires you to get tested before we go on tour, and gives you access to my test results. I pay for the rush test, of course."

He was unbelievable. It was like she'd never said anything at all. Molly thought about what Adra had said: if she wanted to him to stop, if she asked him to stop, he would.

So why wasn't she asking?

"Are you out of your mind?" she demanded. "Why on earth would you think that's something you can *require*?"

Declan locked eyes with her and stood up, slowly, letting her get the full effect of his contracting abs and striated pecs as he lifted himself from the chair. His eyes burned and his lips were pressed into a tight, serious line, and oh holy fuck was it hot.

"Because we are going to have sex," he said. He came around the desk and she was suddenly very aware of the fact there were no longer any physical barriers between them. That she could, if she wanted to, touch him. That she could let him touch her.

And he was walking toward her.

She told her legs to move, and they wouldn't. Stupid legs. Stupid body, fixated on what it might feel like to just say, "Yes."

Too late. He was inches away — inches. Molly felt her lips part, and the thudding, driving pulse in her core reached a fever pitch. Maybe she should just...

Declan took her hand and turned it up, palm facing him.

"Because," he went on, tracing the lines in her palm, as though he were completely oblivious to the fact that she was practically hyperventilating, "You're going to be spending a lot of time in the Clubs Volare, because that's where I like to be. And you're going to see things there that you like. You're going to see things you want to try. And those tests will be *required* there, too."

The geek part of her brain thought, *He used the proper plural of 'Clubs Volare.'*

The rest of her was a little slow on the uptake.

Then: *He's saying you're into BDSM. He's saying you're a submissive.*

HE KNOWS.

Molly tried to yank her hand away, but Declan caught it. The look he gave her stripped her of all pretense. It had been four years since Molly had been naked with a man, and even then she'd always covered up, always had a sheet, a shirt nearby, something. Always some layer, something to protect herself with. She had never, *never* felt as naked as she did now.

"You don't have to hide it from me," Declan said. "I think it's fucking beautiful."

Molly swallowed. The only other man she'd told about her fantasies had thought she was a slut. She didn't want Declan's words to make her feel so good, but they did. They really, really did.

"This doesn't change anything," she said.

Declan narrowed his eyes but said nothing. Then his grip on her wrist tightened and he dragged her over to the desk. There was a contract, a blank line where her signature would go, and his.

"Sign it," he ordered.

Molly stared at it, already knowing that she would. That she would do what he commanded, again. That she *wanted* to. As she shakily began to scrawl her name, she told herself that she would do this, she would give in on this one thing, and that holding out on the rest, on her actual body, would drive him insane. That this really gave her the upper hand.

She stopped halfway. *Be a badass.*

"On one condition," she said, not trusting herself to look at him.

A low, rough sound died in Declan's throat. *Now* she looked at him.

"Did you just growl?"

"What condition?" he barked.

Molly straightened up and cocked her head to the side, feeling good, feeling...she didn't know what. Feeling like she liked this side of Declan. Like she somehow knew how to *be*, like this, knew what was coming, knew he'd do something to wrest power back—and she wanted him to. It made sense to her. The first time a man had ever made sense to her, even if it was in this twisted, crazy, nonsense way.

There was no fighting it. She could keep herself from falling into bed with him—maybe—but she couldn't stop...this.

So she'd have to use it instead.

"What condition?" he said again.

"Total honesty," Molly said. His eyes burned into hers and she forced herself not to flinch, and when she held that gaze, she started to feel warm. "If I'm going to do this, you will give me total honesty. No lies."

A woman who wasn't used to catching the signs might have missed it, but Molly saw him react. A moment when the expression flitted across his face; she'd caught him.

He said, "What makes you think I'm lying?"

"Did you *ever* have a drinking problem?" she asked point blank.

And Declan Donovan was speechless, possibly for the first time ever. It was Molly's turn to smile.

"I know drunks," she said. "You don't act like a drunk, and drunks are always drunks, even when they're sober. And you're a Dom. You're in control, all of the time. You are not a drunk."

He stared at her, and a smile played at the corners of his mouth. Finally, he said, "No, I never had a drinking problem. Agreed. No lies."

Molly bent back over the contract so he

wouldn't see her face, which she was pretty sure could have lit up an entire room. Too late she realized what position that put her in, bent over in cutoffs, right next to him. And then she felt it: his fingertips, dancing on the back of her naked thigh, just teasing, defining the burning boundary where his touch stopped, the boundary she suddenly, desperately wanted him to cross.

She didn't say anything. Didn't move. If she moved, he might stop. If she moved, she'd have to make a *decision* to tell him whether to stop. The only sound was her panting.

His fingers slid up her leg to the edge of her cutoffs, just inside.

Her breath hitched, and she looked down. Her signature ran off the page. She stood up, breathing even harder.

"You are awfully forward," she said.

He grinned, wiggling his fingers in the air. "And you love it."

She blushed. "Well, you've got your signature. Which means I get my interviews."

"I'm not used to having women tell me what to do," Declan said.

Molly thought of Adra and a laughed a little.

"Yes, you are," she said, trying to ignore his hand on her hip again. "Just not with women you *think* you're going to fuck."

It was Declan's turn to laugh. "I'm really a fun guy, you know."

"I've heard rumors about your shenanigans. Apparently it wasn't all the booze, either."

"You want shenanigans? I'll give you shenanigans. I'm gonna have fun with you, Molly

Ward," he said, drawing her close. He leaned in, gently, slowly, trying not to startle her...and then he kissed her on the cheek. He whispered, "You're not immune to me."

And he left her like that, breathless. It wasn't until he was at the door that she could speak.

"Don't think you're immune, either," she called after him.

He laughed.

chapter 6

Declan was grinning like an idiot as he pulled into the Club Volare compound in Venice Beach. He'd practically lived at this place for the last six months, plenty of time to pack in the memories, yet now when he pulled up he thought about Molly Ward—specifically, Molly Ward kicking his ass, and just asking to have hers spanked in return.

He'd been perma-hard ever since that pseudo-scene after the show. Doubly so since he'd gotten her test results—she'd gone and done it, like she said she would. Now he had his end of the deal.

And he should be more pissed off about it. More worried that he'd agreed to that nonsense—no lies. What the fuck did that even mean? Who in the history of public relations had ever told the whole damn truth? Because that's what this was supposed to be, a way to save the band's image without screwing Soren or Bethany any more than either of them had already been screwed.

Then Molly had gone and changed the whole game up, just by being…Molly.

Declan sat in his car for a moment, not quite ready to go meet the guys on the bus, even though he'd been the one to call the band meeting an hour before Molly was due to arrive. They needed to figure out how they were going to handle her. But he just wanted to roll the memory around for a moment, enjoy it again: what Molly had looked like when she finally agreed to do something she'd wanted to do all along. When he'd told her he knew she was into submission. To watch her body respond, and her mind catch up, was such a fucking thrill.

He had no idea what a connection like that would feel like when he was actually inside her. Actually in a scene. It might ruin them both.

Fuck. She had no idea how hot she was.

And fucking *smart*. He was screwed. How the *fuck* did she know he wasn't an alcoholic? What the hell else did she know? And how the hell were they supposed to keep her from finding out the truth about what had happened back in Philly if she'd already figured out one of their biggest lies?

He should be seriously aggravated, but he wasn't. He was excited. So damn excited about the prospect of having a sub that he knew it was dangerous. He knew if he let his dick lead the way he would rush into things, and he wouldn't do that again. He needed to know more about her. Needed to know that she was stable. Sane. Safe.

"Well, fuck me," he muttered. He shouldn't be allowed to feel this damn happy. And, as if on cue, his phone rang.

It was his Uncle Jim, calling him back.

"Finally," Declan said into the phone. "Did you fucking hear from him?"

"Watch your language," Jim said automatically. Declan smiled. Jim swore like a sailor, but it was nice to know the man still considered himself a father figure.

"C'mon, Jim. Please just tell me you heard from Soren."

"I did."

"And?"

"And what he had to say is none of your business. But," Jim cut him off, "he's ok. I can tell you that. And he's dealing with it, so you might have to back off for a while, Dec."

"You know he's like my brother."

"Then you shouldn't have beat the crap out of him and kicked him out."

"You and him are the only family I have." Declan paused. "You're the only ones who know."

"You don't think he knows that? Shit happens. Family sucks. You have to give him his own time."

Declan didn't say anything. There wasn't much to say, except the one thing that scared Declan so much he couldn't bring himself to say it out loud.

Jim heard it anyway.

"I'm looking after him," Jim said. "I'm not gonna let anything happen to him."

Declan exhaled. "Thank you."

The pressure let off, just a little bit, the way it did after a show. Just enough to keep him going.

"Thank you," he said again, and hung up.

The guys were waiting. Time to go face the music.

Brian, the band's bassist, was slumped over the table in the bus's little booth, looking miserable.

"Why are we here *early*, you assholes?" he muttered.

"Why did you get black out drunk the night before we have to leave on tour, you dumbass?" countered Gage.

Erik just smiled. Still not one hundred percent comfortable. Declan hadn't noticed it during the show, so he didn't know if it was a problem yet. But then again, he hadn't noticed much of anything during the show but Molly Ward.

"Dec, c'mon," Brian sighed, sitting up and putting his shades down. Dude was bloodshot.

Might as well just spit it out.

"Molly Ward knows I didn't go to rehab. She knows I'm not an alcoholic," he said, watching them all carefully. Erik looked to the other two, who weren't any goddamn help. Brian was laughing, and Gage just looked at him with disbelief.

"How did you let *that* happen?" Gage asked. "It's been one day. One fucking day!"

"She's smart is what happened," Declan said, glowering. "She figured it out. Knows about alcoholics, apparently."

Which had been an interesting insight, all on its own.

"And that's not all," Declan continued. He sighed. "I promised her I wouldn't lie during our interviews."

Now Brian cracked up. "Oh, dude, come on. You know I have a headache right now, it hurts to laugh."

Declan threw a straw at him, hitting him in the temple.

"This is a joke, right?" Gage asked. "Because I don't see how you're going to keep up this whole web of lies you made us all promise to support if *you're* supposed to tell the truth."

"I'll figure it out," Declan said. "You guys can lie all you want."

"Oh, thank you so much for that," Brian said. "You know this whole thing is your show, man. I still don't know why you're doing this. Come clean and let the chips fall where they may, you know?"

"You know where they'd fall," Declan said through clenched teeth. "I'm not doing that to Bethany. Or Soren."

Brian looked ashamed. "I know, Dec. Sorry."

The group went silent. No one had said they approved or disapproved of what Declan had done—beating the crap out of Soren and kicking him out. They'd all known enough to stay the hell out of it. But there was no denying that it was a decision that had a major effect on all of them.

Erik cleared his throat. "I knew the deal when I signed up," he said quietly. "It's none of my business, and I'll keep my mouth shut."

"Yeah, I guess if we ever want Soren to come back..." Brian said, then looked at Erik. "Sorry, man."

"Don't worry about it. I know how it is."

Declan could already feel a headache coming on. They never talked about Soren, or if he'd come back, or even where he was. Declan had always thought it was because none of them fucking *knew* anything, but it just occurred to him that maybe they did know. Maybe Soren talked to all of them but him. After all, no one but Declan, Bethany, and Soren knew the full story. Maybe Soren could face the rest of them.

Which was bullshit.

Which was dangerous. Declan needed to get in his right mind, his Dom mind, before Molly showed up, because that woman was dangerous, too. Whatever it was he felt with her, it hit him hard, deep, went right through all the usual defenses he had up. Which was fine, he could handle it. But the last time he'd felt anything close to that with anyone else had been Bethany, and he'd been so goddamn wrong about her...

Every memory of Bethany was tainted now with that night. With carrying her, blinded by grief and panic, not seeing Bethany in his arms, but someone else...

"Fuck this," Declan said aloud and stood up. "You all know what the deal is. You all know how to kick ass. Let's get it done."

"Get what done?"

Declan turned to find Molly, in those damn sinful cutoffs and a white tee, a duffel slung over her shoulder and a sly smile on her face.

~ * ~ * ~

Molly could barely handle Declan's eyes on her without melting into a puddle. She was *not* prepared to handle Declan plus three other hot guys. Maybe going from being a social hermit to living in a sexually charged tour bus was going to be more of a challenge than she thought.

The guy she recognized as Brian, the bassist, let out a low whistle, and said, "Good luck with that, Dec."

"Shut the fuck up, Brian," Declan said. He was wearing another black tank, muscles everywhere, flexing while he looked at her. Good Christ, but it never stopped. Molly hadn't ever felt this continuously turned on. She had actually thought there was something wrong with her sex drive until she met Declan Donovan.

The irony burned.

"You going to introduce me?" she asked.

Declan frowned and reached for her, lifting her heavy duffel off her shoulder with no apparent effort and pulling her gently forward. He still kept her close to him. *Am I being marked?* she thought, and smiled.

"So this dumbass is Brian," he said. "This is Erik, who's filling in for Soren—"

Temporarily? she wondered.

"And this here is Gage, our drummer."

All the guys smiled at her and Gage saluted, an odd gesture coming from a dude with plugs in his earlobes. Molly smiled back and waved a little.

And then an uneasy silence settled in.

An awkward silence.

Oh shit, not good. Nooot good. Had she interrupted something? There was obviously something going on that she didn't know about, something beyond the obvious stuff, but she needed these guys to trust her.

"So—" she started.

She got only the one word out before Brian

erupted with laughter.

"So you know he's not really a drunk, huh?"

Gage choked on his beer laughing, and even Erik burst out, covering his mouth and shaking silently. Molly giggled, looking up at Declan, and was relieved to find the big guy smiling.

"Tough to keep secrets on a tour bus, huh?" she said to him.

He leaned down so quickly she couldn't react. "Not as tough as you'd think," he whispered.

That did it. Instant wetness.

Molly tried to blink herself back to Earth and found Brian leering at her. She'd have to set the tone right away.

"Yeah, you know, I actually have questions about that," she said.

Brian shook his head and pretended to zip his lips. Gage shook his head, and Erik just smiled — and they all looked at Declan.

So that's how it was. They all deferred to Declan. She didn't know why she was surprised; the guy was a Dom and the obvious leader of the band. So she was still going to have to crack him to get at the story.

Molly really didn't mind that part.

"You guys know I'm still going to have to write a book, right? With words in it? I'm going to be interviewing all of you, so don't think you'll get off that easily."

"You have no *idea* how easily I get off," Brian said, and ducked when Gage tried to smack him upside the head.

Declan rumbled.

"Ignore them," he said, glaring at Brian.

But Molly only laughed. Brian had broken the tension, and now everyone knew what the deal was. She could work with that. They were all determined to keep something from her, and that was fine. She wished them luck. They were going to need it.

Molly looked up at Declan while Brian and Gage bickered. "Come to think of it, where am I going to be doing interviews?"

She heard Brian snicker. That did not bode well.

"First," Declan said, hefting her bag over his shoulder, "Let me show you to your bunk."

Molly looked up and down the bus. It was...a bus. There wasn't much to see. The area towards the back seemed to have some bunks and a few closed doors, but it was all pretty much open.

Probably she should have realized this. There really wasn't a lot of privacy on a tour bus. Her mind reeled with all the implications of this right up until she felt Declan's hand on the small of her back again, urging her forward.

Did he know it was like an electrical shock every time he did that?

What a freaking habit.

She scurried forward, realizing her nipples would soon be visible through her poorly chosen t-shirt if he kept touching her like that, and not wanting to have to deal with being visibly aroused in front of these guys she just met. Though obviously—*obviously*—she was going to have to deal with it at some point.

"This bunk is yours," Declan said, tossing her duffel into a bottom bunk at the very back, just a few feet from the room at the back with an actual door.

Molly looked at the bunk, which had only a small, thin privacy curtain separating it from the rest of the bus. She thought about the vibrator she'd packed, thinking she was being smart because it was clear that she was going to need frequent relief if she were going to keep her head around Declan Donovan. And then she thought about the fact that at any given moment she'd be basically exposed to four hot men, one of whom was able to get her halfway there with just a look, and all of them stuck together on a tour bus.

It had been so long since she'd had sex, so long since she'd *wanted* to have sex, and since she'd met Declan it was all she could think about. And now she wouldn't even be able to masturbate without turning it into a show.

She might die.

"Is there a problem?" Declan asked.

"It's awfully cramped for two," she managed to squeak out. Then she blushed and looked up at his grinning face.

"For interviews! I meant for interviews!"

"Well, then, madam," Declan said, sweeping his hand out towards the closed door. "Let me show you to your interview room. Also known as my bedroom."

chapter 7

"You're kidding," Molly said.

Declan didn't even try to hide his smile as he held open the door to the back room—his bedroom—for her.

"Nope," he said.

Of course he would get the only bedroom. Of course there would be only one place for her to conduct interviews. Molly shook her head. So not only was she going to be unable to take care of herself when things got too...tense...around Declan, but she was going to be spending a lot of time with Declan.

On his bed.

"You don't have furniture?" she asked.

"There's a chair somewhere," he said. "It's covered with clothes, though."

She could see that. The only clean space in the admittedly cramped room was the bed. And it was an impressive bed. Large. Smooth, soft looking sheets. Molly's eyes swept over a set of metal loops bolted to the wall. And one in the ceiling.

Her heart skidded and she felt a lump in her throat. She knew what those were for. Or at least thought she did. Her *imagination* certainly did. But it meant he'd done those things here with other women.

Of *course* he had. She was an idiot. He was a famous rock star Dom; of course he had subs and scenes and groupies and everything here all the damn time.

Would he do it during the tour? With her in her bunk, right there? Would she have to *listen*?

The thought made her feel sick. Which made her feel mad. She had no right to care at all, and she was only screwing herself by getting carried away like this.

"Hey," Declan said, closing the door behind him. His dark eyes had softened. "Where'd you go? What's wrong?"

Molly shrugged it off, unnerved that he'd picked up on her discomfort so easily. "Nothing. Just…what about when I want to interview the other guys? I guess I'll have to do it in here."

"No," Declan said immediately.

Molly looked up in surprise. "No? Where do you propose I interview them, on the roof?"

"Where I can see you."

"This is you being territorial again, isn't it?" she teased, beyond relieved to have the focus back on Declan. Let him suffer. "The alpha caveman can't even let another man in his bedroom."

"That's not what I'm territorial about," he said gruffly.

Oh God.

Molly felt herself flush, and worse, so many times worse, felt her nipples tighten. Just the way he'd said it, the way she knew he was thinking about her, about *owning* her...

She closed her eyes. She never should have worn this stupid shirt. He could see.

"Look at me," he rasped.

Dutifully, she opened her eyes. It wasn't even weird now when she did what he said, except that it very much was. She was so screwed.

He'd taken another step closer, hulking over her, breathing hard. Looking down at her.

"You're right," he said. "You have to do all the interviews here. But you should know I don't like it. You should know what I'm going to be thinking."

"No," she said softly. "Please don't make this harder."

"No, that's on you," he said. "You're the reason I can't throw you down on that bed and fuck you 'til you scream right now."

"Declan, we don't even know each other."

"I didn't ask you to marry me."

He hooked one finger over the waist of her cutoffs and under the waistband of her panties, against her bare skin. She shuddered, her abs fluttering at the touch as he pulled her forward.

"This won't work if we..." She licked her lips; they were so dry. She couldn't even say it.

"You're wrong," he said, letting his leg come between hers. "But you're going to be the one to admit it."

And then he let her go. Didn't move far, just

separated them. Left her hanging, breathless, panting.

Again.

"I have some rules for our interviews, too," he said.

Molly staggered to the bed and sat down. That was deliberate. He'd put her in this state, revved her up, and then dropped her on purpose. To set rules?

To regain that power.

She looked up at him and smiled. She understood.

"Oh really?" she said. "You already promised no lies."

Declan stood with his arms crossed, legs spread wide apart. She was doing well until she let her eyes drift down. He didn't seem to care that he was obviously hard. Molly's brain ran right off the track when she saw his long, thick bulge pulled tight against his leg, right there at eye level.

"But I didn't promise I'd tell you anything," he said. "Eyes up."

Mortified, she looked up. He was smiling.

Bastard.

Muscled, tattooed, beautiful, sexy bastard.

"Now, if you want an answer," he said, eyes glittering down at her, "you have to give me one."

"One what?" she asked warily.

Declan laughed. "An answer. Just reciprocity. That's all I'm saying. You want a question answered, you answer one in turn."

Molly hesitated. That was actually brilliant. Deviously brilliant. And the beautiful bastard up there seemed to know it. Molly had been totally comfortable with the idea of digging into his life while hers remained protected, of getting Declan to open up about whatever messed up thing had broken up the most profound friendship in his life. The idea of being opened to the same scrutiny left her feeling...

Vulnerable.

Exposed.

Scared.

All things that turned her on when she thought about Declan.

Molly buried her face in her hands. "I am so fucked," she muttered to herself.

"What was that?" he demanded.

"Fine!" she said, frustration winning out. "I can't argue it's unreasonable, and it's not like I have any leverage, so fine. You win. Tit for tat, reciprocity, the whole thing."

Her heart was racing as she said it. There were things that Molly had never talked to anyone about because they left her feeling so ashamed and weak—the way Robbie had treated her, the way his friends had treated her after the lies he'd told. But that was nothing compared to what she'd lost. How afraid she'd felt. How guilty she'd felt to know that it must, in some way, have been her fault. That if only she'd done something... She'd worked so hard to get to a place where she didn't think about it every day, where she could almost pretend that none of it had ever happened.

And now she'd just given the one man she had to guard against carte blanche to find out about all of it. How the hell was she supposed to make sure she didn't get her heart broken if she was going to have to let him in?

Molly glared up at him and said, "This is dirty pool."

Declan bent down, put his hands on her knees, and forced them apart. She gasped as he knelt in front of her, between her legs, putting his face close to hers.

"Bullshit," he said. "You are here to find out the very worst things about me and then make them sound like fucking virtues. I don't know how you're gonna do that, Molly, but I do know you're going to know some bad stuff before this is over. You want me to show you mine? The least you can do is show me yours."

Molly's abs contracted in time with her hurried, shallow little breaths, her body screaming at her, just electric and alive with the nearness of him, of where he was. *Focus. Be a badass.*

"Why?" she said. "Are you actually ashamed? Do you possess the capacity to feel shame?"

The change in him was immediate. His face darkened, his mouth grew tight. Molly could have handled it just fine if he'd been angry, but his eyes looked sad.

"You don't know me yet, Molly," he said softly. "That was a shallow, bullshit, superficial thing to say, and it was beneath you."

She bridled for a minute—beneath her?—before she realized he was right. She didn't know him, didn't know anything about his inner life, didn't know what drove him. Except that something painful had happened six months ago, something bad enough that he had constructed elaborate lies about alcoholism and who knew what else, and she'd just called him shameless.

She *hated* realizing she was wrong when she was still angry.

"Yeah, that was a dick move," she said. Grudgingly.

His hands raced up her thighs to circle around her hips and he pulled her violently forward, their chests nearly touching. She could have stopped him at any time. Could have told him no. Why hadn't she?

"Apologize," he growled.

That was why. The voice, the order: she felt it deep inside. She almost wanted to moan.

"I'm sorry," she said.

He squeezed his thumbs into the crease where her legs met her hips and she rocked a little, involuntarily. Molly grit her teeth, fisted the bed sheet, and glared back at him, determined not to let him get the better of her. She would *not* beg him to fuck her right now, on this bed. She would *not*.

"It's not about shame," he said. "It's about proving to me that you've seen enough of your own shit to understand mine."

She studied his face. There was no pretense there. Just open, honest eyes, a calm certainty. No games, no power exchange.

And the worst part is it made perfect sense to her. The only reason she could even consider the idea of telling Declan the worst things that had happened to her was that she could see, in those eyes, that terrible things had happened to him, too.

She gave in.

"What do you want to know?" she asked.

Now he flashed a wicked smile while his hands

still branded her thighs. "Why do you fight it?"

"Fight what?" she said. It sounded weak even to her.

"How much you want me." He emphasized his point by digging those thumbs in a little deeper.

Oh Christ, was there even a point to denying it anymore? Declan saw right through her. It would be more embarrassing to lie, to keep lying, and admit that she was afraid she couldn't control herself.

He slid one hand up to her waist, toying with the edge of her shirt, as if to prove that she didn't want him to stop.

"Answer me," he said.

An order.

She sighed. Fuck it. Honesty.

"I told myself it was because I wanted to be professional, for the book," she said. "And that's true. But that's not the real reason. That's not the reason I'm scared shitless of the way I feel when you touch me. I fight it because I've been burned by guys like you before, Declan. Badly. Bad things happened. And I'm not doing it again."

Declan moved that hand up from her waist to her face, touching her cheek, her neck, tucking her hair behind her ear. He looked thoughtful and angry all at the same time.

"Somebody didn't treat you right," he echoed.

Molly didn't trust herself to speak.

Declan took her chin in his hand and looked her in the eyes.

"Did he fuck you right?"

Molly gasped. She was stunned mentally—and overwhelmed physically—by the weight of him between her legs, the smell of him so close, the way he brought her physical pleasure just by barely touching her. It took her a moment. And then:

"You want to know how other men have fucked me?" she asked.

Declan growled a little, his brows coming together. Secretly, Molly rated that as a triumph.

"No," he said. "I want to know if you got what you needed. But I already know you didn't."

His eyes roved all over her body, her taut muscles, her aroused nipples, the way she could barely breathe. Yeah, it was obvious. *Fuck.*

And then he got up.

"And you never will if you don't trust a man to give it to you," he said.

And he left.

Molly sat there for far too long. The bus started up with a rumble and she swayed as they turned out of the Volare compound, her eyes staring at nothing while she thought about what Declan had said. No matter how hard she tried, she couldn't find anything wrong with it. He was right.

And now the question that reverberated deep inside was this: could she ever trust anyone? Could she trust herself after everything that had happened?

Could she trust Declan?

chapter 8

Molly. Naked. On her knees.

Declan closed his eyes and stroked himself, his cock so hard it hurt, the hot water sluicing over his hard body in thin rivulets. She was driving him crazy, with those big eyes and those bee stung lips, and that plain, raw desire to submit. Fuck. He would have her. He would have those lips wrap around his cock, those eyes looking up at him, hungry. Yielding.

Until then he had to take care of himself, or walk around with a permanent hard on. He swore he'd match every orgasm with one buried deep inside her. He'd make her come *hard* for every one of these that she missed.

And he knew how obedient she'd be given the chance. Once he had her naked. The idea made him groan, his hand moving faster as the feeling at the base of his cock intensified. She'd beg for it. She'd bend over and take him to the hilt when he told her to. And if he did his job right, it would help her let go of whatever had happened to her.

Fuck.

He kept coming back to those big eyes. What they'd look like when she finally came for him. What it would feel like, looking into those eyes, buried deep inside her, her breasts bouncing with every thrust, feeling her come hard around his cock...

"Fuck!" he roared, his cum covering the shower wall, one hand shooting out to steady him. She was a great fuck even when she wasn't there. "Fucking Molly," he growled.

He couldn't have her fast enough.

Declan took his time toweling off and coming down, wanting a clear head, knowing she'd be right there when he rejoined the guys. That clear head lasted about two seconds after he saw her.

Christ.

A week on the road and already that girl was weaseling her way into everything. Declan didn't mind, but he did find it remarkable. She felt so damn comfortable already, and not just to him. All the guys had gotten used to her.

Yeah, still dangerous.

He'd seen her talking to all the other dudes in the band, even some of the roadies. Doing her detective work. It always seemed to go the same way, too, with her target kind of avoiding her, all nervous because she already knew they were all going to try to lie to her, and then she'd corner them somewhere and get them laughing, smiling.

She was good.

Freaking. Dangerous.

And still Molly hadn't tried to interview him yet. It maybe kinda rankled, a little bit. What the hell did she have to talk about with those other guys? Wearing those damn cutoffs all the time?

He'd actually asked her about that. She had more than one pair. She'd packed multiple goddamn pairs of lethal cutoffs. "It's *summer*," she'd said.

Declan was going out of his mind wanting her. He hadn't jacked off this much in the shower since he was a teenager, and it was never enough. Worse, he'd been thinking about what Molly had told him, that she'd been burned badly by another guy. That bad things had happened to her. Thinking about it pissed him off, but it also made him...fuck, he didn't know what to call it. She'd said it as though it were something to be ashamed of, but to Declan, she'd looked like a grown woman with some baggage to deal with who *owned* that baggage. She didn't pretend everything was hunky dory; she put that shit front and center, and she was dealing with it the best way she knew how at the moment.

As opposed to the other women in his life, who hadn't been able to deal with much of anything and kept on pretending they had no problems right up until everything went tits up.

Molly handled her troubles more like he did. It made him feel closer to her, even if he had no right to feel like that yet.

Again, the whole thing was stupidly dangerous, right there.

Just preshow jitters, he told himself. That was why he had this jumpy energy, why his eyes followed her around the bus, even when he was supposed to be working on new material. She was just so damn beautiful, her hair falling in her face as she leaned over that notebook, writing. The way she tucked one leg under her. The way she made fun of him whenever she caught him looking.

He needed to get either *in* her or *on* stage, one of the two, and he needed it bad. At least he'd get one of those things tonight: first big show on the road. First real test of the band without Soren. They'd played a couple of small venues, like the show at Volare. They'd been warm-ups, and even that had been dicey up until he'd rocked the stage, but this? This was an old venue, Springfield, somewhere they'd played regularly since they started to get big. True blue fans, not handpicked and half famous. Declan stayed away from the news and the gossip, but he knew his fans. Knew most of them were either in love with him or Soren.

Who knew what was going to happen?

"Fifteen minutes!" yelled Davey from the front of the bus.

He caught Molly looking at him. "You checking me out?" he teased.

"No. You nervous?" She grinned. She was curled up next to a window, the sun hitting the highlights in her hair, lighting up her face. More than normal, even.

"Nah," he said. *I'm wound up and you could help me with that*, he thought. But she already knew it.

Molly let her eyes linger on him.

He knew she knew. Knew that it had to happen eventually. They were both only human. And now that he knew she'd been hurt by someone, someone who'd robbed her of a chance to find out who she was — it hit every Dom button he had, knowing he could help her. Declan didn't leave a sub in need. Didn't leave a woman in need, period, but this was different. This was something he knew only he could give her.

"Careful with those looks, Mol," he said easily. "You'll get yourself into trouble you can't get out of."

He laughed when she blushed deep, deep red, then got up to get his stuff together. Too late he thought about how red she'd get over his knee and under his hand, and then he had to jump in the shower again.

Freshly scrubbed and it was all a damn waste. He came out of his bedroom to find Molly looking just as good all over again. In fact, she looked good enough, leaning against that window, legs spread out in front of her lengthwise on the seat, that it took him way too long to read the expression on her face.

He'd seen it before, always when she was checking her phone. Molly looked the way he felt when he was waiting for Bethany to check in and tell him she'd made it through another day.

Somebody had Molly worried. Somebody important.

"Somebody wake Brian up, we're here!" Davey yelled.

Molly's head shot up, and she came to join Declan near the front of the bus while Gage and Erik went to go drag Brian out of his bunk. Declan was surprised to find that she looked kind of nervous. He smiled.

"Ever done this before?" he asked.

"Oh, yeah, tons of times," she said quietly, looking out the windshield. The venue, an old brick factory that had been converted into a concert hall, rose up out of the emptiness ahead. There was already a sea of cars in the parking lot. "Nothing unusual about this at all."

"So you're not nervous or anything?" he said.

Molly just chewed on her lip and kept her eyes on the crowd.

"Don't be a dick, Declan." Brian yawned behind them. "We know you have giant coconut balls made of solid steel, but the rest of us get a little freaked out to see *that*."

There was an army gathering at the entrance to the parking lot. Even Declan didn't expect that, at least not a crowd of this size. They looked rowdy, too. Some of them had Soren signs, some of them Savage Heart signs, or "WE LOVE YOU, DECLAN," and they were on opposite sides of a goddamn police barrier. He could already see some shoving.

"So how big is this show?" Molly asked in a small voice.

"Tiny, for us," Gage said. Even he seemed a little subdued. The crowd only seemed to get bigger the closer they got. "Or it was supposed to be. We're playing smaller venues to build up a buzz, keep it in control until the fans get used to it. But this... Did they oversell the show?"

"Don't say 'it,'" Declan said. "It's Soren. They have to get used to not having Soren around. And they will."

"So what happens now?" Molly asked.

"We go in. We wait. We do sound check. We wait. We kick ass. Simple as that," Declan said. But he was watching the crowd, too. The bus was pulling into the parking lot now, going about an inch a minute, waiting for the crowd to part. He could see actual fights starting. He could hear them, even through the double thick glass of the windows.

"So much for keeping it lowkey," Gage said. "This is gonna be one hell of a show."

Declan, though, was looking at Molly. Then he looked at the crowd, who in his experience would get extra crazy when they found out most of them wouldn't even get in to the show—if they hadn't been told already. Then he checked out the piece of shit security the venue had provided, like eight pudgy guys in cheap black shirts, clearly not enough to do anything in this situation.

"Molly, you sit this one out," Declan said suddenly, surprising even himself with the urgency in his voice. "Stay on the bus."

He might as well have told her to stick to women's work or something else equally dumb. She turned on Declan with such ferocity that even Brian took a step back, and the look she gave him should have turned him right to stone.

Molly said simply, "Fuck. No."

"Do you see that out there?" Declan pointed, irritated even though he knew he didn't have a leg to stand on. He just didn't like the idea of Molly out in that swarm of crazy fans. "You think that's safe?"

"Then *you* stay on the bus," she snapped. "I have a job to do, same as you."

"Can I stay on the bus?" Brian whispered.

"You know she's right, Dec," Erik said quietly. They all turned to look at him. "We're all going to have to make a run for it anyway. At least they don't know I'm Soren's replacement yet," he smiled wryly. "After the show I might need Declan to carry me out, *Bodyguard*-style."

Brian patted their new guitarist on the back while they all laughed. Good. They needed to get rid of that tension. But that didn't change the way he felt.

"Fuck," Declan muttered. He hated being wrong, mostly because it meant he had to freaking admit it. That had been one of Uncle Jim's rules and it was a good one. It just annoyed him this time. He gave Molly a stern look. "Fine. You're right, I can't keep you on the damn bus. But you are staying close to me, you understand? Those people out there…"

"They look crazy," Molly said.

There were warring chants now. "Declan!" "Soren!" It was freaking ridiculous.

"They're wound up," Declan replied. "It can happen. I'm more worried about the lack of security."

And then, just to make sure she understood he was serious, he put his arm around her and pulled her close. He really didn't give a fuck about being half hard, even if they had to run for it. Molly was tense for a second, still pissed at him probably, but then she relaxed into it, warm and soft and so damn female. Declan couldn't argue with that; it felt good to touch her in any way at all. Felt right. He could feel her excitement, her fear, and it brought out that caveman part of him all over again. He had to stop himself from picking her up. What had Erik called it?

"You guys ready?" Davey asked. Security guards had lined a the start of a path from the bus to the performer's entrance at the back.

"You sure you won't let me carry you *Bodyguard*-style?" Declan asked.

Molly elbowed him playfully in the ribs. He was forgiven.

"And give those women a reason to hate me? You must be out of your mind," she said.

The doors opened, and the sound of thousands of screaming fans crashed into them like a flying brick wall.

"Let's *go!*" Davey shouted, and they all rushed out of the bus, toward the line of frightened security guys waving them on in desperation. Declan pushed his way out and then waited for Molly, putting his arm around her again, ignoring the screams.

It was fucking *nuts*.

"Declan, I need you!"

"I wanna have your baby, Declan!"

"Fucking Savage Heart *forever!*"

Molly was ducking into his side under the pressure of the crowd, just the shouting, the craziness of it, the arms reaching for them as they made their way to the door in a scrum of stressed out security guys. Nothing could prepare someone for a fan gauntlet like this, for the way grown adults went crazy in groups. She was tense as all hell, and he looked down to see if she was ok, or terrified, or what, but instead he saw that she was riding the adrenaline just like he was. Looked ready to take the world on, just like he was.

Fuck yes, that is a woman, he thought.

Couldn't tear his eyes away from her face. Which was how he missed it. He only saw Molly's expression: sudden alarm, fear, maybe.

Declan turned just in time to see a bleached blonde woman, heavy black mascara streaming from her crying, crazy eyes, hoisting a bucket over her head as she screamed, "*Murderer!*"

Declan didn't think, he just reacted. He pulled Molly into his arms and hunched over her, spinning them both around so his back faced the psycho, and then he felt it hit his back.

Liquid.

Paint.

Red freaking paint. That was all. It exploded around him from the impact, splattering the security guards and the already riled up crowd, the shock of it igniting the tension and sending the place into pandemonium. The crowd erupted and surged forward, a security guard stumbled and fell, Gage was knocked into Molly. People were going down left and right, swallowed up by the tide of people, trampled under foot. Panicking.

He heard the crazy lady scream, "Soren! Where is Soren? What did you do to Soren?"

But Declan was already running, Molly in his arms, the band following behind him, security going nuts.

chapter 9

Molly still couldn't believe it. Not a drop of red paint on her.

Declan, on the other hand...

"Where the *fuck* is the head of security for this shithole?" he roared.

He was pacing around the dressing room where they'd been herded while the security guys dealt with what was hopefully *not* a full-blown riot outside. Dec clearly hated being cooped up, not being able to do anything. He'd taken off his ruined shirt and put his head under a faucet, though he hadn't seemed to notice that his lower half was still covered in red paint.

Brian, on the other hand, definitely had. He'd been laughing nonstop. "Dude, you have to try to lighten up or we'll all lose it. Or you could stay like that, with the red coating, for comic relief. I'm good with either."

Declan seethed, but they could all see that Brian

was right. That had been *scary*. So close to truly out of control, so obviously dangerous. Molly never would have guessed something like that could happen at a rock concert. They were all basically waiting to hear that no one had been hurt. No one was talking about when they would go on, or what kind of show it was going to be now. If anyone had been trampled, there wouldn't even be a show.

Declan looked over at her for about the millionth time. "You sure you're ok?" he asked again.

Molly cleared her throat. "I'm fine, honestly."

And she was fine because he really had carried her through an actual raving mob. Just covered her body with his, scooped her up like nothing at all, and charged ahead. She could still feel his iron arms around her, his rock hard chest pressed against her, his breath hot on her neck as she'd clung to him. Molly didn't normally let her physical size make her feel weak or incapable, but she also didn't normally hang out in riots.

For a moment, she had been truly scared, knowing she had no way to protect herself if the crowd surged her way. She'd felt completely vulnerable.

And then Declan had been there.

That didn't help with her little self-control problem.

"Hey, buddy, how about a pre-show special, huh?" Brian said, sitting up and clapping his hands together. "Who's up for a pre-show special? Work that tension out."

"Pre-show special?" Molly asked, then immediately regretted it. If she'd thought about it for, like, thirty seconds, she would have figured it out.

Instead she got to watch Gage look ashamed while he grumbled, "You fucking horndog. There's a lady present."

Molly laughed out loud at that. "What about the last two days has made you boys think I'm that kind of lady? I don't care what you do. I'm here to observe, remember? Brian, go get some."

Brian grinned at her, and she hoped she'd pulled it off. It was a little bit of bravado. The truth was that she really, really did not want to think about whether Declan was about to go get himself some pre-show special pussy from some random groupie. Molly already felt queasy at the suggestion.

"C'mon, Dec, you up for it?"

Molly pretended not to watch Declan, but in the next few seconds a freaking UFO could have landed right next to her and she wouldn't have noticed. Declan was still pacing, still obviously pissed off, still lost in thought. Then he snapped to, like Brian's words had just penetrated his brain, stopped, and looked at Brian like he was stupid.

"No," Declan said coldly.

Molly turned away to hide her relief.

"Well, fuck this," Brian said, standing up. "I need to work off the fear of death. I'll catch you guys in twenty."

"More like five," Erik said, sending Gage into a fit of laughter. Brian flipped them off as he left, but it had helped, at least a little bit.

They were all still a little tense.

"Where's Davey?" Declan demanded, wiping

the sweat off of his face.

"On the phone with the label about security," Gage said. "Dude, serious question. Are we going on? I don't want this to turn into a stampede, like freaking Altamount or something. I'd rather we sent everybody home than got anyone killed, man."

"No shit," Declan said. He stood there, drawing all eyes to him just by being. The man was just a presence, covered in red paint, in jeans and nothing else. He would have been a presence even in a freaking clown suit. Definitely when naked, Molly was sure of that. It was just hard to look away, the way he gathered energy around him, the way it seemed like a storm was building around his mood. Declan took a deep breath and seemed to come to a decision. "Ok. You guys stay here, wait for Davey. I'm going to fix this. Molly," he said, giving her that *look*, that commanding, won't-take-no-for-an-answer look, "Come with me."

And he held out his hand.

It was a bizarre sight, the famous rock star, huge, muscled, bare chested and still covered in blood red paint, holding out his hand for *her*. How was he going to "fix" this? How could anyone? And what could he possibly need her for to do it?

"*Now*," he said, and she started. Then his face softened a little. "We're leaving now, Molly. Move."

She was already walking toward him.

"Where are we going?" she asked.

"I'm going to deal with the crowd," Declan said, pulling her toward the door. "And you're coming because I'm not letting you out of my goddamn sight."

The backstage area was like a warren of interconnecting hallways and offices, totally disorganized, and half in a panic because of what was going on in the concert hall and parking lot. There were interns and PAs and even suits flying around on walkie-talkies and cellphones, everyone trying to figure out when the cops would arrive en masse and why the hell they weren't there already. Declan carved a path through them all with that grim expression on his face and Molly was, at this point, along for the ride.

Rationally, she knew this was fantastic for her book.

But mostly she was thinking about what he'd said: he wasn't letting her out of his sight. Did he feel guilty? He'd wanted to leave her on the bus. No telling what would have happened then, but he wasn't responsible for this situation, not in any real way. But he acted like a man who had the weight of the world on his shoulders. Like it was very much his responsibility to fix it.

"Declan, what are you doing?" Molly asked, tugging on his hand.

"Looking for the head of security, the promoter, fucking *someone* who can get me on that stage in front of that crowd with a live mic," he said.

"No, that's not what I meant," she said, stopping in her tracks. He looked back at her, astonished. "I meant why is this your job? What the hell do you think you're going to do to prevent a *riot*?"

Declan actually looked confused for a second.

And then a different expression came on his face, one she was beginning to recognize, the same expression he'd had after the show at Volare, the one he wore when he gave her orders she couldn't refuse.

"It's my job to fix it because I can," he said. Then he smiled at her, the first time she'd seen him smile since they'd arrived. "You'll see. Eventually."

Molly shivered. Somehow she didn't think he was just talking about whatever it was he was about to do.

She was still lost in that line of thought, her body pulling her closer to him, her mind lingering on the memory of his touch, when Declan's eyes narrowed on something behind her.

"Bobby!" he bellowed. "Get the fuck over here and tell me what's happening!"

Startled, Molly turned to find Bobby, a skinny guy wearing a cheap suit, looking about as scared as a grown man could be. He had a phone *and* a walkie-talkie, and both of them were making a lot of noise.

"The police are on their way, Declan," Bobby said. "This is entirely my fault in promoting this event, and I just want to apologize. I failed to take into account—"

"Jesus Christ, Bobby, I don't want to hear that right now. Was anyone hurt?"

Bobby shook his head, his expression still tense. "I think we got lucky there. But they haven't really calmed down, and now the crowd in the hall is even worse, with the rumors and everything. Like a fucking tinderbox. Don't worry, though, we've doubled security for backstage, nothing is getting through, I promise you."

Declan glowered. "You took security away from the fans out there?"

"Well, we had to make sure—"

"What the hell is wrong with you? You know what, fuck it, just make sure there's a wired mic out there and a spotlight in two minutes."

"What?"

"Two fucking minutes, Bobby! Do it!"

Molly watched it all happen in disbelief. He was insane. She could hear the crowd out there, now, screaming, roaring, like a natural disaster just waiting to happen. He was going to get up on stage in front of that? By himself?

"Declan," she said.

When he looked down at her, for the first time, she didn't see Declan Donovan of Savage Heart. She just saw Declan. A man who was...she didn't know. *Something* to her, already, even if she didn't know what, exactly. A man who'd seen through her bullshit and knew things about her no one else knew, even though he'd only known her a few days. A man she definitely did not want to see hurt.

"Please don't do this," she said. He was still holding her hand. She clutched at it now with both of hers.

Declan Donovan blinked.

And then he smiled.

"Molly, it's gonna be fine," he said. "Trust me."

And then Bobby was back with the mic, and Declan told him to go get the rest of the band ready to be on in two minutes flat. He pulled her down the hall to the point where the only thing that separated them from the crowd was a heavy black curtain, and stopped.

And then Declan Donovan threaded his hand through her hair, pulled her tight against the length of him, and kissed her.

chapter 10

The heat of him spread through out her body, from her lips to her tongue, down her chest and through her core, lighting fuses along the way. She lost herself in that kiss. Forgot herself. Let the warmth of his body cover hers until she didn't care about all the reasons this wasn't supposed to happen, or what he was about to do, or anything other than the feel of him on her.

It was the safest she'd ever felt.

And then the hungriest. She kissed him back and felt that rumble in his chest, felt her own hips move for him, felt her arms wrap around his neck. She was out of her mind with desire, out of control completely. It was no longer safe. No longer anything even approaching safe. Declan growled into her mouth, slid a hand down her side, squeezed her ass and pulled away.

"You wait right fucking here," he said.

Molly looked at him, short of breath, mouth

open. No words came.

And then he stepped through the curtain, onto the stage.

The spotlight clicked on and there was a moment of silence, actual silence, when it was just Declan on the stage, striding toward the front with a mic in his hand, still covered in red paint, like all of this made sense to him. And then the screech of the crowd was deafening.

"Quiet!" Declan roared.

They grew quiet.

They actually did.

It was Molly's turn to blink. That thing he did, the way he gave an order that made her obey without even thinking? He'd just done it to thousands of crazy fans at once. And he'd known. He'd walked out there knowing they would just...obey.

"We came here to give you the best you've ever had," he shouted. "But one person gets hurt, one fucking person, and we are *done*. I am not having that shit, Springfield. If you want the best show you've ever had, let me *hear it!*"

The sound nearly knocked Molly off her feet.

Declan grinned. "If you want to be *Savaged*, let me fucking hear it!"

Molly actually covered her ears. She kind of couldn't believe his stage presence. Except that she could, because she felt it, too, she felt it every time she was near the man; he could get her to do things she'd never, ever do. Things she wanted, but things she knew she shouldn't dare do. He could get her to sign a contract saying she'd be on birth control and had no STDs. He could get her to tell him things she'd never told anyone else. He could get her to give in to a kiss she knew would only get her hurt in the end.

And now, right in front of her, was the evidence that it wasn't just her. He could do that to anybody.

It wasn't personal. She had to remember that. She couldn't think it was about her.

That kiss...

"'Scuse me, doll, sorry, coming through," Brian said as he rushed past her, grabbing his bass from the hand of an outstretched roadie with one hand and buttoning his pants with the other. Gage and Erik weren't far behind, and suddenly there were people swarming the stage, setting up barebones equipment, making it all work. A NASCAR pit had nothing on these people.

"Sound check? Who needs a fucking sound check? Let's *go!*" Brian shouted as he ran out on stage to more cheers.

In about a minute, they were set. Erik hit the opening chord of "Ember" and the whole place erupted.

She could see Declan smiling that intoxicating smile. He already had the crowd in the palm of his hand. And then he let loose with that panty-quaking yell and Molly suddenly knew—*knew*—that if she stayed there and watched this, she would be a goner. She just wasn't strong enough to watch Declan Donovan and protect herself at the same time. No one had that kind of self-control. And when she lost control, that was when bad things happened.

"Fuck me," she said.

And then she turned around and walked back

inside to do her job.

***

It turned out that during the first couple of songs of a Savage Heart show was not the greatest time to try to find people to talk to about Savage Heart. Everyone was watching the show. Understandably. Even the techies and stagehands, the people who made everything work, in between doing all the things they had to do, they were just as enthralled as any fan.

Molly couldn't risk it.

It felt physically *painful* to turn away, and she did it anyway.

No way this is good for me.

So she did the only sane thing: She called Adra.

Or she would have called Adra, except that when she looked at her phone, she saw a text from an unknown number.

UNKNOWN: "I'm fine, just busy! – Lydia"

There were about a million things wrong with that. First, Lydia usually signed her messages "Lady," or "bug," because Molly had called her Ladybug for years, even when it had infuriated a much smaller Lydia. It wasn't unheard of for her to use her actual name, but it sounded…weird. Stressed. Not like a casual, fun kind of conversation. Second, an unknown number?

None of that was good.

But there was no answer when Molly called that number, and no voicemail. Lydia still hadn't checked in on Facebook, either, and she wasn't in any of her friends' updates or anything.

Really not good.

And in a weird, sick, terrible, awful way, Molly was almost glad of the distraction, because it brought her back down to Earth. She couldn't allow herself to think that anything was really wrong with Lydia—that was just a no man's land, where her brain shut down completely; she couldn't conceive of anything really happening to her baby sister—but she did really need something to think about other than that kiss. Worrying about her sister was the equivalent of ten thousand cold showers.

So by the time a couple of fans came stumbling backstage, Molly was all ready to put on her professional pants and get down to work. Her preliminary interviews with the guys had been total duds in terms of information. They were all too wary of the whole enterprise and seemed kind of relieved that she knew it was all an elaborate lie because it meant they could just refuse to answer. At least she'd started to develop a rapport with the guys, the kind of thing she needed to paint a portrait of the band. But for the real dirt? She was going to need to talk to the fans.

"'S not the same without him, is all," the male half of the couple mumbled, and helped himself to some of the catering. He was wearing tight black jeans, a ratty old Savage Heart shirt, and a chain belt. He had a Savage Heart tattoo on his arm, and he had his hair dyed blond and messed into chunky, spiky shapes in obvious imitation of the way Soren wore it. Or used to.

His girlfriend, hair dyed jet black, and in a torn up t-shirt meant to show off more than it concealed, didn't seem particularly interested in what he had to say.

"You're sure it's ok, right? They're not gonna be pissed off and kick us out? Because you promised I could meet them," she said.

""S fine. They know me from way back."

These two were perfect.

Now how to get them to talk?

"Did you used to play with them?" Molly asked suddenly. Her voice was loud, startling, and the guy was a little drunk. He looked up at her with alarm, and then, slowly, the flattery sunk in.

"Not, like, officially," he said, all smiles. "You know, just every once in a while, jamming. I'm Ian. This is Sierra. You here with the guys?"

Molly smiled right back. "Yup. I'm, like, their official biographer, I'd guess you'd call it."

"Oh shit, that's so cool!" Sierra sounded suddenly interested. "You spend a lot of time with them?"

"Not as much as I'd like."

"What's Brian like?" she asked. "Is he as funny as he is in interviews? I bet he is. Ian's been promising me I'd get to meet him for like seven months now."

The woman had an unattractive pout. Molly decided there was something she didn't quite like about her. Maybe it was the way Ian looked immediately anxious when Sierra started asking about members of the band.

"Well, there *have* been some difficulties the last six months..." Molly said.

"Fucking tell me about it," Ian moaned. "I still can't believe it. No disrespect to anyone, but it's not Savage Heart without Soren. It's a fucking tragedy, a band like this breaking up. It's a once in a generation band, getting together genius like that, and now it's just...gone."

"Over some stupid bitch," Sierra added.

Molly grabbed at the opening. "Which bitch?"

"No, it wasn't like that," he said, while Sierra rolled her eyes. Molly had to pretend that Sierra didn't grate on her last nerve, but Ian looked back at his girlfriend, an understanding smile on his face. Could he really be that into her? Stranger things had happened, that was for sure, and Molly definitely wasn't one to judge, given her own dating history. "Babe, seriously, I was there. Declan didn't care."

"Whatever, she was a slut."

"Who?" Molly asked again. She was practically on the tips of her toes.

"Bethany," Ian said, shaking his head. "She's a nice person, Sierra. And Declan and Soren are like brothers. They grew up together, even lived with each other for a while when they were kids. Declan didn't give a shit when Bethany started dating Soren, believe me. He was happy for 'em."

Bethany. Molly had a name to go on. She had *something*. She could work with this.

"Still a slut," Sierra said, and crossed her arms.

Molly tensed. Some women loved to use that word. Some men, too. Molly had always hated it, but now she couldn't hear it without hearing the last time it had been hurled at her, and now this was twice in a row, like Sierra was really invested in the whole thing, instead of just...being catty. Molly wondered if Sierra had any idea how much damage that kind of casual cruelty could do. Molly was more than familiar herself.

Ian looked thoughtful. "I guess Bethany's not touring with them this time, huh?"

"I don't think so," Molly said carefully.

"Too bad. Haven't seen her in a while."

Sierra's eyes flashed some jealous crazy, and she grabbed a hold of Ian's arm. "Baby, take me to watch the show so we can be there when they get done. I want to meet Brian right away."

Ian smiled sweetly at Molly and waved as Sierra dragged him off. That boy was obviously smitten, the poor bastard, and Molly knew all about that feeling of helplessness. That's why she was avoiding the stage. She knew better now.

Molly spent the rest of the show tucked away in a little corner on the floor, hidden behind an unused amp, writing out notes on her phone. Not the easiest way to write, but she was lost in it anyway. It was just the subject matter. She could think and write about this band—about Declan—for ages without coming up for air, the material was just so rich, so fascinating. Molly smiled, thinking about how much Lydia would love this when she read it—telling Lydia stories at night, when things were bad with their parents, was how Molly had gotten started writing. There was nothing more natural to her than this. She didn't even notice when the music stopped.

Or even, really, when people started trickling into the backstage area.

She didn't notice much until there were a giant

pair of red-splattered boots right in front of her.

Declan stood over her—towered over her—his chest gleaming with sweat, his abs contracting with every heavy breath, his eyes…pissed off. He reached down to tilt her chin up, his fingers threading through her hair again, bringing her body right back to that ravaging kiss, and said, "Where were you?"

chapter 11

Declan was riled up with nowhere to let it out. She hadn't bothered to stick around. Never mind that he hated the idea of her walking around in a venue that obviously wasn't one hundred percent safe. He'd told her to stay right there and she'd what? Wandered off to take a fucking nap?

He seethed, and reminded himself that Molly Ward wasn't his sub. Not yet. He couldn't discipline her in the way he wanted, but that didn't mean he didn't deserve basic common courtesy. He'd carried her through a mob, for chrissakes, and she'd walked off. He'd kissed her, yeah, but she was the one who'd made it smolder. She was the one who'd made it the best show it could have been.

And now she was there, kneeling at his feet, taking that naturally submissive position, and he didn't know if he wanted to kiss her or throw her over his knee.

"Do you know what I would do to you?" he asked her. "What I would do if you didn't have this stupid idea that we can't fuck? That you can't be my sub?"

He saw the flush come over her, and knew she was feeling just what he was feeling at that moment, the charge he felt from his skin on hers. Just the tiniest touch, and he was fucked. Her soft hair around his fingers, her face upturned toward his...

"Please don't tell me," she whispered. "You know this is...already difficult, for me."

Molly didn't move except to put a hand on his, the one that held her by the back of the head. She didn't try to dislodge his hand, didn't tell him to fuck off. Just looked right back into his eyes.

Oh Good Lord.

"Get up," he said. She did. He bent down quickly and lifted her onto the unused amp so she was at eye level with him and pinned her there between his arms.

"Tell me why you left," he said.

"No," she said right back.

Declan grinned in spite of himself and dug his fingers into the edge of the amp a little bit more, feeling the muscles in his arms flex. He would have a lot to work off later.

He said, "You know I'm going to get it out of you."

He loved how she looked when she was being stubborn. She tucked her hair behind her ear— *God*—and said, "I needed to write."

"Bullshit."

"It is *not* bullshit," she said hotly. "I had a job to

do, just like you did your job when you went out there and…"

Molly faltered, her eyes going soft. He guessed she was talking about how he'd dominated that crowd. Declan had gone out there, high on her kiss, and used her to get his stage mojo back, just like he had at Volare. It worked like a freaking charm. More than that, he was himself again. Dom and performer, all in one. It had saved the show, kept people from getting hurt.

So why did she look upset thinking about that?

"You were just doing your job," Molly finally said, looking down.

"Look at me," he ordered. She did. Immediately. "You helped me do my job."

"What?" she said.

Declan cocked his head to the side. "Don't pull that innocent crap. That kiss."

Weakly, she said, "You kissed me."

"And you made it count," he said, moving his hands to the tops of her thighs and leaning in again, the way he had when she'd been on his bed, so freaking close. He could not get close enough to this woman no matter what he did. He contented himself with looking deep into those big brown eyes and said, "And you fucking know it."

He could smell her.

She put a hand on his chest, lightly, as if to push him away. She didn't. Instead he felt the pinch of her nails as she dug into him.

"Those were extraordinary circumstances," she said.

He shook his head, not bothering to hide his smile. "You doubled down."

"Extraordinary circumstances!"

This close to her, Declan's senses got sharper, clearer. Some part of him had the presence of mind to wonder what the fuck he was doing—was this another mistake? Another danger, something he'd fuck up, someone who'd turn out to be broken in just the ways he couldn't fix? He'd made rules for himself, too, after Bethany, rules he'd meant to keep. But this wasn't that. This wasn't love; this wasn't emotion. This was pure, raw, physical connection, the kind that brought the release they both so obviously needed.

"I need you in the fucking audience," he rasped.

"What?"

"I need you watching in order to do *my* job. And you need to watch to do your job. You can't write a book about Savage Heart if you hide in a corner while we're being Savage Heart."

"I have to watch?" Molly said, smiling. "Is that a new rule?"

"Fuck yes it's a new rule."

That smile just got wider. She said, "What new rule do I get?"

"You don't get any more rules," Declan grumbled, squeezing her thighs. His hands were big enough to span them, get his thumbs someplace interesting.

She made a tiny little sound.

Declan ran his hands up to her hips, her waist, and pulled her a little closer. His lips brushed her temple, her forehead. He let them linger over her earlobe, the line of her jaw.

So. Close.

She trembled under his touch. Her nails dug

into him a little more.

Finally, she spoke.

"Oh God," she said. "Don't."

"Why not?"

"You know why not. I have reasons..."

"They're bad reasons, and you know it," he whispered. "I can show you who you are."

Then he looked down and saw her close her eyes, her face screwed up with conflicting emotions. He could *smell* how turned on she was, but it still wasn't time yet. This wasn't right. She needed to come at him full throttle.

So he kissed on her on the forehead and said, "When you're ready."

Molly buried her face in his chest and inhaled, her fingers clawing at him. She was probably just overwhelmed, but he held her, just because. His dick hated him.

His dick hated the guy who came crashing into their little moment even more. The guy came stomping into their little hidden nook like a teenager, thrashing and hitting the walls, ripping at his hair, and Declan first thought, *Not another psycho*. He put himself between the new guy and Molly until he realized the guy was crying.

And that he knew him.

"Ian?" Declan asked.

"Oh Jesus," Ian said, looking surprised and embarrassed, his cheeks still wet with tears. Dude always got red-faced when he cried. "I'm sorry, man, I didn't mean to—"

"What happened, Ian?" Declan demanded. Ian was a good dude. Ian had hung out with them before, Ian had jammed with them, Ian had been one of the only guys who Soren had actually liked and trusted. He'd said that Ian was really in it for the music, didn't have a starfucking bone in his body, wouldn't know how to do it if someone drew him a diagram.

"You don't want to hear about it, man," Ian said miserably. He wiped his nose on the back of his hand.

"Um, is it Sierra?" Molly said in a tiny voice.

Declan turned around. What the hell? Who was Sierra? And how did Molly know about...whatever the hell was going on?

"She went off to fuck Brian," Ian wailed. "First thing, just went right up to him. He didn't even see me; I was talking to Gage. I turn around and they're walking away, and she's already got her hand down his pants!"

"Who the hell is Sierra?" Declan asked. He was beyond confused.

"Declan," Molly said, shaking her head. "Sierra is—was—his girlfriend. Of seven months, right, Ian?"

"Almost eight," he sniffled. "I knew she had a thing for Brian, you know, she was a freaking fan. Whatever, I get it. But I thought..."

"You thought it was the real deal," Molly said. The sympathy in her eyes nearly killed Declan, and he wasn't even the guy who'd gotten his heart broken.

Ian leaned back against the wall and let himself sink slowly down to the floor. Before he'd looked anguished, angry, upset. Now he just looked depressed.

"She was just using me the whole time, wasn't

she?" he said. He sounded out of it. "She knew I knew you guys from back before you hit. She asked me the whole time, 'When are you gonna get me backstage? When am I gonna get to meet Savage Heart?'"

Declan hated this. He didn't expect anyone to have much sympathy for guys like him, famous guys who could pull almost any woman they wanted, even though it made it impossible to trust anyone. But the worst part was shit like this. Because sometimes you wanted to get laid, and things like this happened. He knew Brian had no fucking clue he was doing Ian's girlfriend right now. But that didn't make it any easier for Ian.

"All right, this isn't happening," Declan announced. He grabbed Ian under the arms and hauled him to a standing position. "Any woman who would do that to you isn't worth it, Ian. Yeah, I know that doesn't make it feel better," he said. "So instead I'm taking you out. Right now."

"What?"

"C'mon, we'll get you cleaned up, then we'll get you drunk."

"Declan," Molly whispered. "Rehab."

Oh shit. Rock stars fresh out rehab probably weren't supposed to go on bar crawls with buddies on the rebound.

Damn.

He stared at her, the girl trying to dig into all his secrets, the one who was supposed to expose him, giving him that conspiratorial little grin.

She just kept getting better and better.

"Ok, Ian, what do you want to do?" Declan asked. No matter what, he was gonna take this guy out and give him something else to talk about besides losing his girlfriend to a groupie fuck.

Ian thought about it for a moment. "Waffles," he said.

~ * ~ * ~

So they had a party at the waffle place.

As soon as Ian started to look a little better, even laugh a little bit, Declan stole his phone and started texting everyone he could think of. Soon the place was full of Ian's friends and acquaintances, all of them excited to be partying with Ian and his friend Declan Donovan. All the employees at the waffle house got in on it, too, and Declan bought midnight breakfast for everyone.

People brought booze, but nobody cared. Declan told her he wasn't going to begrudge Ian a breakup hangover for the sake of bullshit rumors.

And the whole time, Molly kept thinking, *This looks something like a guy you can trust.*

A guy who went out of his way to help out some poor dude who'd been dumped, a guy who used his fame and wealth to make that poor dude feel better, even when he was exhausted after a show, even when Molly knew she'd driven him crazy. He'd driven her crazy, too. She could still remember how hard his dick had felt through his jeans when he'd pinned her up against that amp.

You'll never get what you want from sex if you don't trust anyone to give it to you.

Declan had picked her up and carried her through an angry mob. He'd stopped, said "when you're ready," like he was so damn certain.

NO, these are crazy thoughts. He was still Declan Donovan, rock star. He didn't belong to her, and never would. He belonged to everyone, the way she'd seen him, on stage.

But did she have to trust him with her heart?

Why not her body?

Instantly she felt heat pooling between her legs. Was that possible, though? He'd said he could show her who she was. Wasn't that the same as trusting him with her heart? Letting him in like that, to help her discover...

Molly's spidey sense went off, and she looked around. And then she frowned. A redhead and her brunette friend were, to put it delicately, trying to drape themselves over Declan. It grossed Molly out, and she frowned. She wasn't one of those women who got catty for no reason. Maybe it was the way they were throwing themselves at him with no sense of whether he seemed to be into it. Maybe it was because the brunette had brought her child to this shindig and Molly was judging the crap out of her, fairly or unfairly, or maybe it was the way seeing children always made her a little bit sad. But she smiled to see him disentangle himself, and then went right back to worrying.

Oh man, she was tired.

"Why so sad, beautiful?" Declan asked, slipping into her booth so that she was pleasantly squeezed between him and the wall. There were worse places to be in the world.

"Not sad," she said, wondering if he knew she was lying a little bit. "Thoughtful."

He seemed to watch her. Doing his own thinking. She wished he wouldn't press on her being sad, not tonight, and in a second he seemed to get it.

"You do a lot of thinking," he agreed, and ran his finger through the remaining syrup on her plate. "But since you're too chicken to ask me any questions so far—"

"Hey!" she said, pulling her plate back. "I'm not chicken. And no syrup for men who call me chicken."

He smiled delectably and licked the syrup off of his finger. God.

"I've got a question for you. Who is it you're always trying to call?" he asked.

That threw her for a loop. The only person she was obsessive about contacting was Lydia, but she hadn't known he'd noticed that. What was she supposed to say? Any explanation of why she was so worried would involve telling him about her past. Molly was not prepared to go there right now.

"Too tough for you right now, huh? Chicken," Declan said, pulling the plate back in front of him meaningfully. "I've got an alternative question. How come you're scared to interview me?"

"Who says I'm scared? Maybe I'm just doing research," she said.

"You've interviewed everyone else and avoided it with me," he said, amused. "I think you do want me to tell you what I'd do to you for lying to me if you were my sub."

Yes.

"No, I don't. Look, questions for the other guys are easy," Molly said quickly. "Questions for you are hard."

"Chicken."

And Declan grabbed her hand and pulled her up and out of the booth. That man had become awfully familiar with manhandling her, and Molly just did not have it in her to tell him to stop. She enjoyed it too damn much.

The parking lot was unseasonably cold, and Molly realized they had no ride. They'd come here in Ian's car—Declan had left instructions for Sierra to get a ride home—and now it was just the two of them, out in a parking lot, while a rocking party raged on in the waffle house.

"What are we doing out here?" she asked.

"That's your question?" he teased. "I called Davey. We're waiting for the bus. I'm freaking exhausted, and we have to make time on the road tomorrow. Hey, you cold?"

She was shivering, and not in a good way this time. Her usual shorts and tank top was not cutting it. Declan didn't wait for her to answer, but instead stood behind her and wrapped his arms around her. The contact alone… She didn't know if she was better or worse off, feeling warm and wanting him all at the same time. She sighed and leaned her head back into his chest.

"Why do you keep turning down groupies?" she asked. "Did you know I was watching you?"

Yeah, pretend that's all about the book, Ward.

"No, I didn't," he said, and she could *hear* him smiling. Like he'd won something. "I used to bag all of them. Decided to stop about six months ago. That's a big question, though, Mol. You ready to give me a big answer in return?"

Molly swallowed. In the span of less than twenty-four hours, she had been convinced she was going to die, she'd been saved by the one man who could make her feel...well, the way she felt right now, in his arms, she'd been kissed, she'd partied with a rock star, and now she was facing some difficult truths about herself and what she wanted.

"Maybe we'll save that for your first interview," she said. "But what Brian did tonight, even not knowing... Do you think you've ever done that?"

Declan was quiet. He squeezed Molly a little tighter, and she felt his chin on the top of her head. When he spoke, he sounded different. Pensive. Humbled.

"I must have," he said. "Back when I still... Yeah. But I don't think it's that different from normal people, you know? Maybe just with the volume turned up. People come in and out of each other's lives all the time and have no idea of the damage they do, whether they mean it or not."

Molly turned in his arms, needing to see his face, to confirm the gut feeling she got about what he'd just said. And even more, to see whether not Declan Donovan, the guy who kept secrets, would let her see what he was feeling.

He did. He didn't tell her more, but he let her see that, whatever it was, it hurt him. The light was bad out there in the parking lot, but he didn't shy away, and she could see the pain in his eyes. That there was some wound there, something that wouldn't heal, something that he carried with him. Was it Bethany? Was that what had happened six months ago in Philly?

But Ian had said that Declan hadn't cared when Bethany started to date Soren. There had to be something more. Something deeper…

"Declan…"

"The bus is here," he said gently. How had she not noticed a freaking tour bus drive into the parking lot? Molly swore. She could actually lose time with Declan. "You can interview me tomorrow. Tonight let's just watch *This is Spinal Tap* and go to sleep."

She raised an eyebrow.

"You have your own bunk," he said, tightening his arms around her with a smile. "You come near my bed, and you won't be doing any sleeping."

A few things happened after that. After coming aboard to find Brian shame-faced and sorry, and everyone so welcoming that it felt like a family already, after all they'd all been through together, Molly noticed when Declan suddenly stressed out and reached for his phone. The lines didn't leave his face until he'd checked it and evidently saw what he needed to see, and she realized that this was why he'd noticed her stress about getting in touch with her sister. There was someone Declan worried about, too.

And then while watching the movie, Molly fell fast asleep on Declan's chest, waking only when he kissed her forehead, picked her up, and carried her to her bunk.

chapter 12

Molly dreamed of Declan.

She was backstage, waiting for him, wondering when he would be done with the show, if he would be with someone else. So sure he would rather be with his fans, with all those other women, that nothing she felt with him could be real; he wouldn't ever choose her. But then he surprised her. She didn't know how, but she knew it was him suddenly standing behind her.

It was *his* hand on the small of her back.

His hand that went farther now, no longer gentle, groping her ass, pushing between her legs...

His hand that held her still, his hand that reached around, found her breast...

She moaned, and then they were back in the office at Volare, and she turned to face him and her clothes were gone. Just...gone. She didn't know how, but he had done it. He'd taken them. She heard that growl, and then he clasped his hands around her wrists, forcing them down to her sides, baring her to him, naked. Powerless. His.

She had that thought, that exact thought: *He can do whatever he wants with me.* And it spread through her body like wildfire, and she suddenly wished he would...

And then he spun her around and he was bending her roughly over that desk, telling her, "You're mine," her whole body thrilling to the words, her breasts pushed into the desk where she'd signed his contract, his hand thrust between her legs, spreading them, his hand on the back of her neck, holding her there...

When he entered her, she came so hard that she woke herself up, panting, covered in sweat.

And totally disoriented.

She had actually come in a dream. Just from freaking dreaming about him. She was still...oh God, still with the aftershocks.

What the hell was that?

Molly lay there, wide-eyed, tangled up in sheets, wishing to God she had a real room with a real door, and wondering what the hell all of that meant. She'd always had a thing for rough sex, for being...well, controlled. Dominated, ravaged, whatever. She'd always had fantasies, *tons* of fantasies, my God, fantasies so much kinkier than that dream, but never about anyone she actually *knew*. Never something potentially real. But that? That was definitely Declan. In fact, it hadn't even been a particularly kinky dream; it was the fact that it *was* Declan that made it so hot.

The idea of Declan owning her. Having total control over her body. Taking her? Oh God, yes please.

She knew she had to stop thinking about it, or she'd need another orgasm, and she had never found it easy to be quiet once she got going. But not thinking about it was practically impossible. This, right here, in this little afterglow, thinking about Declan dominating her, this was the only relief Molly got. She hadn't even realized how much she needed a break until right now. Outside her little cocoon of a bunk, wrapped up in dreams of Declan, there was the real world, with all those real responsibilities, with all the pressure of getting it right or having everything collapse around her. Her plans for the future, getting out of Pleasant Valley Park, getting Lydia out. But in here, she could give it all up to Declan. Dream Declan, anyway.

Molly groaned. It was clearly time to start being responsible again. And she was clearly screwing herself over with these kinds of thoughts.

And she had very nearly had gotten a hold of herself by the time she knocked on Declan's door, hoping to use his shower—until he answered the door in nothing but boxer briefs.

"First interview in ten?" He yawned, leaning against the narrow doorframe and rubbing his face. He was so big he filled the entire doorway, to the point where it looked like a miniature door for hobbits or something. The effect was just a wall of tanned, tatted muscle, moving slightly under his skin as he stretched, reminding her of a wild animal, something that was about to pounce.

Molly gulped.

"Yeah, sounds good," she said. "Mind if I use

your shower again?" She hated using the guys' shower.

Declan ran a hand over his head and looked at her, wide-awake now. He looked at *all* of her.

"Be my guest," he said slowly.

She could *feel* his voice on her body. Oh, God. Oh God, oh God, oh God.

Molly took a very, very cold shower. By the time she was cooled off — at least momentarily — the bus had stopped for a minute and someone had gone and gotten breakfast sandwiches. She smelled them as soon as she stepped out of Declan's room, and was hit with hunger pangs. She was ravenous. Sex dreams were kind of a workout.

Molly smiled a little bit to herself as she made her way to the booth at the front of the bus. There was something kind of fun about knowing she'd gotten off, however unintentionally, while everybody else slept. Like she'd gotten away with something.

Except that maybe she hadn't.

Gage seemed on the verge of laughing. Brian looked at her with something like open awe and jumped up to get her a breakfast sandwich from the communal bag in the middle of the table, which was suspiciously unnecessary. Erik was red-faced and silent, chewing furiously on his bacon, egg, and cheese.

And Declan…no one should be able to smolder this early in the day. Or look at her like…what, was he mad? No, that was ridiculous. But there was something going on. That tiny muscle on his jaw bulged out and his eyes were glaring at her, burning holes in her shirt. If he kept doing that, she was going to be in trouble all over again. She'd had more time to think about the previous day now, the kiss, the way he'd carried her, the way he'd looked out for Ian. One by one, her reasons for resisting Declan's advances were crumbling, and it scared the shit out of her. And now they were all acting as though they'd...

Molly was afraid to ask. She'd never had quiet orgasms, but who knew if that extended to dreams? There were some things it was better not to know. She'd just grab her breakfast and then go hide in the baggage area for the rest of the tour, no problem.

But Declan snapped first.

He jumped up, grabbing the breakfast bag with one hand and Molly's arm with the other.

"We'll eat during the interview," he said gruffly. "Come on."

And he hauled her off to his bedroom.

They'd wolfed down their food in silence, Declan staring at her as she ate, Molly trying to get herself into a professional headspace. This was difficult to do while sitting cross-legged and barefoot on Declan's bed. The man had very expensive sheets. Sheets that felt very, very good against her bare legs. Sheets she knew he'd been in, not too long ago, possibly while naked.

Not like he was wearing much now. Just jeans. Was the man allergic to shirts? The air conditioning on the bus wasn't great, but in Molly's opinion that should be balanced against the threat of a shirtless Declan. She could only retaliate with cutoffs.

Molly cleared her throat and flipped through

her notebook one more time. She was never going to be more ready then she was now.

"You ready?" she asked, trying not to sound nervous.

Declan got up from the lone chair and started to pace. "It's your show, sweetheart. Shoot."

Molly took a deep breath. She'd had to be very careful when selecting the topics for this. For the first interview she didn't want to press too hard, too fast. He was too ready for that, too guarded. She had to come at him indirectly, kind of sneaky, and eventually win him over. She should be entirely focused on wearing down his defenses. Instead she'd found herself wondering what questions she'd need answered to feel like she could trust him, what answers he could give that would get her to break her own rules. By the time she was done crafting questions, she wasn't entirely sure what the purpose of this interview was.

"This is already personal," she said, and when she heard the words out loud, she knew how true they were.

"No shit," Declan said.

"Why is that?" she asked, glad to drop the pretense.

"I don't know," he said. "I just like you, that's all. We click. But that's not a bad thing, Molly. I can like you and want to fuck you at the same time and not have it turn into some crazy drama neither of us can get away from. You should know I don't do that kind of thing, in case the whole contract thing didn't make that clear."

"I should, huh?"

"You know you should."

Declan gave her one of those stares, and she broke. She looked down. Licked her lips.

She said, "What kind of thing is it, exactly, that you don't do?"

"Relationships, commitment, obligations—whatever you want to call it," Declan said. "Because I'm bad at it, and because guys like me can't have that without some kind of drama. Write that down."

It had been in the contract she'd signed—something about sexual contact not implying any commitments and a non-disclosure agreement for both signatories—but she hadn't really connected the dots. It had seemed like an abstraction, a formality. But he was telling her it applied to her, personally, directly.

Maybe another girl would have been offended. But Molly was terrified of getting involved with Declan, of losing control of her emotions, her life—again. He was telling her that wasn't going to happen for either of them.

He cocked his head and said, "I've never told a reporter that before."

"I'm not a reporter."

"You're still writing it down."

Declan started to prowl around the bed, back and forth, making Molly feel like she was being cornered. Herded. Hunted. It was making her feel decidedly other than professional. Was that what she'd wanted to hear? Did promises of not getting involved actually mean anything?

"So what kinds of things do you do?" she asked.

He looked at her. "Arrangements. Contracts.

Don't pretend you haven't thought about it," he said, growing impatient. "What's your first question?"

Was he nervous? Jumpy? He seemed on edge, jittery, his muscles flexing as he walked, his arms pumping, his shoulders rolling. He looked as worked up as Molly had felt after her dream, as she was starting to feel now, just watching him.

"Did they all hear me?" Molly asked.

Declan stopped short, took a breath, his abs contracting in a long, sexy wave. "Yes," he said huskily. "Is that your first question? Because then I know what I'm gonna ask you first."

"No," she said in a small voice, shrinking into a tiny little ball. "That didn't count."

"This room is soundproofed. I'm disappointed I didn't get to hear you," Declan said, planting both hands on the edge of the bed and leaning toward her. "To see you. What were you thinking about when you came?"

"That didn't count!" she said, scrambling back on the bed, as if she could get away from his presence. From how much she wanted him. From how incredibly embarrassed she was; did he *know* that she'd dreamed about him? It was impossible, but he always seemed to know these things, like she was just too easy to read. Desperately, she looked at her notebook. "Here, this is my first question: Was Soren there when..."

She trailed off. She couldn't read that. Damn it. This was hard, too hard. She shouldn't have led with that, especially not because she was running from her own embarrassment, because she was flustered. Another dick move on her part.

But more than that, she didn't want to ask him about his mom's death because she cared about him. About what affect that might have on him. And on what he thought of her.

Already, even without sleeping with him, she was screwing up because she liked him. Because he was a good guy. But there was so little information out there about Declan's life when he was kid, so little that it was kind of suspicious. About all anyone knew was that his mom had died when he was young and he'd moved in with his best friend's family—Soren's family—before his Uncle James took him in. And that was when Soren and Declan had started playing music together.

She had all these questions she needed to ask, all these things she needed to find out, and yet she hated the idea of being the one to bring up something painful for him.

"Oh my God, I suck at this," she murmured, running her hand through her hair. "I am actually, legitimately terrible."

"What are you talking about? You're amazing," he said. Declan studied her, the muscles on his arms standing out as he supported himself on the bed. He hadn't gotten up from that about-to-pounce position, something Molly was very much aware of. He said, "What are you afraid to ask me?"

"Not afraid," she said grudgingly. "I just don't like the idea of hurting you."

Whatever Molly expected, it definitely wasn't deep, rumbling laughter. But Declan, for some reason, thought that was hysterical.

"Baby, you can't hurt me by asking me

questions," he said. "You're sweet, but you can't. What's hurt me is already past. Talking about it doesn't make it any worse."

Molly frowned, feeling more like an idiot than he could possibly guess. She'd made that assumption because, for her, talking about the things that had hurt her definitely *did* make it worse. Molly didn't pretend her past didn't exist, but there was a time and a place for dealing with it. She'd gotten so good at repressing all that stuff when she needed to, just to be able to function — which was basically all the time — that she assumed that that was how everyone dealt with painful things, and that forcing them to the forefront of his mind would mess with him. Well, fine. Declan didn't have that problem. Declan was invulnerable. She went down her list, took a deep breath, and said it: "How did your mom die?"

Declan didn't hesitate. Didn't blink. He said, "She killed herself."

Molly felt her heart break just a little bit. Maybe more than a little bit. Slowly. Along one deep, guilt ridden fault line, one that promised to become a painful scar, the kind of thing she'd think about later when she already felt bad. She'd never wished she could take something back so much.

"Declan, I'm so sorry."

His eyes were soft, and his voice gentle. "Don't be. It's not your fault. It's just something that's a part of me now. I told you because I wanted to."

"Soren was there?"

All the gentleness left his face. Declan's lips pressed together, and his jaw tightened. He nodded. "Yeah. Soren was there. Soren's the only one who knows about all of it."

"And he still was able to do something so bad in Philadelphia that you lost control and hit him? And then kicked him out of the band?"

Silence.

Declan drew his brows together and frowned. Then he climbed up on the bed, moving toward her until she was backed up against the headboard, and he kneeled in front of her.

"That is the only time I have ever lost control," he said, very quietly. "Soren was the only person who could've gotten that reaction out of me, and only with what he did. It will never, ever happen again."

Molly's breath came fast and shallow, her whole body on alert. He was so close, and he had brought it up, he was talking about what happened six months ago. She didn't know which thing excited her more, but she was tense, taut, pulled tight. Wanting more. More of Declan, inside and out.

She licked her lips and said, "What did he—"

"You already asked your question," he said, cutting her off. "My turn. But first—do you understand what I just said? *It will never happen again.*"

Molly had never seen him this intense. This demanding. Declan's stare was never anything to mess with, but now she didn't think she could look away if she tried. This was the one time she'd ever seen him need something from her. Want, yes; desire, all the time. But *need*?

He needed her to know that he wouldn't lose control.

"I don't think you would, with me," she said.

And she really didn't.

Why was she so certain? She had no idea why as she watched him exhale, the muscles in his shoulders and chest roiling over each other, his neck tense.

"I wouldn't," he said. His voice was rough. "My turn. Who is it you're always trying to call?"

Molly felt her heart lurch. She could do this. She *would* do this, and she would find out if she could be like this with him, be vulnerable, and not lose herself, not lose her heart and her mind…

Oh God, was she really thinking about doing this? Letting Declan show her who she really was… Was he right all along? That it was inevitable?

"Molly," he said, his tone a warning.

"My sister," she said. "My baby sister."

"Why are you so worried?"

"My dad got custody when my mom died a few years ago. Lydia turns eighteen in a few weeks, but she's financially dependent on him. And he's an asshole who won't let me talk to her."

Declan seethed.

"Why?" he demanded.

Molly took a deep breath. *Just get it out.*

"Dad was always an asshole, but then he got saved, too, so he became a religious asshole. *After* he left us, conveniently. Not sure how that blind spot works for him. Anyway, apparently I'm an ungodly slut because I got pregnant four years ago." She averted her eyes. "I lost the baby."

Declan's eyes softened and his shoulders went slack. Molly just couldn't look at him. When he reached up to tuck her hair behind her ear, to brush her cheek, she tried to hide her face. She did not want to cry. She did *not* want this to be...

"There's a whole lot there," he said.

No kidding. Molly had tried to tell herself it was a good thing when she'd had the miscarriage. Robbie had just started parading his new girlfriend around, everyone hated Molly because Robbie told them all she was a cheating slut, she was a teenager who had been crying about being pregnant for weeks. She was sure her life had been ruined. So when it happened, she hadn't understood why this hole had opened up inside her, why she suddenly cried for the lost future she'd been so afraid of, why every time she saw a child...

"I can't," she said, choking. "Not now. Please."

Declan just put his arms around her. "Nope, not now," he said. "Eventually."

Eventually. He was so goddamn certain! Molly blinked back tears and tried to figure out why that made her feel relieved instead of angry. Declan just...said it was going to happen, and so it was. She didn't need to worry about it. Didn't need to stress, didn't need to be, once again, the one to carry all the weight...

"Oh Christ, that's so messed up," she murmured into his chest.

He pushed her back, against the headboard.

"What?" he asked.

She sighed. There was no point in trying to hide it. She was tired of that.

"There is a part of me that likes it when you do that, when you tell me what I'm going to do. Because then I don't...I don't know...I don't have to think about it. You have no idea how much I stress about whether to tell people about that, about how they'll see me, about how I'll see myself, because I don't even know what it means, or...and I usually am so good about not thinking about it. But then you say that, and suddenly I don't have to be—"

He smiled. "In control."

He didn't know the half of it.

She said, "You don't see how messed up that is?"

"No," he said, that deep voice resonating right through her, penetrating to her core. "Because it isn't messed up at all. It's a fucking safety valve. If you let it be."

Molly pressed her legs together and gripped the sheets. She tried not to think about how close he was, about how much he'd crowded her, about the weight of that stare...

Stay focused.

"What's your safety valve?" she asked.

"Performing," he said, coming a little bit closer still. "And this."

There was no use pretending she didn't know what 'this' was. What it might be.

"Oh," she said, trying to figure out where to look. If she looked up, into his eyes, she'd be lost. He could get her to do whatever he wanted. She already knew that. She'd lose all control of the interview, of...everything. But he was so close, now she was stuck staring at his chest. His abs.

Not much easier.

"It must have been hard during the last six months, when you couldn't perform," she said. "You must have—"

"I didn't do anything," he said, his voice thick.

"I need a sub who can actively consent, who can actually use their safeword. Being famous makes most women too compliant. I've been fucking frustrated."

"I don't know if it's all the fame's fault," she said, digging her heels into the bed, pushing herself back as far as she could go. He was like a hypnotist. Maybe she could look down. Oh God, that little trail of hair...

She said, "What do you need release from?"

"Same as you. Bad memories."

"Of what?"

"Look at me, Molly."

The command cracked the air and pierced her brain, forcing her head up. He looked different. It was like when he was on stage, or like he had looked in that office at Volare, like there was almost a freaking aura around him.

"This ends now," he said. "No more running, no more fucking pretending. We're doing this honestly."

She breathed a little faster. Didn't trust herself to speak, didn't know if her body could say no, didn't know if she could make her mind say yes.

"You remember what I told you on the dock?" he asked, his fingers tracing the line of her jaw.

She would never forget.

"You told me I'd beg," she breathed.

"Now," he said, grabbing the waistband of her shorts and pulling her down the bed, dragging her with him so she was on her back, lying in front of him while he straddled her. "Now is when you beg. Tell me what you want."

Fuck.

Molly closed her eyes. She could do this. She had to do this. If she didn't, she'd always, always wonder...

"I want you," she said.

"Eyes open," he ordered. "Be specific."

Molly ran her hands through her hair and tried to cover her face. He grabbed her wrists—oh God, she thought of that dream—and pinned them on either side of her head, this huge man looming over her, on top of her...

She groaned and pressed her hips into his.

"I want you like this," she panted. "I want you to...dominate me."

"*Specific*," he said again.

He held both of her thin wrists in one large hand and trailed a finger down the center of her chest, between her trembling breasts.

"What was your dream?" he said again. "You don't answer me, and I swear to God I will spank you before you even sign a contract."

She squirmed. *Spank her?* The throbbing between her legs intensified.

"You," she said. "It was you, taking me. You tore off my clothes, and..."

Molly stopped. She couldn't believe she was saying this. The last time she'd said any of this to someone it had been Robbie, and then later, when he wanted everyone to believe she was a slut who had cheated on him and gotten pregnant, this was how he convinced them. He told them all about the things she wanted in bed. Every time she showed herself to someone, it blew up in her face.

Declan seemed to know, seemed to read her. Again.

"Do you trust me?" he said.

"Yes."

"I trust you," he said. "God help me, I trust you. You're my sub. Say yes, and you're my sub."

Molly felt it rise up from deep within her trembling body, something she just couldn't fight anymore, something that felt right for the very first time. "Yes," she said.

Declan fisted her shirt in his hand and tore it clean off.

chapter 13

So goddamn beautiful.

Molly didn't even know. Had no idea.

She lay under him, cheeks flushed, eyes wide open, lips wet, parted, panting. She wore a white lace bra, the pale skin at the tops of her breasts beginning to flush, her chest heaving. She looked stunned, either that he had actually ripped her shirt off, or that she'd liked it so much.

And then she moaned as she rolled her hips up, into his aching cock, and he clenched his fist even tighter around her ruined shirt. Holy. Shit.

He couldn't take her yet. First he had to stop. Had to explain the rules. Had to wait for the bigger stuff. It felt like trying to stop a freight train. He settled on top of her and breathed deeply.

"This is about testing limits, Mol," he said. "You liked that."

"Yes," she whispered.

Still scared, her eyes still wide, still darting

about, her mind still obviously racing.

He bent down and kissed her. He found her stiff, nervous at first, but as he gently sucked that bottom lip he felt her begin to bloom underneath him. Slowly she unfurled, relaxing into it, until she was straining against him, her kiss hungry and hard. He wanted to bring her that release as often as he could. It had the same effect on him. Quieted his mind, let his body rule. He pulled away before he could fall into it — he needed to keep his head.

Now her eyes were softer, but still focused. She looked melted into the bed, but he could feel the heat coming off her.

He had never wanted anyone so much in his life.

"You are my sexual submissive," he said. He was breathing hard. "We're gonna talk about what that means later. There will be a contract. Terms. Right now, you obey. You answer me honestly, you tell me what you're feeling, and you do what I tell you, unless you need to safeword out. Understand this one thing: I am in control." Fuck, he was rushing. "Your safewords are red, yellow, green, like a stoplight. Do you know what that means?"

"Oh Jesus, Declan, yes," she moaned. She was writhing underneath him, ready to explode. She had no idea how much he wanted to cut loose.

"Do you know when to use them?" he said. "If you're ever —"

"Oh fuck, Declan! Have I ever been shy about telling you what I think?" she shouted, trying to rise up at him, her eyes shining, her skin glowing, her entire body asking to get fucked.

Declan grinned, and tightened his grip on her

wrists.

"Don't start being shy now," he said, dropping her shirt and yanking down her zipper. "And don't try to top me from the bottom, not unless you want a bright red ass."

A muffled sound escaped her, a kind of shocked giggle. She looked deliriously happy, feverish, like a dam had burst and now she was just ready to go. He stripped off those cutoffs and let his hand roam back up the inside her leg, feeling the soft, supple smoothness of her skin, watching her shudder and shake with every touch. She looked half there already, her eyes lidded and far away. That wasn't going to fly. No way he was missing this. He needed to see her, and she needed to be seen. That much was obvious from the way she tried to hide away what she was.

He stroked her between her legs, outside her panties, coaxing another moan from her. They were damp, and he inhaled sharply at the thought of how freaking wet she was.

"These come off," he said roughly, tearing at her underwear. She lifted her hips and shimmied, biting at that plump lower lip again, and kicked them off. "And this," he said, unhooking her bra.

She was naked.

Molly Ward, naked, in his bed.

He took a moment just to look at her. Her limbs long and tan, her stomach and breasts pale, everything soft. Her nipples a darkening pink, already tight and erect, just asking to be pinched and sucked. Fuck yes.

"Fucking amazing," he muttered. She was gorgeous, soft, wet. He got between her legs just to look at her, and the insecurity crept back into her face. Nervousness. Discomfort. He already had her at a disadvantage, naked while he was clothed, but that was the point. This wasn't equal. She was his to enjoy.

And she was a little afraid of it. Afraid of being that vulnerable. Afraid, and aroused.

"Nuh-uh," he said, sliding his hands up her legs, her stomach, over her breasts. He gave them a playful squeeze, then leaned over her, his face close to hers. "That's what this game is, sweetheart. You let go, and you're mine. I'll make you forget about every other man who's ever hurt you. You're done with that. And you gotta know what I see when I look at you. Watch me."

"What are you—oooh," she gasped.

He'd slipped just one finger inside her. Just one. So wet, so soft, so tight around him. He let her wrists go as he moved his finger inside her, and she pressed her fingers into his shoulders, bearing down on him inside. Gently he placed his thumb on her clit and her hips jerked while her eyes got that faraway, frightened look, like she was too overwhelmed by what was coming and wanted to run away.

"Declan—"

"Shhh," he said. And he slipped his forearm under her, lifting her to a sitting position without ever taking his finger away. "You're scared."

"It's been...a long time," she said. Every time he moved his finger she got stuck on a word. "Maybe I'm just..."

"Finish your sentence."

For the first time since she'd said yes, she looked

away.

"I don't know if I can come with you watching me," she said. "I don't know if I can come with you. With anyone. It was never that easy with anyone else, and now…" She shrugged. "I don't know, Declan, I'm kind of a mess. Every time I start to let go, I feel like everything's going to come crashing down around me. Great pick for your sub, huh?"

She gave him a sad smile.

Declan could have killed whoever it was that did this to her. All the people responsible, every single one, the whole world, whatever. Instead he put both arms around her and pulled her close, onto his lap, until her nose was practically touching his.

"You're perfect," he said, and kissed her until she put her arms around him and sighed. When she felt supple and warm and just as lost in him as he was in her, the boundaries between them starting to blur to nothing, he took her hands in his and lifted them above her head.

"Hmm. What are you doing?" she murmured.

Wordlessly, Declan slipped one of her wrists into a soft leather cuff, then the other. Then he held her while he sat up on his knees and attached the line connecting the cuffs to the hook he'd had bolted into the low ceiling.

"Showing you there's nothing wrong with you," he said. Molly tested the cuffs, and saw she was truly restrained, her weight in his lap and her legs wrapped around his waist while her arms were above her head, suspended from the ceiling. She looked at him, smiling and worried all at the same time.

"What are you doing?" she whispered.

"You can't move," he said simply, running his hands up her sides, smiling to see her shudder. "You can't run away."

He brushed her hair out of her face with his left hand then gripped a fistful of hair, holding her head in place. "You can't even look away."

"Declan," she huffed, and her abs contracted as she pulled on the cuffs, her breasts right at eye level. Too tempting.

"I'm going to make you come," he said, "and there's not a damn thing you can do about it."

He took one rosy nipple in his mouth and lathed it with his tongue, sucking until it was hard and pointed. Molly ground her hips into him helplessly, and gasped when she felt his rock hard cock.

"That's for later," he murmured, moving to the other breast. "All you can do right now is let go."

"Oh God, Declan, what if—"

"Shut up," he said roughly, pulling slightly on her hair. She gasped again, bit that lower lip. "No more speaking unless spoken to, unless it's your safeword."

Her eyes glinted up at him, that ball busting look he'd loved so much, back in the beginning. She rocked her hips against his cock—Jesus, was that good torture, knowing he had to wait until he'd shown her what she could do—and said, "Yes, sir."

Oh that did it. He held on to her hair and thrust his hand between her legs, finding her even wetter than she'd been before, even sweeter. He ran his fingers up and down the length of her folds, teasing a low, comfortable hum from her throat.

"Tell me how that feels," he said.

"It feels — oh."

Molly jerked her head as he abruptly pushed two fingers inside her. She twitched around him, breathing irregularly while he sought out her g-spot and curled his fingers against it. If he went for her clit directly she'd short circuit and burn out. Declan was going to build something deeper.

"I'm going to fuck you right here, later," he said, moving his fingers in and out, around and around, pressing against that spot. "You're gonna take all of me."

"Fuck," she muttered. "Fuck."

He pressed his palm against her mound and rolled it with the rhythm of his fingers, making her swollen flesh slide against her clit, her legs shake, her arms strain at the cuffs. He looked down to see her abs contracting up and down, up and down, as she rocked her hips into him, her body picking up the rhythm even if her mind was all over the place.

"Look at me," he said. "Nowhere else."

Molly pressed her lips together and nodded, her eyes shining with bright tears, locked on him. He let her hair go, knowing she wouldn't move, wouldn't disobey an order, natural submissive that she was, and let his hand trail down her back. She arched at his touch, gasping, her inner muscles clenching. She was so damn sensitive, how could she be afraid she wouldn't come? That she wouldn't let go?

She needed permission.

Declan picked up the pace, the realization making him insane. He would tell her to come, and she would, and he fucking knew it. He had the most beautiful woman he'd ever seen thrusting on top of his hand, looking into his eyes, begging him to give her what she needed, and it was almost more than he could bear.

"You are so fucking beautiful," he said. "Everything about you, Molly, is beautiful."

She blinked, and those tears gathered on her eyelashes, trembling while the rest of her shook. He put his free hand on her hip, his thumb pressing into the muscles right above her pubic area, and added another finger inside her. Then he pushed aside her folds, put his naked thumb on her clit, and gave her an order.

"Come for me."

He stroked her everywhere once, twice, watching those big brown eyes get even bigger, and then she screamed, her muscles bearing down on him, drawing him in deeper while she came all around him. She pulled on those cuffs while her legs squeezed around him, nearly pulling herself up, running away from it again. He held her fast and kept going, watching her face, feeling everything she felt. She kept coming, so much stronger than he would have guessed, and when the look of surprise on her face finally passed into bliss and she slumped over, her head against his, she murmured, "Thank you."

She had no idea what was coming next.

chapter 14

Oh my God.

Her body was boneless, weightless, full of light and sparkling air. What the hell was that? How had that even...? At some point he'd uncuffed her wrists and thrown her arms around his neck, holding her up against him with his arms, and she'd just lain against him without the strength to do much of anything besides wait for her vision to go back to normal.

He'd looked her in the eyes the whole time.

Molly would have sworn that would have killed it, would have made it impossible to get off, made her feel too vulnerable and exposed in a way that she was still scared to feel. But then he'd ordered her to, and it was like there was no choice.

Oh God, it had been so good.

She giggled into his neck, thinking about all the other things she fantasized about, thinking maybe, maybe...could she tell him? And he'd think it was beautiful? He'd demanded honesty. She couldn't deny him that.

She probably couldn't deny him anything anymore. Not after that. She laughed and nibbled at his ear, grinding herself against him just to feel the impossible hardness of his cock again. This was like a vacation from real life, from the limitations of being a real person—there was no way normal people felt like this, this free, this happy, not all the time—and now that she had a taste there was no way she could fight it anymore.

"That was incredible," she said into his ear. She couldn't stop herself from smiling.

"I told you to keep your eyes on me," he said, gently peeling her off of his body. His eyes were shining, but he was shaking his head. "I was already thinking I owed you a spanking for all the crap you put me through the last few days. Don't push it."

Molly was on her back again, with Declan kneeling between her spread legs. Every time he brought that up—spanking, like actual spanking—she felt a little thrill of excitement and simultaneous disbelief. There was some part of her that just did not believe he would do it, but if he did...

She smiled at the thought. She hadn't quite come down from that orgasm, and thoughts like that were going to send her right back to lalaland. In theory.

Anyway, he was wearing way too much clothing. She'd felt that monster underneath her. She wanted to get a look at it before she felt it inside her, maybe find some way to equalize things between them even a little bit, since she was still naked. She could feel her natural embarrassment start to creep back at the edges, and to fight it off she sat up quickly, determinedly, and went for the button on Declan's jeans.

He caught her hand.

"What part of 'I am in control' was confusing to you?" he asked her. Now it was Declan's turn to smile. "I tell you I'm thinking about spanking your ass red and you pull this topping from the bottom crap again. I think you want it."

Molly's jaw dropped as every embarrassed, humiliated neuron in her brain fired at once. "No," she said.

But also yes.

Oh, help me. Yes.

Declan still had hold of her hand in his. Now he looked down at her nipples, already turning hard again, traitorous little pieces of flesh that they were.

"You have a safeword," he said casually. Unconcerned.

And then he pulled her with him while he sat on the edge of the bed.

Molly laughed lightly. Laughter had always been a nervous reaction for her, the thing she did when she didn't know what else to do. It had gotten her in trouble so many times already.

And now Declan scowled.

"Over my knee," he ordered.

"You're not serious," she said. "I mean, I know...but you're not serious."

Slowly, Declan pulled her toward him. She could see he was enjoying this. So was she, even if she couldn't quite believe it. Didn't want to believe it? She'd thought she was done fighting this, but there was something in her that just hadn't given in.

"What did you think domination meant, Mol?" he said with that same casual tone.

She didn't say anything. What was there to say? She had agreed. She had a safeword. She just didn't want to say it. And yet she couldn't imagine going through with...

"You're still resisting all of it," he said simply. "That's gonna stop right now."

She was kneeling at his side now, and he reached across with his other hand to grab her other arm.

"One more chance." He was grinning. "Over my knee, Molly. Now."

Why was she resisting? Just a stubborn, knee jerk reaction? Molly thought back to the elation she felt when he had her restrained, his fingers working in her, what had happened when she realized it didn't matter if she fought it. It had been incredible. And here she was again, fighting just because the idea of giving up control made her stomach flip and her throat get tight and...

Molly hated that feeling.

He helped her along.

"No more warnings," he said, and pulled her over his legs. She felt off balance, clumsy, as he adjusted her weight and held her down. She felt her weight press her skin into his rough jeans, felt the hugeness of his erection press against her belly, and tensed.

Declan put his hand flat on her back and rubbed, murmuring appreciatively. "Everything about you, Molly. Just perfect."

That made her feel a little better. She was so exposed, so...diminutive, in this position, but the fact that he wanted her—that was a kind of power, wasn't it? She arched her back a little, feeling the warmth spread again, loving how much he wanted her, loving that she could feel it.

"Nuh-uh," he said, and an arm came across her back, holding her in place. She couldn't move at all, except maybe to flail her legs, and that wouldn't do jack.

And it turned her the hell on.

"Oh my God," she said.

Smack.

His open palm smacked against the meatiest part of her ass, sending waves of pleasure straight through to her core, and Molly gasped.

"You gonna fight it anymore?" Declan asked.

"No," she said.

Smack. Her thighs shook together and her clit throbbed.

"You gonna try to torture me some more?" he asked.

Well, he wanted honesty.

"Maybe," she said.

Declan laughed, full-throated, deep, rough. He slid his hand up her thigh and toyed with her entrance, saying, "We're gonna see about that."

Smack.

Smack.

Smack.

She gripped at his leg, the bed, anything she could try to get her hands on. He had her helpless, and it was making her insanely hot and insanely ashamed all at the same time. She wanted nothing more than for him to fuck her—finally—but this was too much. She didn't know if she could admit how much she liked this, loved this, needed this, to herself, let alone anyone else, but her body wouldn't let her lie. She was still fighting it, and she was losing. She didn't want to, but she didn't know how to stop, even while the pressure built up inside her.

She groaned, half in pleasure, half in mental agony.

Declan stopped. His hands roamed all over her back, her sides, the backs of her thighs, gently, like he was feeling his way. She knew he could feel how wet she was all over again, but she turned her head, buried it away.

"You need to come again," he said. It didn't even need to be a question.

"Yes," she mumbled. She was one big, painful ball of confused tension, but she still couldn't look at him.

He noticed.

"You're still fighting," he said at last. "Thinking too much. Don't worry, baby, you'll get there. But right now you need a little help, huh?"

"Mmmph."

He slapped her ass and she jerked forward, a reminder of what he'd just done. Not hard enough to really hurt, just hard enough to sting. She felt herself get even wetter.

When he spoke, it was with that voice. That commanding voice.

"On the bed, Molly. Face down, ass up."

Molly shivered. Face down, ass up. It was so…

Degrading? Hot?

She was on fire with it. She opened her mouth to say — what? Raise a political objection to words that turned her on almost as much as his hands on her body?

"Molly. Now."

That voice. She was back on the bed before she even knew what she was doing, on her knees, staring at that pillow. She knew he was behind her. Could feel it. Slowly, she lowered herself down to her elbows, her knees bent, her ass so high up in the air it felt...obscene.

Oh God, another turn on.

And she didn't have to see him. Didn't have to show him her face.

She hung her head and wondered why it was she needed this so badly. Needed to be shielded, right now, while at the same time so primitively vulnerable. And all that thought, all that bullshit anxiety, going on at the periphery of the pulsing, throbbing sensation that filled her core.

She didn't even think about a condom until she heard the crinkling of a wrapper. And that was insane, that she of all people wouldn't think of that...but then both of them were taken care of, and he still knew that she would need that in order to not lose her mind.

"I'm putting a condom on," Declan said from behind her. "And then I'm going to ride you hard."

He reassured her.

On both counts.

Oh, what the fuck, how did he know everything? How did he know she'd need a condom, how did he know she needed to retreat to the privacy of this position, to rough sex, to get taken hard from—

He plunged into her without warning, filling her with heat, stretching her until she cried out, gripping the sheets in front of her. She pulsed feverishly around him, aching for him to move, afraid that if he did she would burst.

"Oooooh," was about all she could manage. His fingers dug into her fleshy hips and held her there, impaled on him, waiting for her to get used to the size of him.

"Oh fuck, Declan," she panted. It was just on the edge of what she could handle, just on the edge of overwhelming, and she thought she would drown in it. He pushed all other thoughts out of her mind, leaving only him, inside her, about to...

He slid out, slowly, dragging the head of his cock across her most sensitive nerves. Just as she'd been on the brink of being overwhelmed by his intrusion, now she was aching from his absence. She angled her hips up, not even thinking, just a primal, animal response, and his fingers dug into her.

"Mine," he said, and drove into her again.

And again.

And again.

She was screaming already, wailing, not even knowing what was happening to her body, able to do nothing but ride the sensation of whatever it was he was doing to her, whatever it was that was happening inside her. She couldn't move, could only take it while he fucked her hard, fast, rough. The pulsing, throbbing thing he'd put inside her expanded up and out and exploded, splintering the world and shattering her self, who she thought she was or had to be.

All that was left in its place was pure happiness.

Her cheeks were wet with tears when she came back down and realized he was still inside her, unmoving now, waiting for her. His big hands stroked her backside as he pulled out of her slowly, murmuring to her. He rolled her over on her back, gently, so gently, and lifted her legs around his waist as he moved between them.

He was looking directly at her, and now she could handle it. From this place he'd put her in, this calmness, this blissed out sense of certainty, she could handle it.

"Look at me," he said, his voice hoarse. How had he held out? "Look at me, Molly."

She put her hands on those huge shoulders, let herself feel the warmth of his skin, the power of the muscles moving under her, and looked him in the eye.

This time he entered her slowly.

Inch by agonizing inch.

Holding her with his gaze.

By the time he was fully seated in her, she knew: she was his.

Every stroke, every sensation, every moment; he wasn't just fucking her. It was the intimacy that left her breathless, unable to speak, unable to do anything but let him in. Over and over again, she let him in.

He held out until she came again, calling out her name as he fell on top of her, sweating, exhausted, spent. She could barely remember her own name, but she knew one thing: he'd known what she needed, and when she needed it. He knew to fuck her rough, then soft, then hold her. Make love to her.

And that word scared the shit out of her.

chapter 15

Molly was a cuddler and he freaking loved it. More than that, she'd draped herself over him like the world's tiniest, sexiest blanket, and had promptly fallen asleep while Declan stroked her back.

He couldn't keep his hands off of her. Even when he had an idea for a song, the first time in a goddamn age he'd felt like he could write, he'd had to think about it before he scrounged for something to write on. He'd *felt* it when he'd lifted his hands from that soft skin.

But fuck it, a *song*.

Half a song. But still better than nothing. Declan hadn't written anything since kicking Soren out, hadn't wanted to even think about it, hadn't looked at pen and paper. He didn't need a psychology degree to know why he suddenly felt inspired. He'd just watched the most beautiful woman on the planet push through her own fears and come for him, as his sub. If his sub could be brave enough to do that, he could write a damn song.

Plus he had the muse naked and smelling of sex right here in his bed.

He was careful not to wake her. She was so light it was easy to hold her cradled to his chest while he rummaged on the nightstand for his notebook. He caught sight of her face and stopped.

Everyone looked peaceful while they slept, but Molly...Molly looked happy. She'd looked like that while she came for him, too, and surprised to feel it coming on. He was going to put that expression on her face every day.

It was her. Fuck him, it was her that did it. Declan had damn good instincts, and he knew his sense of danger wasn't wrong. Molly was... He felt that pull, all over again, only this time stronger than he'd ever felt it before. And that physical connection he'd known was there since day freaking one had been beyond anything he'd ever dreamed of. He'd *known* what she was feeling; he'd *felt* it. He had no freaking clue how that was possible. Every time she'd come it'd torn through him, leveling him. There was nothing normal about it.

It was more than that, though. He'd actually felt it when she was afraid, freaking out, felt safe, or whatever, and he thought—felt—like he'd known why she felt those things. He understood what scared her better than anybody, how terrifying it was when the world spun out, how exhausting it was to keep everything going. How she needed a release from that. And while he was used to reading people, it had never been quite like that. Never so raw.

It shook him.

Whatever. He had to get over it. He knew how this shit ended. And he didn't get involved, for good reason, and he'd promised her that. Promised *himself* that. This D/s thing would be amazing for both of them, she'd get the world out of it, she'd get a book. And Declan would get used to the fact that he'd lose her eventually.

"Mmm," she said, burrowing her face into his chest just a little more. The way her body shifted against his, all smooth, soft curves, got him going all over again. "What're you doing?"

"Writing."

Molly looked up, propping her chin on his chest, her brown eyes looking very, very interested. "A song?"

"Yup."

"Can I hear it?"

"When it's ready."

She accepted that way too quickly. He'd expected to have to fight her off, the way he normally did, and that it would end with her pinned under him and him inside her, the way it inevitably would if she teased him while naked and in bed. Instead his beautiful new girl was looking down, tracing tiny little patterns in the ink on his chest. His Dom instincts kicked in.

"Freaking out because you finally gave in?" he asked.

"Maybe a little bit," she said quietly. "But it's passing, I think."

She slid her hand over his chest and down his abs, so low his cock jumped, then back up to his neck, his face. He let that go. Plenty of time for instruction later. "This helps," she said.

He grinned. "Good."

"Um, Declan?"

"Yeah."

"How did you know?" she asked, taking even more interest in his ink now. "That I needed you to..."

"Take you like an animal from behind before we—"

Declan saw her look away and felt her tense before he even got to the end of that sentence. So the intimacy was still tough for her. It wasn't going to change overnight. Something to work on.

He said simply, "I felt it."

"Felt it?" she said, looking up with a smile on her face. "Like, you are the sub whisperer?"

"Not with all subs," he said, smoothing her hair out. She rolled fully onto him, her breasts pushing into his abs, his half-hard cock pushing into her belly, her legs between his. He made a mental note: He'd make her scream again before she left this room.

Declan held her hair and made sure she was looking at him.

"Not with *any* other sub. Just you. But the rule is you fucking talk to me when you feel something like that. I don't know why I got it anyway, but it's not safe, to rely on something like that, and I'm not playing games with your safety. Or mine. You fucking tell me when you feel something like that in the future, you understand?"

Molly licked her lips. Afraid and aroused. And brave.

Man, she was a woman.

"Yes," she said.

"You liked getting spanked too damn much," he said. "Next time I'll have to do it in front of an audience or something if I want to get my point across."

Oh, *that* got a reaction. He'd never get tired of how big those brown eyes could get.

Molly wiggled her hips, just enough to tease his rapidly hardening cock, and Declan tightened his grip on her hair.

"Careful," he warned.

She was smiling. "So how does this work now?"

"Now you get more rules."

"Do you get more rules?"

He smiled. "No."

"Hmm. I dunno about that," she said, though her body said otherwise. Molly seemed to know it, too. She tried to look stern. "I have a job to do."

Declan tried not to laugh.

"Think of it this way," he said. "Domination and submission explores your stuff. Interviews explore mine. Your mind is your own, except when you're naked."

She scoffed. "As if it would be any other way."

Declan sat up suddenly, hauling her up with him so that she straddled his erection. He made sure she could feel it nestled in her folds. She groaned slightly.

"That's one of the reasons I like you, sweetheart," he said, moving her hips for her to wet his cock. "The reason I trust you as a sub. Your mind is your own. But your body…"

And he flipped her over onto her back, pinning her arms above her head, letting her feel the weight of him between her legs. She was so slick, moving against him mindlessly now, making tiny little sounds while he held her down.

"Your body is *mine*. Always. At any time. Mine."

Her breasts rose and fell rapidly with her shallow breaths, and he could see her fighting to keep the thread of the discussion. Damn, he loved to screw up those complicated, intellectual thoughts of hers.

"But not during interviews," she finally managed. "Otherwise this will always happen, and I won't get anything I can use, and I'll be a huge failure, and I just cannot…"

Declan growled. It made sense. "Not during interviews. But there'll be a time limit, because fuck me, Molly, but if you think I can handle being alone with you in this room for too long without being inside you, you're insane."

Her breath hitched.

Big brown eyes. Rosy pink nipples. Wet lips.

Damn.

He reached for the nightstand again. "Put this on me," he ordered gruffly, giving her a condom. "And say thank you."

Her fingers shook with excitement and he had to help her. It was…he never thought he'd use the word 'adorable,' but Jesus, that's what it was. He was going to take that adorableness and turn it inside out before he was through. As soon as they got the condom rolled down he pushed her down, flat on her back, grabbed her legs, and hauled her down to him. Then he lifted both of her legs up to her head and sunk slowly into her, as deep as he could go.

That's when she said thank you again.

~ * ~ * ~

Molly felt like she was hallucinating. She'd never come that much or that hard in her entire life. She'd never even allowed herself to hope that she could experience anything like that with anyone else, and then *bam*, one after the other. Declan freaking Donovan.

She actually *might* be delirious from the whole thing. He'd barely given her any time to rest, only to check in, see what she was feeling. As if he didn't already know. He was right, though: she needed to actually say it, even if the idea made her feel kind of queasy with anxiety. Still, she felt completely, unreasonably safe.

And satisfied. Oh God, so satisfied. And yet she still wanted more. That shouldn't be possible, should it?

He hadn't even left her in peace in the shower. Instead she'd felt a hand come between her legs, and then she was pressed up against the shower wall, wet and slippery and screaming.

She'd barely had time to think. And that, honestly, was a good thing. Molly didn't trust her brain with this, not even a little bit. That same anxious tendency to try to control for every little contingency that had gotten her through the bad times would only screw her up now. Overthinking this would just…she could already feel the panic. And yet, when she let Declan guide her in this one area, she felt…serene.

Maybe this was exactly what she needed to

write this book. And to move on in her own life. Maybe this was exactly right.

For now.

She just had to make damn sure to protect her heart. Like, for example, not getting weirdly jealous about whomever it was Declan texted every day. Which was absolutely not what was happening. Molly just had a professional curiosity. There was still so much she didn't know about Declan and what had happened to break the band up that anyone important to him was a possible lead. Anyone who had known Declan before he became famous, anyone who might have seen him develop those walls he'd built so high around himself.

Someone like Soren.

Molly watched Declan on his phone, oblivious, that look of worry on his face. She'd ask him about it eventually. Find out who it was. Strange that she felt ok about asking him about his mom, but somehow she knew that this, whatever was happening with the person he texted with, this was a tender thing. She had a hunch it was because his mother's death was in the past—as much as it could be, anyway; Declan felt like he'd dealt with it, the way he'd talked about it. He'd said it couldn't hurt him anymore. Molly wasn't sure she believed that, but she had a feeling that whatever situation kept him tied to his phone for a few minutes each day—that still had the power to hurt him. And she didn't want to contribute to that.

She had to wonder about what he'd said: domination was a release for him. Was it a release the same way submission was apparently a release for her, at least so far? The only tangible, meaningful thing she knew about his past kept floating to the forefront of her mind: his mother's suicide.

Jesus. Yeah, that was a big one. She couldn't even imagine, feeling that kind of loss, that kind of abandonment. How would that shape a man? Is that where he learned to watch people so intently, so carefully? How to read people?

Molly felt a tiny twinge that maybe Declan's ability to read her moods and thoughts was tied to the most traumatic incident of his life rather than some innate magical connection, but she quickly snapped out of it. *Don't be so selfish.* Whatever experiences had shaped Declan in the end he had chosen to become the man he was. Molly firmly believed in free will.

And she *definitely* believed in Declan's will.

And she trusted him.

Oh, fuck it.

"Who are you texting?" she asked.

He looked up sharply. "You're already working on question credit," he said. "That's gonna have to wait until you earn some more."

"Evasive," she said, propping her head up on her elbow. She was wearing one of his shirts and her cutoffs, though it looked like she was wearing nothing at all, the shirt coming to mid-thigh. She kind of liked the effect. She could tell he did, too.

"Women who test the rules," he said, giving her that wicked smile. "Get disciplined. And you're probably a little sore already."

She was, in fact.

And she kind of loved it.

So much so that she'd kind of forgotten that they

were on a tour bus, in the middle of a tour, with a bunch of other guys on the bus. Right up until it stopped.

chapter 16

Molly hadn't realized how close they were to the next show, another surprise showing at one of the first clubs where Savage Heart had ever played in Hoboken, New Jersey. She also hadn't realized how close they already were to New York City—and to the original Club Volare.

Declan had said they'd go there. And now she'd be there as a sub. *His* sub.

How on earth was she supposed to think about anything else?

She'd better figure it out. She only had so much time to corner the rest of the guys and try to get as much out of them as possible, and that time was running out. Now was actually kind of a great opportunity—they were stopped at random buffet restaurant somewhere off the highway in Ohio before they headed on to New Jersey.

Ugh. The guys.

They obviously—obviously—all knew exactly

what she'd been doing in Declan's bedroom for...God, how many hours? She'd avoided them, going straight to her bunk to get a shirt and then just kind of hiding, and now, at a freaking buffet line off I-70, was the moment of truth.

Never mind that she hadn't totally figured out how she felt about everything. Declan had blown her apart, and she was still putting the pieces back together, trying to figure out what it all meant, or if it had to mean anything. But now she had to do it in front of an audience, too.

The guys were all heaping their plates as high as they could. All of them millionaires, and all of them still excited by all-you-can-eat buffets. She shook her head. At least Declan wasn't there—he was talking to a roadie about something involving equipment. For some reason, she really felt like she had to navigate this alone. She didn't even know how she and Declan would interact in public now, but she needed to set a tone for herself.

Molly took a deep breath and braved the salad bar.

Brian—being Brian—was the first to say something, taking precious concentration away from the shrimp pyramid he was carefully constructing.

"Long interview, huh?" he said, smiling evilly.

Gage coughed. "You must've gotten his whole life story. I mean, you're done, right?"

Erik, poor, sweet Erik. He gave her a look of picture perfect innocence and said, "You must have enough for a book now."

Then he smiled.

"You guys are all assholes," Molly said,

laughing in spite of herself. She stabbed at some cherry tomatoes, a motion she found weirdly soothing, given her embarrassment. She knew her face was at least that red.

"It's about time," Erik said.

"We do not need to know any details," Gage said, inspecting some ribs. "You know, whatever kinky shit you're up to, don't feel like—"

"Speak for yourself," Brian said. He looked genuinely offended. "I need some fucking details."

Molly threw a cherry tomato at him. "You know, Brian," she said, as sweetly as she could, "you're about due for another interview."

He grinned back. "One of your special interviews? Sign me up."

"Never in a million years, Brian," she said, nudging him over to a secluded booth. "Now get your ass over there."

***

Brian was leering at her.

Well, of course Brian was leering at her. He was Brian. Molly was pretty sure he had a compulsion to leer.

"Is it really so incredible to think that I had sex?" she asked him.

"No," he said. "It's incredible to think that it wasn't with me."

Molly popped another tomato in her mouth and considered this. She didn't know how Declan would react to a statement like that. She and Declan hadn't actually discussed exclusivity or possessiveness or whatever beyond the way he'd made his feelings about what belonged to him abundantly clear.

Mine.

She felt a shadow thrill, just the remembrance of Declan's massive dick sinking into her, and tried to hide her smile. He could turn her on remotely now, no touching required. Just memory.

"You gonna talk like that in front of Declan?" Molly asked.

"You think I'm suicidal?" Brian laughed.

"So you don't want me to tell him you were hitting on me during an interview?" she said.

"Oh shit, Molly, I was kidding," Brian said, looking vaguely worried. "I don't know what you two have going on, but I know it's not normal groupie shit."

"Normal groupie shit?"

"He would care, is what I'm saying. Not like with…"

Brian caught himself and tried to trail off, like it didn't mean anything. Molly's brain went into high alert. "Not like with Bethany?" she guessed.

"Ah, shit," Brian said, hanging his head. He picked at another overcooked french fry. "Yeah, not like with Bethany."

"What happened with that?"

"Nothing. It wasn't a big deal. Declan had a brief thing with her, nothing serious. He broke it off, and then she and Soren had a thing. Everyone was cool with it."

Brian was possibly the worst liar Molly had ever seen. Like, he redefined 'shifty.' He was squirming in his seat like he had a skin condition, and his eyes looked everywhere but at Molly.

"This has something to do with why he kicked Soren out, doesn't it?" she asked.

Brian threw up his hands. "No idea. Not saying anything. Invoking *omérta*."

"Ok, let's try something else," Molly said, stealing a french fry. Brian put mayo on them. She might as well try it. "Do you know anything about Declan's family?"

The mood changed. Brian gave her a serious look, which, coming from him, was particularly disorienting. He turned his plate so she could get at some more fries and looked at her, hard.

"Listen to me. You need to ask Dec about that."

"He told me about his mom, Brian," she said quietly. "I'm asking you your opinion."

He crossed his arms. "Feels like you're asking me to betray a friend."

Molly stopped. Maybe she was. That hadn't been her intent, but she could see how it might feel that way. Even look that way.

"Ok, wait. No. I'm not trying to get any family dirt that Declan wouldn't give me on his own. I'm just… I know Soren was there for him then, and I'm trying to understand the two of them, that's all. How they worked, how they looked from the outside, before everything went to hell."

Brian was quiet for a second. He pointed at the fries that they were now sharing. "You like the mayo?"

"Yeah, but don't tell anyone. It's like eating a heart attack."

"I know, right? Gross, but fucking delicious. I picked this up in Amsterdam." He slathered another fry in mayo and chomped on it. "It was

Soren who turned me on to it. You know, I didn't really think this tour was going to happen? Dec said we could keep it going without Soren, but the minute it all happened, I thought, fuck no, it's all over. We're done. I just couldn't imagine Declan without Soren, or Soren without Declan. And I was right, too."

Molly cocked her head. "What do you mean?"

"Declan was messed up until right before that first show at Volare in Venice," Brian said. "A fucking *mess*. And then...something set him right."

"Something."

Brian crossed his arms. "Yeah. Something. Not saying any more, because contrary to popular opinion, I am not a total idiot."

"Oh, c'mooooon." She smiled.

But Brian just shook his head. "He's not the same, obviously, he's different. But you've seen the shows. He's got something working for him, that's for damn sure. Something different. I didn't think it could happen. I mean, it's not the same, we all miss Soren, but...Dec's got some mojo back. And so we didn't have to cancel the tour."

The tour had almost been cancelled? Molly tried to process this information. She couldn't quite conceive of Declan being forced to do anything he didn't want to do, of being wounded, damaged enough that it would cost him his music. It frightened her.

"Brian," she said, suddenly serious, suddenly thinking about the fact that they were talking about *Declan*, the guy who'd just turned her world upside down so sweetly, so savagely, the guy she couldn't bear to think about hurting. And this, this was something that hurt him every day. "What happened?"

"You ask me that like you think any of us really know," he said. It clearly scared the crap out of Brian, too. He was only playing with the fries now. "Here's the thing. They were like brothers, right? Brothers fight and shit, but you never question whether they're gonna be around, you know? Until now. Soren's family history wasn't anything like Declan's shitshow, but it's not like it was *happy*, either. Declan is Soren's family, too. Or was. You gotta think about what's big enough to undo something like that."

"What would be big enough?" Molly asked. "For you."

"If it were me?" Brian looked genuinely surprised by the question, like it was something he'd never thought of before. "I guess...shit. Something that made me question everything I knew about them, you know? That made me think they weren't the person I thought I knew."

Molly stared at him. "You've been through that before."

"Lots of people have."

"What do you think changed between Declan and Soren?"

"I don't even know, Molly, I don't go there." He was lying, and Molly felt bad for him. This was a terrible position to be in. He said, "This band is my life. I'm not gonna rock the boat."

"You know part of the story," she said. "It's hurting him, right? Having this big, gaping wound?"

"It hurts everybody."

"Don't you want to help him?"

"Them? Yeah. I'd like to help them both. Doesn't mean I can."

Brian was avoiding her eyes again. Molly thought about it. Brian was a goofy, womanizing, drinking rocker with a surprisingly sensitive streak and a desire to see everyone get along. He'd felt so bad when he'd found out that Sierra was Ian's girlfriend that Declan had had to convince him not to call Ian and make it worse with effusive apologies. She bet he was a middle child.

"Are you in touch with Soren?" she asked.

Brian froze, fry in the mid-dip. "Why would you ask me that?"

"Oh my God, you are. I can tell, Bri. You'd make a really shitty poker player."

Brian's mouth flattened into a grim line. He leaned forward and lowered his voice.

"Don't you fucking tell him, Molly," he hissed. "I'm serious. I have a hard time figuring out what to do in this situation, and I've known them both for ten fucking years. Soren doesn't tell me anything, anyway. It's not like I know where he is."

Brian trying to be tough looked a lot like Brian being scared.

Molly took his hand. "This is tearing you up a little bit, huh?"

"Jesus, yes," he said. He gave Molly a good squeeze, then took his hand back and ran it through his oily, shaggy hair and cracked a thin smile. "It almost feels good to tell someone. Too bad it's you."

"What does he say?" she asked. "Soren, I mean."

Brian fumbled for his cigarettes, glared at the No

Smoking signs plastered everywhere, and stuck a cig between his lips, just for the feel. He looked at Molly and sighed.

"Mostly he asks if Declan's ok."

Molly caught her breath.

It was just then that Declan came striding into the restaurant. He would have turned heads even without the little bell that rang whenever anyone opened the door. In torn up jeans and a t-shirt, the man was just as tall, tanned, and muscular as ever. Molly was just as stricken as every other female in the building.

But she was the only wondering if the dominating rock star and general force of nature was really, underneath it all, ok.

chapter 17

Declan smiled when he saw Adra calling on his personal line. How did she know already?

"What's up?" he answered.

"I haven't heard from you is what's up!" Adra cried. "Either of you! What the hell is happening?"

"That is pure torture for you, isn't it? I should tell Ford."

Volare L.A.'s Dom lawyer, Ford, and Adra, a sub and agent/whirlwind/all around press guru, were forever finding reasons to work together while denying that anything was going on between them. Ford had helped Declan negotiate the legal fallout from kicking Soren out, and Adra had taken charge of the image stuff, and the whole time they generated a level of sexual tension that could have powered half of California.

"Ford has nothing to do with it," Adra said after a moment. "And you know it's torture. Now, will you please—"

"Adra," he said, silencing her. "Did you do this on purpose? Try to set me and Molly up?"

"No! Why, did it work?"

Declan chuckled. Adra the meddler, always trying to help everyone else, going so far as to mess with a Dom's love life.

Sex life, he corrected himself.

"Are you mad?" Adra asked. "Did something happen? Look, that wasn't the only reason, obviously. I mean, she's an incredible writer, it was just…I mean, this was a bonus, right? Right? Oh my God, tell me."

"Maybe I'll tell Ford," Declan mused. "He'd probably have opinions on your meddling. And I know he's got opinions about that new spanking bench."

Silence.

Well, that was interesting. Maybe those two were finally…

"It's none of Ford's business," Adra said curtly. "Maybe you could talk to his new sub. Now are you going to stop torturing me already?"

Damn. It really wasn't any of Ford's business if the man was that dumb. Declan would never cease to be amazed at the way some men couldn't see what was right in front of them.

"Yeah, Molly and I have worked out an arrangement," Declan allowed. He smiled when Adra squealed. "Or, actually, we're in the middle of working out an arrangement. Nothing written yet. Aren't you worried about how this is going to affect the book?"

"No. Are you worried that now you're going to have to start telling the truth?"

Declan frowned. He could see Molly through the restaurant window, poking at a salad, and the idea of lying to her made him sick. And it was true: one of the tenets of a D/s relationship was honesty. He wouldn't mess around with that. But there were some things that weren't his to share, not properly. He shouldn't even have told Adra.

"I won't lie to her," he said. "She already knows rehab was bullshit. But you know I can't tell her what happened with Bethany and Soren. If she finds out, I can't do anything about that, but it's not mine to tell, Adra."

Adra just sighed. "I think you're more involved than you think, but what do I know. Listen, I'm actually calling about the baby shower in New York. Lola wants you to come."

"The what?" Declan blanked. Baby shower? That was a chick thing, right? He knew Lola was pregnant and all, and he had lots of plans for Molly that involved Volare New York, but he'd never really put 'baby' and 'Volare' together in his head.

"Yeah, I don't think it'll be, um, typical. Probably more adult themed than is usual, anyway. I think Lola just wants an excuse to throw a party. But the point is, she wants you there. You're part of the Volare family now, so not optional, unless you want Lola on your ass. And I want to see Molly."

Declan winced. Molly at a baby shower? He didn't pretend to know what that might be like for her, but it couldn't be all wine and roses with all the memories it would bring up. He wasn't entirely sure he liked the idea of that, especially not if she was already in an emotionally vulnerable state from exploring her submissive side. On the other hand, it could be exactly what she needed. She couldn't go through the rest of her life *only* associating children and pregnancy with her own pain or it would drive her insane.

"I'll think about it," he said, without further explanation. "I'll talk to her and call you back."

"Soon."

"Yup," he said, and hung up.

He looked at Molly again.

Damn it, she was a light, even through the dirty glass of a highway restaurant. He hated to see anything darken that, but that was part of the point, wasn't it? She had some stuff to deal with. She had some things she needed to do, a new way to be. He was helping her.

So what was the big deal?

Maybe he was just caught up in his own bullshit. This place they were playing at next, it was one of the first places he'd played with Soren way back in the day, before Savage Heart even had a name. It was just the two of them, lying about their ages, plus whoever they could get to help out. The first night Declan's car wouldn't start, and they'd lugged all their gear on first the Long Island Railroad and then the freaking PATH train all the way to Hoboken just to play this little club. And it had been *awesome*.

Declan had his own memories to contend with, that was for damn sure. He'd been brooding about it on and off since they'd booked this show. The whole place was wrapped up in memories of him and Soren, building the band. It had been his whole life. Before his Uncle Jim, Soren had been the only person who had made him feel at home, sneaking him into the Andersson family's basement when Declan's mom was really bad, learning to play, to write together, Soren fucking picking him up off the ground after he'd found his mom...

Declan stopped, breathed, flexed his fists.

Adra was right, to some extent. He was involved in what had happened that night, with what Bethany had done, what Soren had let happen. It wasn't like it hadn't affected him; it had fucked him up royally for a while. Declan had to accept the possibility that maybe he wasn't talking to Molly about it for more than just noble reasons. The woman had a tendency to see right through bullshit, after all. Maybe he was worried she'd see through his.

Maybe he was worried he'd been wrong to kick Soren out this whole time.

"Fuck me," he muttered.

Declan got that sick feeling, that bullshit that had nearly ruined the tour. He always knew the Hoboken show would be the hardest for him, but damn, he did not expect for it to hit him like this. Especially not after he'd had Molly. Not after she'd said she'd be his sub. He'd felt invincible since that moment, untouchable, invulnerable. It had only gotten better when he'd seen he was right, that submission had helped her, had actually gotten through all those defenses she had up all the time. That she'd been *happy*.

Nothing could compare to that. No memory, no matter how shitty, could top that.

And now he watched her through the restaurant glass and saw that look again, that sad, worried, empathetic look, the kind of thing that made him want to move worlds to put a different expression on her face. Whatever she was thinking about, whatever she was talking about, it wasn't a happy thing.

He frowned. Not on his watch. And she was ready for him as a Dom. For what he needed, right now.

Declan walked into the restaurant and ignored everyone else. He was used to being recognized. Didn't matter. There was just Molly now, sitting in that booth, looking right back at him with the same need he felt.

And something else, too. Something that looked like…concern.

"Hey man, we were just finishing up," a man said. It came from the other side of the booth. Brian.

Declan hadn't even noticed him.

"Good." Declan looked at Molly. "On the bus. Now."

He saw her try to suppress a smile, put on her serious face. She couldn't quite manage to hide the way his order turned her on.

"This is an interview, Declan," she said.

"It's over, though," Brian said hastily, getting up. "You know it is. It shoulda been over before it even began. Remember our deal, though, Molly."

"It's not an interview anymore," Declan said, not even caring about whatever deal Brian had made with Molly, or what he'd told her. Which was a good thing. If they'd just been having lunch, his possessive instincts might have kicked in, and Lord knew he was already fired up.

"On the bus. Now."

Molly waited until Brian was well out of earshot, looking up at him with those eyes the whole time, giving him all sorts of ideas. Then she said, "Yes, sir."

He was sure she put some extra swish in her hips on the way to the bus.

He was sure she knew what he wanted.

Could she possibly know why?

Fuck me, total honesty.

Declan nodded at the driver, who was smoking a cigarette out in front of the bus, and closed the door behind him. The driver would know not to come knocking. Hell, everybody would know. Declan didn't care if they were late getting back on the road. Some things were more important. Like having another hit of Molly Ward.

She walked right up and jumped on the table they all used, giving him an innocent look. "What was it you wanted?" she asked.

He growled.

"You know what it is I want," he said.

She smiled.

"But first, tell me why you looked worried when you saw me," he demanded.

Molly opened her mouth, stopped. Frowned.

"Molly," he said. "Tell me. The rule is honesty. Don't test discipline before we even have a contract."

That got her talking.

"Are you ok?" she asked, point blank.

Declan just had to stare at her for a second. She was asking *him* if he was ok? What the fuck, was she psychic? It was only about thirty seconds ago that he'd been wondering the same thing himself, whether or not he'd screwed everything up with Soren and the band, whether he'd been wrong, and here she was, vibing on it.

"I don't know," he said. "I'm finding out."

"Like me."

"Like you."

Molly stared back at him. Declan didn't think he was alone in finding this strange, whatever went on between them, however you might explain it. Her chest was rising in quick, shallow little movements, her hands gripping the edge of the table. She wanted him.

He needed her.

Declan moved forward, put a hand on each knee and spread her legs slightly, tracing a line up her the inside of her thigh until he hit the fringed edge of her cutoffs.

"You're going to wear a skirt at the next show," he said, his voice tight, controlled. "If you don't have one, a roadie will go get you one. But I need to see you up front in Hoboken, and I need to know I can have you at any moment. I need to know I can stop the show, haul you off, and be inside you in less than ten seconds if I need to."

"If you need to?" she asked. Her voice was tiny, wondering.

"If I need to," he said, slipping his thumb inside her shorts. Fuck. She was wet. "Or if I want to. Now strip."

The command took a moment to register. He was pleased to see that when it did, she didn't hesitate to jump off the table and pull her shirt over her head and shimmy out of her shorts. Molly only looked once at the door, nervous, before she shrugged off her bra.

Declan couldn't help himself. He reached out and held her breasts, loving the weight in his hands, the way her nipples peaked so readily at his touch.

"Panties," he said gruffly.

Molly was red-faced already, bending only slightly to get them over her hips. She gave one last anxious look at the door and then gasped when he pinched her nipple.

"Put this on me," he said, fishing a condom out of his back pocket. He was never going to be without them now, not until—if ever—she got comfortable going without. He wanted nothing more than to feel her all over him, skin to skin, but that was something that was going to have to wait.

She wasn't as nervous as she'd been before. For someone who'd gone from zero sex to sex on demand, she was handling it pretty well.

And the look she gave him as she pulled down his fly...

"Fuck," he grunted, and grabbed hold of her hair. "Quicker."

Now she was nervous. He saw her swallow slightly when she saw the size of him up close, and he thought about what he could do with those lips. What he would do with those lips.

Just in time she got the condom rolled down, and he pulled her up and threw her on the table, loving that shocked little giggle she gave as he grabbed each of her ankles.

"Ask nicely," he said.

She groaned. She hated having to talk. That's why he made her, even if it drove him absolutely freaking crazy, just having to look at her, spread in front of him like that...

"Please," she said. "Please fuck me, Declan."

He pushed into her so hard she moved backwards on the table, a little gasp escaping her lips. He growled and grabbed her hips, pulling her back onto him as he surged forward, and Molly arched her back with a scream as he filled her completely. Ruthlessly. It still wasn't enough. It was never enough for him, not with her.

Declan pounded into her while she struggled to regain her breath, her pussy clenching around him, her hands searching for something to hold. Molly finally put them above her head, pressing into the side of the bus just below the window overlooking the table and booth, and threw her head back with a cry.

He reached for her breasts, bouncing beautifully right in front of him with every stroke, and greedily kneaded the flesh in his hands. Molly tensed, nearly pushing herself up, moaning, and Declan responded with a hard thrust and a vicious pinch to both nipples.

Molly came even more viciously. It shocked her eyes wide open, her pussy clasping down on him like a vise, so much so that he had to pause and hold back. She rose from the table, her abs straining, her mouth open in a silent scream, looking at him in wonder.

Holy fuck, he thought.

He pushed her back on the table and fucked her with wild abandon, taking what he wanted from her, until she was slick with sweat, her eyes wide and unseeing, sobbing his name as she came around him, again and again and again.

When he finally collapsed on top of her, Declan was already thinking of all the things he was going to do to her with that information. All the things he could do when they finally got to Volare. All the things he could with the proper equipment.

"I am going to make you hurt so good," he said into her chest.

He heard her pleasurable sigh, felt her hands in his hair. If he could stay buried in her forever, it would be fine by him. He knew he'd have to deal with his responsibilities too soon—the show, the band, and, most importantly, Molly herself. He'd have to talk to her about the baby shower. He'd have to find out more about her, figure out what made her tick, help her discover what she liked.

But for right now?

Fucking heaven.

chapter 18

Molly couldn't stop smiling. She felt like an idiot. No, she probably *was* an idiot for agreeing to this ridiculous situation. How was she supposed to be a hard-nosed investigative…biographer, or whatever was her official job title, if she was also submitting sexually to Declan Donovan? It wasn't a theoretical question; how was she supposed to do her job—any job—if she was constantly having sex?

Constantly getting fucked. And fucked *well*. With always the possibility that he'd demand sex at any given time.

Yeah, no wonder she couldn't stop smiling.

And now she was wearing this tiny, itty little bitty skirt, the kind of thing she was sure showed her ass every time she moved, and she was wearing it with the knowledge that she was wearing it *for him*. It made everything she did erotic. Like foreplay. Every time she moved, every time she felt the fabric lift in the breeze…

She was in her own little X-rated fantasy world. Too bad she was also standing on a sidewalk in Hoboken, getting in the way.

It was chaos once again. A local radio station was supposed to announce the show only an hour before Savage Heart went on, but the news had leaked. Either the club itself, or the opening act, or the police—clearly someone had gotten the proper permits this time; the police had closed down an entire block behind the club for their bus and the vans and trailers of the smaller bands. Anyway, someone had opened their mouth. And Hoboken found out.

It was a mob scene. Almost as bad as Springfield. Only this time, the cops were prepared; the mob was on the other side of heavily reinforced barricades. They'd broken out now in a drunken chorus of "October Moon" and it didn't seem like they'd stop anytime soon.

Meanwhile, the roadies had to set up and the guys had to get ready. The cops wouldn't let her within ten feet of the barricades, and everyone else was too busy for an interview. So Molly was standing in the middle of the street while everyone else had a job to do and the world frothed with fan mania around her.

Well, almost everyone. One dude kept staring. Kept sneaking looks. The kind you could actually feel slime across your skin.

And now he was back.

"So are you with one of the bands?" he said. He was skinny and tall, older than Molly thought at first glance, just looking at the studded belt he wore and his mangy faux-hawk. He had some wrinkles around the eyes, the mouth. Nicotine stained teeth and sallow skin. None of that was so bad, except for the creepiness.

He had sidled up to her. An actual sidle.

"I don't think they'd let me back here if I wasn't," she said.

"You know Savage Heart is playing tonight," Faux-Hawk said. He gave her a crooked smile. "I could probably get you in to meet them."

Molly stifled a laugh. She didn't want to be rude, but that was funny.

"You know," Faux-Hawk said, coming close enough to touch her hand with his, "if I thought you were nice."

No longer funny.

She recoiled from that touch, knowing just what he was offering, or rather demanding, from her. Immediately she heard Robbie's voice in her head, calling her a slut, and it made her furious. She'd almost thought she was free of that. She'd had so long now without feeling that way, without feeling dirty, without feeling bad about the things that made her feel good, and this asshole comes along and...

"Back off."

It was Declan. Always Declan. Showing up like he had that first day on the dock at Marina del Ray, except this time he was furious. Tall, thick, muscled, contained caveman. Molly felt his heavy arm come around his shoulders, and this time she gratefully leaned into him, wanting that protection. Not so much from the idiot with the faux-hawk—she could handle him—as from her own thoughts. Nobody got protective of sluts. She hated that she even thought that way, it was such a double standard; she didn't believe women could be "sluts," except when she felt like one.

Faux-hawk tried to play it cool. "Oh, hey, Declan, what's up? I'm with Radio Riot, and—"

"Not tonight you're not."

"Well, I'm not, like, *in* the band, I help them out, but sometimes—"

"I said get the fuck out," Declan repeated. His voice had that deep, bottomless timbre that was both supremely controlled and deeply intimidating. Molly freaking loved it, even if it made her feel, in a primitive way, a little afraid. "You think you can insult my woman and then come chill out at the show? Get the fuck out before I throw you over that barricade."

My woman.

Faux-hawk seemed to focus more on the physical threat than Declan's declaration of...what? Ownership? Possession?

More?

No. No. Declan had specifically said that he didn't do relationships or commitments or whatever. She had to keep that straight in her head. She had to make sure she didn't forget that she wasn't allowed to fall in love for her own sake, either, or she would be well and truly fucked.

"Your sub, you mean, right?" she asked.

She was still plastered to his side, feeling small and protected and feminine against the hard masculinity of Declan. It felt good.

"You wanted me to announce your sexual preference to that piece of shit?" Declan asked.

He actually looked confused.

"No!" Molly said. No, that...that had not come out right. Her brain was fried again, being near him, feeling the heat of his body, smelling him. She needed, like, note cards to talk to him like this. A PowerPoint presentation. *Something*. She would need to add a "no contact" rule for interviews, or she was doomed.

"Molly," he said, slipping his hand down to her waist and turning her to face him. The intensity of his gaze shocked her into the moment. "You are *mine*, Molly, while you're my sub. I meant that. Do you remember that?"

Molly looked up into those dark, deep eyes and remembered the feel of him, burying himself inside her. *Mine*. Oh God, yes, she remembered.

"Yes," she said.

Declan put his hand to the side of her face, and she couldn't help but lean in to his touch. Gruffly, he said, "I can't help what I am. Any man who comes near you is asking for trouble. Any man who disrespects you like that is damn near suicidal. And any man who touches you is fucking dead. Do you understand?"

She nodded. She understood. She understood how good it felt to have Declan get stupid and possessive over her, she understood how wanted she felt, how cared for. And she understood that it came with a condition: *while you're my sub.*

"Lenny!" Declan shouted. It snapped Molly out of her morbid thoughts and right back to the chaos at hand. A big, burly guy with a crew cut and a few military looking tattoos lumbered over. Declan's hands were still planted on her body, and he turned back to look her in the eye while he spoke.

"Lenny, you stay on Molly the whole show. You get her anything she wants, you make sure she's in the front row, and you don't let anyone, *anyone*, touch her until I want her. You know the signals, right, Lenny?"

"'Course."

The signals? What the hell? Was it actually true that rockers had secret signals with their security guys to pick out hot chicks from the crowd to bring backstage?

Wait, *Declan* had signals?

Before she could say anything, he'd crushed her mouth under his, and any thoughts she had about Declan and groupies and jealousy fell back to let Declan himself take charge. His kiss was hard and ruthless, and it shocked Molly's body alive like no one, like nothing, but Declan could. She felt it race through her skin, her muscles, her core. Before she knew it she was moaning into his mouth, her hands searching out his chest, her hips pressing into him.

She was useless against that onslaught. Helpless. She was angry, jealous, and she had no control over her own body.

Declan's hands gripped her by the arms and he pulled her away, gently biting her lip as he did so.

"Get ready," he said.

And then he left her with Lenny. Just walked away, imperious, dominant, not needing to hear her response.

And she was pissed all over again. Turned on and pissed off. Molly had a vague notion that she was pissed off for stupid reasons, that maybe she was inventing crap to get pissed off about because she was scared, but in the sea of conflicting emotions that Declan Donovan inspired, that was at least one that didn't scare the crap out of her.

Fine. She'd sit in the front row and be pissed.

"Lenny, can we go inside?" she asked.

Lenny answered by taking her arm. Which was just as well, because Declan had kissed her in full view of the crowd behind the barricade, and the reaction was, um, harrowing. Molly covered her ears and ducked.

It was inside, in the VIP area, where Molly finally found a way to do her own job. This was good news because, aside from the obvious reasons, it gave her an excellent reason to stop thinking about that annihilating kiss, and how she was both annoyed and profoundly disturbed to find that, fine, she was jealous.

She must have looked nervous, pulling at the hem of her short skirt, not touching her drink, eyes darting around. And it was true, she was freaking out a little, but mostly for reasons having to do with the fact that no one was supposed to get jealous over non-involved, purely physical arrangements.

But she wasn't about to share that with Mickey.

Mickey was one of the owners of the club, a dude in a shiny suit with lapels from the eighties and too much gel in his thinning hair. But he was nice. Kind. Considerate, in an old-timey, Frank Sinatra kind of way. He'd brought her the drink she hadn't touched, and he kept coming by to check on her—she figured at Declan's request. Lenny was just a silent, brooding statue of intimidation.

"C'mon, sweetheart, why so blue?" Mickey said, sitting down on the low couch next to her. "Declan tells me to make sure you have a good time, and you look miserable. How can Mickey help?"

Molly's mind went into overdrive. This was one of the first clubs they ever played. And Mickey was definitely old enough to have been there.

"You know, you can totally help, Mickey," she said, turning a bright smile on him. "I just have so many questions. You knew them in the very beginning, right?"

It was Mickey's turn to smile with evident pride. "I gave those boys their first gig. Hometown boys, how could I not?"

Her mind raced. "Out in Montauk, right?"

"Ridgeback Township," he said, leaning back and stretching out his arms. This was obviously a story he liked to tell. "Middle of fucking nowhere. Nothing going on. I come to Jersey, do ok, come back for my mother's chicken parm, and these boys are playing my nephew's basement for a high school party. Blew me away. I had to have them here before anyone else got 'em."

"Mickey, listen," Molly said, leaning in. "You know Declan and Soren really well, right? Better than almost anyone?"

"Yeah," he said, frowning.

"Do *you* believe Declan was in rehab?"

Molly had the much bigger, tougher, macho guy pinned. He wasn't about to get up and run away, and yet he looked like he was being sweated by cartoon gangsters. He may have actually loosened his collar.

"Because the thing is, Mickey," Molly went on,

tasting her drink. Gross. Too sweet. "I know he wasn't. Declan doesn't even drink. But the whole world thinks he had a problem, because he was photographed at that expensive celebrity rehab place in Malibu. One of those telescopic lenses or something, I don't know. Pretty sketchy. But he was definitely there. So I'm thinking maybe he was visiting someone?"

Mickey gave her some very skillful side eye. Then he laughed softly.

"Ah, shit," he said. "Those are very specific questions. You two more serious than I thought?"

Molly cringed. She hadn't *meant* to mislead him, but she hadn't gone out of her way to tell the truth, either. She kind of hated lying. She sighed, knowing she just wasn't going to be able to keep the tough-nosed investigative muckraker thing going.

"Um, I'm not just with the band. I was hired to write a book about Savage Heart after Declan kicked Soren out. You know, tell the story? Only no one will actually tell me the full story outright, so I'm kind of...piecing it together."

Then she smiled brightly.

Mickey stared at her. He looked disappointed.

"I thought you and Dec were, you know," he said, waving his hand around in the air. "I mean, I was happy for the guy. He's never introduced a girl before."

Molly blushed deep enough to bring Mickey's smile back. "It's complicated," she said.

"Ha!" Mickey laughed. "Knowing Dec, I bet it is. Listen, you seem like a nice girl, and more importantly, my boy looks happy with you. So whatever. None of my business. I'll tell you one thing—yeah, I think you're right, he was visiting someone."

Molly hesitated only a moment.

"Was it Soren?" she asked.

"What?" Mickey looked genuinely shocked, then...pissed, maybe? He put down his drink and smoothed the front of his shirt. "No, it wasn't Soren. Lady, you don't know those boys at all if you think it could have been Soren in that place. Neither of them touch nothing, not ever. Both of them got real good reasons for that. You want to find out about Dec's personal life, you ask him. My money's on the girl he had before..."

Mickey stopped. Maybe he had noticed how Molly had flinched at the reference to Declan's "personal life," like it was something she was very much not a part of, or maybe he just caught himself before he started talking about Declan's previous girlfriends—or 'arrangements.' Or hell, maybe he'd seen Molly's reaction to that, too. All that jealousy she'd told herself she could handle came roaring back to life, and she knew, of course, that he was talking about Bethany. Bethany, who had jumped from Declan to Soren and somehow still had a hold on both men.

"Listen, forget about it," Mickey said, standing up. "You talk to Declan, ok? He's a nice guy, I'm sure he'll tell you if you ask nicely. And you better get up front now, anyway. Declan said he wanted you up where he could see you. Lenny, you got her?"

Molly bristled a little at that, them talking about her like she wasn't there. But it reminded her of

Declan, too, in that Dom mode, and the familiar warmth pooled between her legs. It wasn't fair, what he did to her, even when he wasn't there.

"Miss Ward?" Lenny said, gently putting a hand under her arm. The lights in the main part of the club had gone down. The show was about to start.

She was being…delivered.

Dammit, why does that turn me on?

Then the first chords rang out, and she remembered.

chapter 19

Front row. Small stage.
Savage Heart.
Declan.

All of Molly's annoyance and frustration, her insecurity and jealousy, all stuff she knew she didn't have a right to be feeling — it melted away in the heat of Declan, on stage. She was grateful. It was almost like being in bed with him — he drove out all the messy, stressful, unhelpful thoughts, and left room only for being. For feeling.

It was like that first time she saw him on stage, at Volare Venice, only more so, because now when he sang to her, when he *looked* at her, she knew *exactly* what he would do to her. What he could do to her. She knew what it felt like to have those hands on her body, to have him inside her, controlling her, telling her to come when he felt like it. She *felt* every line, like his tongue on her skin, every beat like a thrust.

She was powerless before him, again. Like he was her puppet master. He had her practically coming right there. She couldn't keep from moving, from sweating, from nakedly wanting him. And he *knew* it.

And she wasn't the only one, either. The women around her—why did all promoters have to pack the front rows with crazed female fans?—were going absolutely batshit. The stage was littered with panties, bras, things even Molly couldn't identify, and she'd lost count of the obscene screams, the promises. Every time it made her want to step up and claim what wasn't, technically, hers.

But Declan kept singing to her.

It all went to hell about the time some deranged redhead managed to break through and climb half on stage while Declan was singing. The woman clawed at him, screaming incoherently, while Declan carefully disentangled himself, waiting for security to show.

And he never lost eye contact with Molly.

That was when the crazed fans noticed her. And recognized her, from Declan's public kiss out by the bus. Molly knew they'd figured out what was going on, and that she was Declan's...something, because of the shouting, and then the collective wail that rose up. Declan looked at Lenny, made some kind of signal, and Molly didn't even have time to react. She was half-carried out of the club, away from the screaming insanity, and into the street.

It looked like a totally different place than it had before the show.

Still with the bus, the vans, the trailers, all

parked side to side, making a network of tight little hallways between them, nooks and crannies everywhere. Still with people milling about, smoking cigarettes, trying to look cool. Still some cops. But most of the crowd—and the police, and the press—had migrated to the next block over, where the front entrance of the club was located, either because the cops had herded them there or because they thought they had a chance to get in.

And it was dark.

Molly felt the summer breeze under her skirt and remembered to be outraged. She was not a piece of chattel.

"Lenny, *what* the hell—"

But Lenny kept her moving. She knew she couldn't be pissed about being hustled out of harm's way, but, well, she was.

And more pissed when she realized she was being taken back to the bus.

"Oh, hell no, Lenny, not the bus. I have my own job to do, this is bullshit."

"Sorry, miss," he said. "Got the signal."

"Are you freaking kidding me?"

He was not.

There, leaning against the bus, in the shadow of the van parked next to it, was Declan Donovan.

"Thanks, Lenny," he said.

The sight of him still stunned her. Bare chested and sweating, his tattoos swirling around the ridges and planes of muscles still tight from performing, his eyes practically glowing...

"How did you get out here?" she asked.

"The basement's connected to the next building over." He was staring at her. Hard.

"What about the crowd?"

"Fuck the crowd," he said, pushing off from the bus. "The singer from Radio Riot's handling that."

He was walking toward her now.

"You didn't have to—"

"They were about to tear you apart," he said.

"Yeah, but security could have—"

Declan's hand closed around her wrist and he pulled her against his body, silencing her.

"And I needed to have you," he said.

Molly stopped breathing. She burned everywhere he touched her, and her pulse thudded in her head like she was about to pass out. Every sensation, every thought from when he was on stage came flooding back to her, and she felt a hungry absence inside her.

"Now," he said, his voice rough. "Here."

Oh my fucking God.

Molly's heart pounded in her chest as she looked around, suddenly aware of how not alone they were, of how much noise even the remaining hangers-on were making. She couldn't see anyone, but she could hear them, knew people would start looking for Declan Donovan soon.

Declan pushed her back against the side of the looming bus and she let out a small moan. He pushed down her tank top and bra, exposing her breasts, taking a nipple between his forefinger and thumb and squeezing.

"Oh, God," she groaned.

"Nobody can make me sing like that," he rasped.

He took her chin in his other hand and kissed her violently. His tongue pillaging her mouth while his hands roved over her body, anywhere, everywhere, increasing in urgency. Molly let her hands explore his back—oh God, his back, muscular and hard and writhing—while he found the hem of her skirt and yanked it up over her hips.

He paused for a second, as if in surprise, hands on her panties. Then he slid his hand between her legs and grabbed her sex.

She actually yelped.

"Take these off," he grunted.

Molly leaned back against the bus, panting, blinking into the dark, searching for his eyes. Hesitating. Not because she was unsure, or because she didn't want this, exactly this, but just the last vestige of insecurity, of feeling bad about wanting this...

She heard him growl. Heard the sound of his zipper. His grip tightened and she nearly came, clutching at his arms, not sure if she could stand.

"That's an order, sub," he said. "Panties off."

That sense of relief flooded through her, leaving nothing behind except how much she wanted him. Yes. This. Panties off. Molly hooked her thumbs into the waistband and stripped them clean off. She barely had time to step out of them before Declan had her back up against the side of the bus, his hands cupping her ass, lifting her as if she weighed nothing at all. She sighed, throwing her arms around his neck as her legs went around his waist, and then she gasped as he impaled her in one fluid stroke.

Molly couldn't do anything but hold on, wide-eyed, while Declan slammed into her, fucking her mercilessly against the Savage Heart tour bus while roadies and groupies and whoever loitered around, just out of sight. Her first orgasm came upon her with almost no warning at all, and she bit into his shoulder while she shuddered around him, unable to stop herself, to stop him, to stop the next orgasm from coming over the crest of the first, one after the other, pounding her into complete submission.

She wasn't quiet by the end. How could she be? But she didn't care anymore. Declan was just never satisfied, pumping into her until she had nothing, nothing left, until she was sure she would pass out. When he finally came, even Declan's knees buckled slightly, and he fell against the bus, one hand still supporting Molly. Which was good, because she wasn't sure she could stand on her own. She wasn't sure she could speak, either.

Molly didn't even remember about a condom until Declan took it off of himself, tied it up, and threw it away. She was horrified that she hadn't even thought about it.

"When did you put that on?" she asked.

"Before you got here," he said. "I meant it when I said I might have to fuck you in the middle of the set."

"No kidding," Molly said. She looked down—she looked obscene. No other word for it. Boobs exposed over the top of her bra, skirt hiked up over her ass, obviously looking freshly fucked. "Look what you did," she said.

"Makes me want to do it again," he said.

There was a beat where he seemed to actually contemplate doing just that—was that even physically possible?—and then he shook his head violently. "Damn," he said. "I have to finish the set, or believe me, Molly, we wouldn't be done here."

Declan touched her face briefly, softly, before covering her breasts, fixing her skirt. He kissed her sweetly, then bent down, picked up her forgotten panties, and put them in his pocket.

"C'mere," he said, and picked her up just as easily as he had before.

"Don't you have to go back to the show?"

"Yeah, but you're gonna wait for me on the bus," he said, punching in the door code while Molly clung to his neck.

"Hey, wait—is that Lenny?" she hissed. She could see a familiar, massive bulk standing about twenty feet from the front of the tour bus, out of sight from where they had just fucked, but still weirdly close.

She felt Declan smile more than saw it.

"I had him and another security guy make sure no one bothered us," Declan said. "No way I'm going to let some random chucklehead get anywhere near you."

She swatted ineffectively at his shoulder, and he laughed as he climbed the bus stairs, Molly still in his arms.

"Good to know you liked thinking you could get caught, though," he said, apparently not intending to put her down. "Gives me lots of ideas."

Molly squeezed him a little tighter. "Ideas?"

They were finally in Declan's bedroom. He carefully lowered her onto his bed and now she could see him smiling.

"We'll be staying at Volare in New York," he said. "You're going to wait here for me, naked, legs spread. I'm going to finish the show. And sometime later tonight, we'll be at Club Volare. And then, baby, I have some things I want to do."

***

Amazingly, Molly fell asleep after that. Naked. With her legs spread.

She had amazing dreams.

Still, none of that could change the fact that Declan had worn her out. She wondered about that as she was drifting off—how on earth did he have the energy to go back on stage and finish a performance? Molly felt like she was made of Jell-O by the time he'd put her on his bed.

He was a freaking animal.

What would a man like him dream up at a place like Club Volare?

Images of leather and lace and restraints and even metal floated through her mind as she fell in and out of consciousness, luxuriating in the feel of his sheets on her naked body, in the knowledge that she was there for him. Dreams and reality started to mix together into one continuous, unrecognizable state. She thought, for the most part, that she was awake, until Declan's touch actually awakened her.

She wasn't lying on her back, legs spread. She'd curled up and gone right to sleep. And Declan had just gotten into bed to be her big spoon.

"Oops," she murmured, turning to face him.

He kissed her forehead. "You were tired."

This, in itself, was new. So new. Being held by him felt…

No, stop thinking. Don't ruin it. So Molly snuggled in deeper, instead, nuzzling into his chest. Declan's arms tightened around her. And she let herself just feel good.

"Why are you so good at taking care of me?" she asked.

He didn't answer except to run his hand up and down her back, his face buried in her hair.

"I do that, too," she murmured, feeling close to sleep again, and maybe a little too lost in the freedom of nearly being nearly unconscious. "With Lydia. My friend Shauna does it with everyone. Funny. The only people I know who take care of people like that never had anyone to take care of them."

She felt him stiffen slightly, then hug her a little bit tighter.

"My mom and I always tried to take care of each other," he said, finally. "I'm better at it now."

He wasn't wrong. The next time she woke up, he already had her bag out and was pulling some sweats on her.

"Go back to sleep," he said when she tried to get up. Then he scooped her up, cradling her in his arms, and said, "I need you rested for when you wake up."

Molly smiled into his neck. "Why's that?"

"We're at Volare."

chapter 20

Declan had never needed much sleep. He'd learned to do without when he was a kid; the nights he needed to stay up and be vigilant, and somehow he'd just never really gotten out of the habit.

But all he wanted to do was go sleep next to Molly.

He just didn't want to be far away from her. And, truthfully, holding her while she slept was just as peaceful for him as burying himself deep inside her, in its own way. It meant he actually slept. And slept well.

Weirdest fucking thing.

But now they were at Volare New York, and Molly was still worn out—something that gave him some satisfaction—and there were people he hadn't seen in too damn long. There were about a million things to be worked out before the big show at Madison Square Garden: when he was going to see Uncle Jim, whether he'd bring Molly along. And tonight, there was equipment he wanted to get.

And Adra had a damn big mouth.

"Why are you all looking at me like that?"

Chance Dalton, the guy who'd given him his membership at Volare L.A., Lena, Chance's girl, Lola and Roman, who ran the New York club, and Adra were all sitting around the lounge, smiling. It was borderline creepy.

"I hear you're having an excellent tour," Roman said, without a trace of irony.

"Aw, fuck, Adra, you really told them?"

Adra just clapped her hands.

"C'mon, buddy, she was never going to keep that quiet," Chance said, picking up another beer. "We're all going to meet her at the shower?"

Lola held up a hand. "You did tell her it's not an actual baby shower, right? Not my style. I want to see Doms and subs having a good time."

Declan ran a hand through his hair. Damn. He still needed to talk to Molly about the baby shower. He'd been trying to gauge her response, her readiness to deal with it, but it wasn't like they'd had a lot of time. And most of it had been spent fucking.

"Depends," Declan said. "I don't know if she can make it. I'll find out. You guys weren't waiting around to grill me, were you? 'Cause I gotta be honest, I'm just headed out to get some gear."

"Good for you," Lola said, trying to get up with her giant belly. Roman put a hand out and gave her a look, then got up himself.

"Good for Molly," Adra murmured.

"I will show him where it is, Lola," Roman said. "You sit."

"I'm not *helpless*, Roman."

"No, you are my wife." The big Spaniard kissed Lola back into the couch until her arms went slack on the cushions. "And you are carrying our child. You will put your feet up, and I will show our guest around. And I will bring you a golden apple or the last Siberian tiger or whatever else you may want while I am at it."

Lola tried to hide her smile. Declan had never seen anyone quite so obviously in love. "Peeled grapes," she said, ruffling the very distinguished Roman's hair.

"You will pay for that later," Roman murmured just loud enough for everyone to hear.

Chance laughed.

Maybe others did, too.

Declan, though, was just kind of stunned. That's what it looked like. Love.

It didn't seem so strange anymore.

~ * ~ * ~

Molly couldn't remember the last time she'd slept so well, and she didn't even know where, exactly, she was sleeping. Just that it was with Declan. At Volare New York. She'd let him carry her inside through a secret VIP entrance, and he'd had someone turn most of the lights out ahead of them so they wouldn't wake her all the way up. He'd gone somewhere and come back a little while later with some bags, and since then it had been just wonderful. They shifted together and held each other, and just *fit*. Like they'd been sleeping together for years.

Somewhere in the back of Molly's mind all of her danger alarms were going off again, all at once, but it turned out that having to be strong through years of traumatic crap with no one around to help her had a silver lining: that ability she had to push down painful stuff until she could deal with it later? Turned out it also worked at silencing danger alarms. Because dammit, she was enjoying herself. And she didn't want to stop.

So she'd burrowed deeper into the hollow between Declan's shoulder and his neck and let her sleepy eyes open very slowly.

Well, she opened them slowly until she realized she had a view of the biggest morning erection she'd ever seen. Then they flew right open. It was ridiculous. The bed sheet looked like a circus tent.

"Oh my God," she said.

Molly couldn't help it. Her hand just…went. She smiled as she let herself linger over his abs, touching him lightly, the way he'd teased her, marveling at how soft his skin was, even when it was stretched tight over so much hard muscle.

Declan woke up when she was oh so close and caught her hand.

"Nope," he said. His abs were contracting in hypnotizing ways.

"Why?" she asked.

"Gotta talk." He sounded strained. Secretly, Molly smiled.

Then he rolled her on her back and trapped her there, spreading her legs and positioning himself perfectly. She groaned.

"I can't concentrate like this," she complained.

"It's payback. You'll concentrate like this, or I

won't let you come for hours."

Molly stuck her tongue out at him and Declan ducked and nipped it. She squealed from the shock, and then felt herself get incredibly, incredibly wet. If he didn't let her come after this she might die.

"Ok," she said. "I'm sorry. I'll listen. I'll concentrate."

Declan grinned, shifting so that he spread her legs even farther. "Damn right you will. And you gotta tell me the truth, Molly."

She was starting to think this was something serious, and she frowned. "Of course I will, Declan."

"Lola is having a baby shower. You've been invited. It's not a usual baby shower, whatever the hell that is. I think it's just gonna be another crazy Volare party, but I said I didn't know if we could make it." His dark eyes were soft and serious, and he brushed her cheek with one hand. "We can go anywhere you want. It's New York, there's stuff to do. And I figured you'd want to see my Uncle Jim, so we could go do that instead."

"Are you asking if I can go to a non-baby shower baby shower with you?"

He thought about it. "Yes."

There was something about this man that was just unbelievably sweet. Molly doubted that Lola had only just now extended the invitation. Declan had been thinking about this for a little while, clearly worried about how it might affect her, because babies. And yet this was the guy who'd just ordered her to drop her panties and fucked her senseless against a tour bus.

Molly thought about it. She thought about how

much energy she'd spent over the years pushing that particular pain down, and she thought about what Declan had said when she'd asked about his mom—it was in the past, and talking about it couldn't hurt anymore. She wanted her past to be past, too. Maybe that meant not running from the present.

"A baby shower is a happy thing," she said. "I'm happy for Lola. And I should be there if she wants me there. I want to be there, with you."

"You sure?" he asked.

"I'm sure. I just..."

"What?"

"I don't totally want to talk about it right now?" she said, giving him her most innocent look while grinding her hips into him. That massive erection was pressed into her thigh and she could almost, almost...

"I'd much rather talk about this," she whispered, her voice dropping. "Or maybe not so much talk..."

Declan laughed out loud, rolling his hips so his dick rubbed against her wetness, making her moan. "What did I tell you about topping from the bottom?"

Oh yes.

"That you'd make my ass red," she panted.

"I have plans for you this morning," he said, his voice already husky. "Now you're going to have to wait a whole lot longer before I fuck you."

"No," she said. "Please, Declan."

But Declan sat up, forcing his legs under hers, and grabbing both of her hands. He shook his head. "You can beg a whole lot better than that, baby."

And then he reached over the side of the bed and came back with a bag. Molly stared at it. That's what he'd been doing last night. Collecting...equipment. She licked her lips.

"Put out your wrists," he said.

His voice had changed. Deeper. Harsher. Just the sound of it...

Molly tried to hide her giddiness and obediently put her wrists out. She was both excited and afraid, and the fear was like at a scary movie, sort of. Safe. Just a hit of adrenaline, the kind you could revel in. A *massive* hit of adrenaline.

What would he do to her?

He cuffed her wrists and then pushed her back down on the bed, stacking the pillows under her bottom. Before she knew it the cuffs were secured to an attachment in the headboard—of course there'd be an attachment in the headboard here—and she was at an angle, her legs spread like she was being served up to him.

She couldn't help it. She giggled. "Shouldn't I meet your friends first?"

He answered her with a swat to her right nipple, then her left. The sharp pain lashed out into sharper pleasure, like her nipples were connected directly to her clit, and she gasped. What had that been?

Declan held up a riding crop.

Oh my God, a riding crop.

"There's more than one way to make your ass red, Molly," he said. "I think you need a blindfold."

She gasped. Of all things, that seemed somehow the most extreme to her, not being able to see what was coming. While restrained. While at his mercy.

Molly felt the wetness begin to spread between her legs, and Declan raised an eyebrow. He looked down, and deftly slipped one finger inside her while she groaned.

"Yeah," he said, taking the time to lick her off of his finger. "A blindfold. Don't move."

It was a struggle to stay still while Declan's huge body moved above hers, between her legs, while she knew his thick, heavy erection was so close, but somehow she managed. She thought it was practically heroic on her part.

Especially because as soon as she couldn't see, everything—*everything*—became more intense.

His breath on her breasts.

His weight on her thighs.

His touch, brief and tantalizing, on her stomach.

The feel of leather cuffs, slipping around her ankles. The way he spread her legs even further, anchoring the cuffs to the corners of the bed, making sure she was truly immobile. Imprisoned.

His.

"God, that's pretty," he said. "Let's see you move."

She felt something teasing at her entrance, something hard, plastic—not him. What was it? She had no idea, and it kept pressing, pressing...

She moaned. She moved her hips, straining against the cuffs.

He chuckled.

"Do you want to come?"

"Yes!" she said. She could already feel herself building up, getting frustrated. It was amazing, nothing short of a miracle, that this was something he could do to her—turn it into a game, whether or not he'd let her come. Just a few weeks ago she'd been unsure if she'd orgasm with a partner ever again, and now she was basically his plaything.

That made her even hotter.

"Please," she said.

"Nah," Declan said. "Maybe later. First…"

Molly felt cold metal brush against her nipples and gasped. She had *no* idea what…

Then she felt the teeth closing around her nipples and cried out. In surprise or in pleasure or both, she didn't know.

"Nipple clamps," Declan said. "Feel the chain between them, then going down your stomach, between your legs?"

"Yes," she breathed.

"That's a lead. It's mine." One set of cold, metal teeth closed around one nipple, then the other. The bite was just enough to sting continuously, something she couldn't shut out of her mind.

"I control it," he said, and pulled on the chain. The nipple clamps pulled tighter and Molly groaned, the fire shooting straight to her center, demanding to be quenched.

"Yes," she moaned.

"Be good," he said.

Molly was very, very tempted to be bad. Instead she bit her lip and nodded.

Then: she squealed.

He was pushing something into her ass.

Something very well lubed, but still *something*. She felt more lube, cold and thick and gooey, and Declan's voice cut through all the sensation with a simple command: "Relax."

Immediately she did, and pushed down.

Whatever it was entered her with the little pop she remembered; it had been so, so long since she'd had...

"It's very small," Declan said. "But powerful."

And he switched it on.

Molly's body jerked up, not at all ready for the sensation of a vibrating butt plug. She already felt full with the intrusion, a delightfully dirty sensation she loved feeling for Declan, but now that it *moved*...

Her brain, her nerves, her body—none of them knew what to do. She was writhing, groaning, until she felt Declan's weight on her. Steadying her. Holding her.

"Let it flow through," he said from somewhere above her, and pulled on the nipple clamps, the fire adding to the vibrations, spiraling up into her until she arched. His lips covered hers in one of those brain-melting, consciousness-destroying kisses, and she was done. Her mind shut off, her body turned on, and the rest of her was somewhere nearby, floating in bliss.

He kissed his way down her neck, between her breasts, to her stomach, her belly button. His hands gripped her thighs and she heard him inhale deeply, and then she felt his hot, hungry mouth between her legs, and she arched again, screaming, crying.

Nothing had ever felt so good.

No one had ever eaten her like this, like he'd die without her, like what she held between her legs gave him life. The vibrations from the plug melded with his strokes and left her dizzy. He drove her right to the edge and then pulled back, leaving her with the vibrations of the plug, and a deep, deep need at her core.

"Beg," he said, and pulled on the nipple chain.

Molly screamed. "Oh God, *please*, Declan!"

"Please what?" he said, leisurely, not letting up on her nipples, grazing her clit with his finger.

"Please let me come," she wailed. "Please don't stop, please."

He smacked the side of her ass, one finger dipping in and out of her while the plug buzzed madly on. "You can do better than that."

She shook her head, struggling against the restraints in a blind frenzy, needing to move, needing him *now*. "Fuck me," she gasped. "Please, Declan, fill me."

She heard a soft growl and then he pushed two fingers into her while she moaned. Then three. Then four. She felt full, so full, like she couldn't possibly take any more, Declan filling her completely, fucking her completely.

"Now you can come," he said, and put his mouth on her. He sucked her clit in his mouth and made her come with so much force that she nearly expelled everything.

Her throat hurt.

Her hamstrings hurt.

Everything, everything ached with the force of that orgasm, and it was still coming. Still overwhelming. Still a force ripping through her, leaving her with no choice but to submit and let it flow.

He held her. Drank her. Dominated her. Loved her.

"Oh God, you," she remembered moaning, and

didn't want to have to explain it. Was thankful, now, for the blindfold, because she had no idea what was happening to her both inside and out, and she didn't want him to see, the way he always saw through her.

Which was of course when he took the blindfold off.

"Look at me," he said gruffly. She had no choice.

Molly remembered thinking she could lose time, looking at him. Into those dark eyes. Right then, she would have given up all the time in the world. She'd never felt so accepted, so cared for, so...

No.

She pressed her lips together and held them while he looked at her, his cock poised right at her entrance. Silently she shook her head, feeling tears gather at the corners of her eyes, and finally said, "Please."

Declan held her face, wanting her to see him, to know he felt the same, while he filled her in one long, slow, punishing stroke.

Molly let the tears fall, and came again, and again, and again.

chapter 21

Seeing Molly in his uncle's house was freaking weird. It was weird, and it was nice, and it felt good, and that made it weirder.

She was totally at home, too. Just shootin' the shit with Uncle Jim, teasing them both, talking about going fishing on Jim's boat. What the hell?

Even with their morning play, Declan and Molly had been up and about earlier than anyone else who was staying at Volare for the baby shower party thing. Apparently everyone else had had a late night rather than an early morning, but that was just fine with Declan—he'd rather spend time alone with Molly anyway. The guys in the band were all off doing their thing in the few days they had off before the big Madison Square Garden show, Club Volare was sleeping it off, and he had her all to herself.

And she'd insisted on seeing Uncle Jim, once she found out Declan was planning on visiting anyway. She had about a million reasons that all made sense, and she said it was in the book contract, which he hadn't read in ages. What was he going to do, say no?

Well, come to think of it, he could. But Declan had some perverse curiosity about what would happen when Molly met Uncle Jim, like worlds colliding. Part of him thought it might change something when Molly finally saw him fully stripped of fame, since Jim did not tolerate any of that bullshit and always liked to let that be known.

And it did change something. It made everything more real.

And now Molly was laughing with Jim, like she was part of it. Part of this home, this life, this history. It was blowing his freaking mind.

"Molly, you here on business or pleasure? What's the deal, you going to grill my ass?" Jim said, getting another set of beers from the fridge.

"You would love that, huh?" Molly laughed.

"I've been getting ready ever since Dec called," Jim said. "I want to see what everyone's so afraid of."

"Then maybe now that we've met, you'll let me call you when Declan's not here?" she asked. Declan marveled at the expression on her face. Sweet, but lethal.

Jim looked back at Declan. "You know you're screwed, don't you?"

"I've been told," Declan said, finally pulling back a chair. "How do you know about all this stuff with Molly and the book?"

"C'mon, how do you think?" Jim scoffed. "Brian."

"That fucking gossip."

"And don't ever let him change. Besides, I think I could take you, young lady. No offense."

"Oh, I'm sure," she said casually. And smiled.

But Molly was toying with the label on her beer bottle, tearing it off piece by piece and collecting the casualties in a neat little pile. And she kept looking sideways at Jim. For some reason, Declan went on high alert. She was planning something...

"Hey Jim," she asked, sipping on that beer. "Who has the second toothbrush?"

Uncle Jim actually sputtered. Declan did a double take, but was the first to recover.

"Jim, are you getting laid? Are you fucking serious?"

Jim coughed some more beer, and Molly narrowed her eyes. She didn't know Jim well enough to appreciate what a freaking happy miracle this was—there weren't many gay men this far out on the island, and even fewer in Jim's age range, though maybe at some point, that didn't matter anymore.

"Yeah, I'm getting laid," Jim said, glaring at Molly. "Truce?"

"Truce," she agreed.

"Jim, come on. Fucking spill."

"It's not serious," Jim said, getting up to clear the empties. Declan got a weird vibe—was his uncle avoiding his gaze? That would be a first. "He's a state trooper. Lives kind of a long ways away, so, you know."

"Toothbrush," Declan said.

Jim just grunted.

Something wasn't right there. Declan looked at

Molly—she seemed to get it, too. Which was weird all over again. Had he really only met her a few weeks ago? This woman who was the best he'd ever had, sitting at his uncle's table, drinking beer like she knew she belonged.

"Hey," Jim said, waving a hand across Declan's field of vision. "I asked you a question."

"What?"

"How's Bethany?"

Declan was still looking at Molly, which was maybe the only reason he saw her flinch. It was how he felt, too: like a crinkle had just come into an otherwise perfect day. Why would Jim bring Bethany up now? When he knew—or should have known—that Declan couldn't give him a full answer?

"She's fine, Jim," Declan said. "Doing fine."

"Good," Jim said, and gave Declan a look. A steely look, the kind Declan used to get when there was something important that he had forgotten. "Didn't I tell you it'd be fine?"

He had.

Over and over again.

It didn't change anything. Declan was still going to watch his phone. He was still going to make those calls.

Declan stood up, ready to be back on his own with Molly, ready to be somewhere else—feeling like that for the first time in his uncle's house.

"We gotta get back," Declan said. "Baby shower."

"Yeah, ok," Jim said, drawing Molly into a big hug. "But you're not getting out of fishing with me. Can you come the day after your last show at the

Garden?"

Molly looked at Declan. "Can we?"

What was he going to do, say no?

~ * ~ * ~

They settled into silence in the car on the way back. Molly told herself it was just as well; she had a lot to think about. She should be thinking about the book, about what she was going to ask Jim, the man who knew more about Declan and Soren than anyone, about whether Jim had been telling the truth about his trooper boyfriend—there was a spare bedroom that didn't look so spare anymore, which wasn't really a boyfriend thing—about how she was going to deal with the party tonight at Club Volare.

But all she could think about was Jim asking Declan about Bethany. And how she'd felt that morning, when Declan was inside her.

The two things were not a great combination.

And they hadn't talked about it yet. Not that she wanted to—God, did she not want to—but Molly kind of figured that Declan might be all over it. And instead he was pensive.

About Bethany?

Molly cringed and mentally tried to slap herself. She had absolutely no right, no right whatsoever, to be jealous. To feel...she didn't even know what she felt. Hurt? She had no right to that, except of course that she did. Because whatever was going on between her and Declan didn't feel like it followed the rules. Not his rules, not her rules, not the rules of logic.

Two people supremely in control of their lives, and they'd ended up like this. Who would have guessed?

"Hey," Declan said. Molly had lost herself in looking out the window as they raced down the Long Island Expressway in the muscle car that Declan had rented. He was right—it was fun to drive, and be driven in. And it was beautiful out there. A clear summer day, sun glinting off the water, sailboats dotting the bay.

"Molly," Declan said, a note of warning in his voice.

"Yeah, sorry," she said. "Just thinking."

"I bet," he said, downshifting. There was no traffic, though, no one else out there in the middle of a weekday, so there was no reason to slow down. Declan continued, "So you gonna tell me about the crying this morning?"

"Oh, damn," Molly said. She'd totally jinxed it.

"Come on, you knew you were going to have to tell me about crying during sex," Declan smiled. "Don't even try it."

"Can I not, though? Really, just this once," she pleaded.

Declan laughed, then switched to Dom voice, which got a laugh out of her even as it really did pull at her. He said, "No. Tell me. Now."

She sighed. Fine. No fighting it.

"I don't totally know," she said, pulling at some of the stray threads on bottom of her skirt. "It's just...you make me feel."

"Feel what?"

"Just...feel. Really *feel*. And every time, it's overwhelming, and I don't know what's going on, and then...I cry. It feels amazing. And it's kind of terrifying."

He didn't say anything for a minute. Just worked the muscle in his jaw, his neck. Molly was still looking at him when she realized they'd pulled off the highway, down a short road, and into a little parking area overlooking an old, eroded beach. Theirs was the only car.

Declan pulled up right to the edge of the lot, looking over the ruined remnants of sand dunes, reedy grass, markers telling people not to walk on the dunes. Farther out there were long-legged birds hunting for fish in the shallows, seagulls diving, all of this nature going about its business totally oblivious to the human beings nearby.

It was still, and peaceful, and frightening, because it meant there were no distractions. There was just what Molly had just told him. And whatever Declan was about to say.

He put his seat back and turned to face her, his expression so serious she wanted to laugh because it made her nervous.

But his eyes were kind. Caring.

Worried.

"You enjoy it," he said carefully.

"I don't just enjoy it," Molly said, utterly unable to keep anything from him when he looked at her like that. "It's...God. I don't even know what to call it. It's revelatory."

Declan didn't gloat, didn't preen or anything. He knew what it was already. He just sat across from her, looking like a freaking god, being attentive and understanding.

What was a woman supposed to do to defend

against that?

"Then what terrifies you?" he asked.

Oh shit. She was tearing up again. Again!

"Seriously?" she said, wiping her eyes. "I don't cry for *years*, and now I'm like...Jesus."

Declan reached across her to get to the glove compartment, his arm brushing her breasts, and she gasped a little bit. How she could have both reactions to him, emotional and physical, at the same time—it wasn't fair. Her brain couldn't process it. Or maybe it was her heart.

"Here," he said, and offered her a tissue.

She stared at him.

"You brought tissues?" she asked, incredulous.

Now he smiled. "Of course I brought tissues."

"You would," she said, laughing while she wiped away tears.

"Molly," he said, touching her chin with one finger, guiding her toward him. "Why didn't you cry for years?"

"Oh boy," she said. This would take a minute. "I don't...I guess the short version is that it was all too much. I told you about the...the miscarriage."

There. She could say it without melting into a puddle of tears. Progress.

"Well, the guy I was with, Robbie, was a real dick. Told everyone I cheated because I was some sex-crazed kinkster, got a new girlfriend, turned his entire crew at the park against me. They...they were pretty hard on me, and then I lost the baby. They still all think I'm a quote unquote cheating slut, still hate me, still treat me like shit. They even started in on Lydia before she left, which is why I don't...well, it doesn't matter. I'm getting out of there, thanks to you."

"Thanks to yourself. You got this job, I didn't give it you," Declan interrupted, his voice stern. Then he softened. "Keep going."

"Well, Robbie made sure I was totally ostracized. I lost the baby, and then...my mom died. All in the same year. Just all this stuff. It was so much loss, all at once, and I just...I don't know. Shut off. Went hard. Turned to stone." She shrugged. "It helped. It meant I could work through school and get good grades. And now all I have is this job, and Lydia."

"When was the last time you heard from her?" he asked.

This surprised Molly, but it shouldn't have. Of course he'd been paying attention when she'd wandered off with her phone.

Well, there was no prettying it up. Little sisters were little sisters. It wasn't like Molly was a part of Lydia's daily life anymore, not with their dad watching over her.

"I got a few texts," Molly said, looking at her fingers. "But they were kind of bullshit. I know she's hiding something. It's just so weird, you know? Like, I don't care if she's dating a guy or whatever. I just want to show up at dad's place the day she turns eighteen with keys to our own apartment and an empty suitcase for her to pack. I just..."

Damn. The waterworks started again. Molly did her best to hold it down.

She took a deep breath, clenched her fists, and said, "I'm going to do right by her. I am not fucking that up, too."

"Molly, look at me," Declan said. His voice was calm, strong. Certain. And his face... Lord help her, but she found comfort there.

He waited a moment, then he fiercely said, "You *never* did anything wrong."

Why did it sound different, coming from him? Why did it sound weightier, more real?

Why did she want so badly to believe him?

"I know," Molly said, smiling a little bit. "But knowing that isn't the same as *knowing* that, you know?"

"Uh huh," Declan said, running his hand through his sexy ass hair. "Fuck yeah, I know all about that."

Declan closed his eyes for a good moment, and when he opened them again, he looked at her, clear, calm. Like something had been decided.

"I'm going to tell you something," he said. "Something I haven't told anyone besides Jim. Or maybe Soren told Jim, I don't remember."

"Wait," Molly said, taking his hand. She just...she needed to touch him. Needed to feel the calluses, needed to know he felt her, too. Especially with what he was about to do.

She said, "Declan, this isn't about the book. Honestly. You don't have to—"

"Quiet," he said, and squeezed her hand. "Forget about the book. I don't give a shit, honestly. You can put this in it if you want, but that's not why I'm telling you. I'm telling you because you're you. You get that?"

Molly was pretty sure her heart stopped.

"Molly?"

"Yes," she whispered. His hand was hot in hers.

"I left my mother alone that night," Declan said, his voice never wavering. "I'd known she was off for at least a week, the way she used to get. I don't know, she'd be diagnosed with something now, probably. But I was just so fucking tired of it. Twelve years old, and just...done. So I went out with some kids and drank some beers and threw some rocks at shit down by the boat dock back in Ridgeback. Just a stupid night, you know?"

Molly knew what was coming. How could she not? She knew how it ended, knew that sixteen years later the little boy in this story would grow up to be Declan, strong, confident, successful Declan, and yet she couldn't help but cry for him.

"I found her when I got home," Declan said. "I tried to carry her to the bathroom, to get some cold water on her, but I couldn't make it. I was a late bloomer," he said, as though he needed to explain. "It wouldn't have helped, probably. She'd taken everything she could find, probably just after I went out, and I was gone all night, so there wasn't anything anyone could do. She'd been dead for a while."

"Oh God," Molly whispered. "Declan."

"I don't remember much after that, to be honest. Soren was with me. He was the one who got me out, I think, called the cops."

Declan paused, frowned. Soren. Soren was still a deep, fresh wound underneath all of those layers of scars. But he pushed ahead, looking up intently into Molly's eyes, wanting to make sure she heard whatever came next.

"The point is that I blamed myself," Declan said. "I still...I'll never not wonder what would have happened if I'd stuck around that night. If maybe she would have cleaned up eventually, or...I don't know, something. Maybe somewhere down the road. But I know, like you said, that it's not my fault. But that isn't even close to *knowing*."

Molly couldn't grip his hand tightly enough. She kept thinking to something he said back in Springfield, when she'd asked him why it was his job to calm the crowd—he'd said it was his job because he could do it, where others coulnd't.

She looked at him now, sitting across from her in this rented car, having just shared something so intensely personal in order to make *her* feel better, and wondered.

What kind of man is this?

"You feel responsible for everyone, don't you?" she asked him.

"No," Declan said. He hadn't taken his eyes off of her. "Just some."

This was not a man who would ever let someone in pain slip by him. This wasn't a man who would wash his hands of a situation, think it wasn't his problem. He had contracts for his lovers, saying he wouldn't get involved—maybe that was because otherwise he *always* got involved.

Very quietly, Molly said, "Was Bethany in the hospital for drugs and alcohol? Or something else?"

Declan took a deep breath. He didn't look upset. In fact, he almost looked...relieved. His eyes sparked a little, his shoulders relaxed, his thumb brushed against the back of her hand.

All he said was, "It's not mine to tell."

Molly felt it coming on, that feeling, that

drowning, overwhelmed feeling she'd get when Declan tied her up, or coaxed her over an edge, or pushed inside her—except now he was sitting across a car, looking at her with the sense of wonder she felt. She just wanted to be close to him. Closer. Wanted him, for once, to feel the thing he helped her to feel all the time, to not be thinking about any of the people he worried about, to simply get to *feel*.

Molly wasn't thinking about Bethany, or jealousy, or her book, as she climbed over the gearshift. She was just thinking about him. Just looking at Declan as she hiked up her skirt, just wondering if she'd be able to do it, if she could give that release to him, all on her own.

He didn't move for a moment.

Didn't seem to breathe.

Then he exhaled long and slow, his hands moving up her thighs, pushing her skirt up around her waist. He never broke eye contact as he fished a condom out of his pocket—she smiled; of course he had a condom—and gave it to her. He was unnaturally still while she put it on him. Like a man held rigid, on the edge of…something.

Molly saw that her own hand was shaking as she let the back of his seat down. While she positioned herself over him. While she slowly, slowly lowered herself down, gasping at the first touch, at the feel of him sliding through her folds, as his erection pushed back at the first resistance from her body. Her mouth fell open, breathing fast. She'd never felt him like this before, looking him in the eye while she slowly sank down around him.

Declan's fingers dug into her hips. He was

breathing fast now, his chest rising, falling, his veins popping out of his neck.

He seemed so much bigger, going slow. She was almost drunk on it, on him, on watching him. She couldn't take it any longer, and when she leaned forward to kiss him, he surged upwards, into her, all the way to the hilt, and they both cried out.

Molly held on, her mouth seeking his, her body knowing better than she did, and rode them both over the edge.

chapter 22

They were woken up by overly polite knocking on their door at Volare.

Or at least Declan was woken up. Molly curled up, made some kind of absurdly adorable snuffling noise, and opened her eyes when she reached for him and he wasn't there.

They were doing a lot of sleeping together.

They'd both been exhausted when they had gotten back from Uncle Jim's and had decided on a nap. Declan figured it was the stress of a tour and the constant sex, but truthfully it felt like more. Whatever happened in the car on the way back from Uncle Jim's had taken everything he had. He wasn't sorry. He just didn't know what the hell was happening.

Neither did Molly. They didn't try to talk about it, to name it, or to categorize it, which was good, as far as Declan was concerned. He didn't know what was happening here yet, and he didn't want to jinx it by telling it what to be. He'd already gone further than he should have, broken his own rules. Whether he'd gone too far...

"What's up?" he whispered as he cracked open their door. It was Adra.

Smiling.

"Ok, normally I wouldn't disturb you two," she said, grinning as Molly threw a pillow at the door. "But you're late. The non-debauched portion of the baby shower has begun."

"Non-debauched?" Declan asked, yawning. "Why would we go to that?"

"Ignore him," Molly called out from behind him. "We'll be right there."

Adra raised an eyebrow.

"Excuse us," Declan said politely. "We'll be a little bit late."

Declan closed the door only to find Molly grinning and barely holding up enough sheet to conceal herself. Declan had made a rule that she wasn't allowed clothes in this room—and it was a damn good rule.

"You did that on purpose," he said, feeling himself harden in his hastily pulled on boxers.

"Maybe."

Declan grabbed the edge of the bed sheet and pulled, stripping her down to nothing.

"Goddamn," he muttered. He would never, ever get tired of that.

He climbed onto the bed, watching Molly's smile broaden, thinking she'd gotten away with something. Declan just shook his head and pinned her naked body underneath his.

"You know what the worst thing I can do to you

is?" he said.

Molly's eyes got very, very large. "No."

"Make you wait," he said, and kissed her, deeply and thoroughly, while his hands roved over her body. He teased her nipples, her ass, her thighs, and ground himself against her clit until she moaned—and then he stopped.

"Oh God, you were serious," she panted.

"You are going to *pay* for that," he growled, tearing himself off of her. He was left with his own aching erection. "Get dressed. Be ready in five."

"Where are you going?"

"Cold shower," he said ruefully. He didn't even mind when she laughed.

Sometimes being a Dom was hard work.

His shower, though, left him feeling contemplative. The weirdest thing about all of that was how natural it all felt. It was easy. Fluid. With no respect for the boundaries that Declan normally set up with subs. By the time they were ready to go, Declan was glad, for once, that Adra stopped by to kidnap Molly—there was some kind of girls' thing that had nothing to do with him.

"Where do the boys go?" he'd asked.

"They're not banned, you know," Adra said. "Go wherever you feel like, just let us have our fun grilling Molly on our own for, like, twenty minutes."

"Should I be scared?" Molly asked.

"Probably," Declan grinned. "Is Ford around yet? I have to talk to him about Savage Heart stuff anyway."

Declan didn't miss the shadow that passed across Adra's face, and neither did Molly. He hadn't been wrong about what he'd sensed over the phone—that was a fresh wound for Adra.

"I think he's upstairs, on the terrace," Adra said. "No idea if he's alone. C'mon, Molly, there are mimosas."

Declan didn't think he'd ever seen Adra move so fast. That was a situation that could get weird, quick. Adra and Ford were the twin pillars of Volare L.A., with Chance heading up the place. And it was Adra and Ford together that had helped Declan through the darkest moments after what went down in Philadelphia with Soren and Bethany. He felt loyalty to both of them. He didn't want to see either of them unhappy or hurt.

Declan brooded.

And thankfully, when he did find Ford, smoking a cigar on the upstairs terrace, the man was all alone.

Looking like someone had just run over his dog.

"What the hell is wrong with you?" Declan asked, falling backwards into the chair across from the normally put together lawyer. Normally hanging out with Ford made Declan feel like he was contributing to the balance of the universe; where Declan was all rough edges, jeans and tats, Ford was blond and chiseled and wore tailored suits. They'd clashed at first, but in the end they'd figured out that they understood each other. And now Ford was obviously not himself. Rumpled shirt, disheveled hair, a scowl—something was up.

"Nothing," Ford said, shaking his head.

Declan decided to let it slide—temporarily. There was uncomfortable stuff to get out of the way first.

"So did you find him?" Declan asked.

"Yeah," Ford said. "I found him. Or at least found a representative authorized to speak on his behalf. And his representative, who, by the way, asked not to be identified, asked me what the hell a lawyer wanted with Soren Andersson. Very cranky."

"Jesus. This whole thing…"

"So do you want me to make an offer? They have to know why your lawyer is contacting them, and I got the sense they wouldn't be amenable to a deal. You'd probably have to pay out the nose for the rights to those songs."

"I don't care about the money," Declan said.

"What do you care about?"

Good question.

"Declan, should I make an offer for the full rights to those songs?" Ford said.

It was something Declan had put in motion almost immediately after he'd kicked Soren out of the band, when he'd been enraged with the image of Bethany, limp in his arms, still fresh in his mind. It was the closest thing he could think of to severing ties completely with Soren. And now it seemed…childish. Probably because it was childish. Angry. Just a way to hurt Soren.

"No, hold off," Declan said, sighing.

"Ok, honest question," Ford said. "Do you know what you're doing?"

"No idea," Declan said. "First time in fucking ages I'm lost at sea. How about you?"

Ford said nothing.

"Dude."

Ford glared.

"Not buying it," Declan said. "I saw Adra already, man. You have some other sub? That you brought here?"

Ford closed his eyes. "Yeah, that hasn't worked out. I let her go. She has her own room; she'll be doing her own thing."

"Don't think that's gonna make a difference to Adra. I do feel tempted to kick your ass for that," Declan admitted.

"Adra and I are not anything," Ford snapped. "Adra doesn't want—"

Ford stopped himself, obviously with great effort. Something had obviously happened, even if nothing was currently happening.

Declan knew all about that.

"Declan, believe me, I'm not going to hurt her, not ever, not intentionally," Ford said finally. "It's more complicated than it looks, so just…stay out of it for now, all right?"

Declan swiped Ford's whiskey, taking a sniff. "Yeah, that's fair. Complicated is complicated. It's not like I'm one to talk right now, you know? What is this, Green Bonnet?"

"Good nose," Ford said. "I got a bottle smuggled in from Ireland."

Declan laughed. "Smuggled?"

"Sounds more fun that way, right?" Ford grinned, pouring Declan a finger. "So you know all about complicated, then. Things getting real with Molly Ward?"

Declan swirled his whiskey and laughed softly. "Hell yes," he said. "Things are getting mighty real."

Declan fell silent. That's what it was, wasn't it?

The Dom/sub dynamic—one of the things that made it perfect for him was that it existed outside of real life for most people. It was a walled off garden of sex and power, and that was just fucking perfect for a man like him, who wouldn't put his own damaged bullshit on anyone if he could help it. More than that, he didn't want to deal with the kinds of women who were drawn to a man like him—women like Bethany. Because it ended up being the same dance again and again, reliving the same painful drama over and over.

But Molly somehow transcended all of those limits. Molly was the perfect sub for him in ways he didn't yet truly understand, but she didn't stop there. She kept going. She was in his thoughts all the damn time.

If that wasn't real, Declan didn't know what real meant. But that was also terrifying. Declan was man enough to admit when he was scared, and if he was falling for Molly Ward—well, everyone should be scared, because obviously the apocalypse was coming. The day Declan Donovan put himself in a position where he might one day hurt someone...

Declan slugged his expensive, illegal whiskey and stood up.

"Ford, I gotta go do a thing," he said.

Ford raised his glass. "Be fleet of foot, and...whatever the rest of that saying is."

Declan barely heard him. Because the thing he had to do was Molly. Just Molly. He needed to see her, be with her, smell her. See for himself, once again, if he was really losing his mind.

~ * ~ * ~

If Molly had any lingering reservations about how she'd handle a baby shower, they were quickly dispelled by what counted as a baby shower for Lola Theroux. It really was just an excuse for a party that a pregnant lady happened to be hosting. Or presiding over. Something. Molly couldn't quite figure it out—she'd assumed Lola was Roman Casta's sub in their marriage, but Lola herself was one commanding woman. Maybe there was more to that situation than met the eye.

Interesting.

And Molly herself had been quickly embraced. Like, literally, embraced. This was a huggy crowd, and Molly was surprised to find that all the hugs really did melt away the social anxiety she hadn't realized she'd been carrying around with her. Because these people, they were all...well, if they weren't all rich, they were all definitely successful. And she was Molly Ward from a trailer park.

And none of it seemed to matter.

No wonder Declan liked this place.

Ugh. Just thinking the man's name made her clench. He'd wound her up expertly just before sending her out to this party, and she'd never quite come down. It was torture—just like he'd intended.

The bastard. So why was she smiling about it?

Because you...

Her mind blinked back to that moment in the car, just before she'd taken him inside her, when the look in his eyes had been just...pure gratitude. Gratitude to *her*, when she had him to thank for everything, everything. She'd felt something move then. Something big.

Molly forced herself back into the present. Whatever it was, that big thing—that thing she refused to name even though she damn well knew it was—that was not something that was going to be good for her, in the long run. That was something that, if she let it, if she let her expectations and dreams and feelings run wild, was going to get her poor heart shattered all over again.

She knew what Declan was. She knew what the deal was when she signed on. She was just going to have to take him for what he was.

In the meantime, she needed to figure out how to do her job. And it was starting to look increasingly like she had an impossible conflict of interest.

"Hey, Silent Bob," Adra said, bearing down on her with champagne flutes in hand. "You are not mingling. Why no mingling?"

Molly was standing next to a couch, just a little outside the main circle of friends that had gathered, probably looking lost in thought. Still, though.

"Silent Bob?" Molly looked aghast. "*Silent Bob?*"

"It was all I could think up on short notice," Adra said, waving it off. "They can't all be winners. Seriously, what's up?"

"Declan. I mean, obviously…Declan."

"Obviously." Adra sipped her champagne. "You going to elaborate on that?"

"Um…not yet?" Molly ventured. "I'm just still figuring it out. Or, I dunno, coming to terms, or something. But there is one thing I need to talk to you about. The book."

Adra looked incredibly unworried for a woman who'd sent her an extremely large check for the book in question. "Go on."

"Don't you see?" Molly said. She looked for something to nervously pick at, like those trusty old beer bottles at Uncle Jim's place, and came up empty. Might as well drink the champagne. "I mean, I *care* about him. And it changes everything. I'm not even doing this for the book anymore, if I'm totally honest. Like, I'm looking into what happened with Soren and Declan, and I think I have it almost figured out, but I don't know if I can *write* about it! Because I'm not doing it for the book."

"Why are you doing it?"

Damn.

"I'm doing it for Declan! I just... Look, I know there's something big there, something that's still hurting him. And I am a problem solver by nature, it's just who I am. I get shit done."

"A baby badass," Adra agreed.

"Baby nothing," Molly said fiercely. "It's like I can see this giant hole in his life where Soren used to be, and I just want to help him fix it, the way he's helped me with...other things. But that might mean that the book isn't what it was supposed to be, not entirely. Because I don't know how it will turn out, and if it's a choice between what will help Declan and what will sell books... You can only serve one master, you know?"

Adra burst out laughing. "Yeah, I am familiar with that rule."

"I didn't mean it that way," Molly said, blushing. "I just..."

"Yeah, you kinda did," Lola said from the other side of the couch. Molly blanched. At some point all those ladies had stopped talking and started listening. They'd all heard her. Everything.

And they were all...smiling?

"Yes," Lena whispered, and did a little fist pump.

"Ok, wait, what?" Molly said. "What's going on?"

"We couldn't help but overhear," Lola said. "It's just that we like Declan, too. We want good things for him. That's all."

Adra said, "Look, if your story becomes part of Declan's story, that's what you write about. Don't worry about it. Just do what comes naturally, and your talent will win out."

"If *my* story..." Molly wouldn't let herself quite finish that thought.

And Lola's smile lit up the room. And that was it. No more angst, no nervousness, even though Molly knew enough to know that both Lola and Lena had had bad experiences with the press. They all just kind of trusted her.

Molly couldn't quite wrap her head around it. She was so used to dealing with all the people back home who hated her, who thought she was a cheating liar, who were so ready to believe Robbie, that the idea that she'd be just...welcomed—it was hard to process. She kind of sat there in a daze while more women arrived—someone named Stella, who shined like a little ball of happiness, and a few others—and Molly felt enveloped in a warm blanket of acceptance.

And then she looked up and saw Declan leaning

against the far wall, looking at her. Wordlessly, he put out his hand and Molly stood up to take it.

chapter 23

In a room full of women wearing expensive designer threads, Molly was a freaking star in a little black dress from Target. They all loved her, Declan could tell, and it was important to him that they like her, the women of Volare who'd been so kind to him when he'd needed it. He realized now he'd almost been nervous, apparently for no reason. Molly was rocking it. She had them all in the palm of her hand.

But when she thought no one was watching, her face changed. Something on her mind. Something heavy. Happy and scared, all at once. Except Molly didn't need him or anyone else to help her sort it out; she wasn't sitting there like a little girl lost. There was nothing panicked or helpless about her, just a small furrow in her brow, like this was just another problem she was going to solve.

That was the moment when Declan realized he didn't have to worry. Molly wasn't like Bethany.

Molly wasn't going to fall the fuck apart if Declan screwed up; she wasn't in love with him. Because that was how he worked, and he knew that now. He wasn't afraid of caring about Molly. What kept him up nights was the idea that a woman he cared about would need more from him than he could give and he'd fail her. That was why he kept things impersonal in his arrangements.

But Molly...he wasn't sure Molly would ever need him like that. He wasn't sure she'd ever need anyone like that. She was the strongest woman he'd ever met.

And that meant he was free to feel, too.

Molly looked at him. He reached out his hand and beckoned. She was already getting up and walking toward him, her sandy blonde hair teasing at her face, her body moving in all the right ways. Declan decided he'd have to reconsider his punishment strategy in the future; no way was he ever doing this to himself again.

"Hey," she said. "I was thinking about you."

Declan let his hand fall on her stomach, moving around to the small of her back in that way he knew drove her crazy. He didn't even talk, just pulled her close to him, wanting to feel the warmth of her soft body.

She felt the hardness of his and made an appreciative little noise.

But Declan watched her face. There was more there than just lust.

"What's on your mind?" he asked.

Molly looked down, that little line appearing between her brows again. She opened her mouth, closed it again. Declan decided to help her out and tilted her face up to his.

"Tell me," he said.

"I don't know if I can write the book the way it should be written," she finally said.

"You're the only person I want to write it. You're the only person I trust. It's you or no one," he said.

"But—"

"You," he said slowly. "Or no one."

Molly put her hands on his chest and fingered his shirt, the beginnings of a smile playing at the corners of her mouth. "Ok," she said.

"That isn't the only thing on your mind," he said. He loved that he could read her, and he hoped to God it never went away.

"No, it isn't," she whispered. "But the other thing isn't ready yet."

Declan frowned and tucked a tendril of hair behind her ear. He didn't like to think there were things upsetting her. He wanted her to know everything was ok, that he understood that things were different, even if he didn't know how. But she wasn't ready.

He would wait.

"It will be," he said, and kissed her.

They had maybe a quiet moment like that before everything stopped. And then they were reminded of where they were.

"May I have your attention please?"

It was Roman, walking in like he owned the room, which, to be fair, he did. Following him were a bunch of guys Declan recognized and some he didn't. There was now a good mix of Doms and subs walking around of both genders, people mingling, flirting. Some playful swats with crops here and there. Declan hadn't even noticed the party getting bigger.

"My wife has decreed that there will be games for your amusement," Roman said, "Though she will, of course, be for my amusement only."

Lola tried to look annoyed and failed spectacularly.

"Sign-ups over there!" Chance shouted, and the crowd flocked, all except Adra, who was clearly relieved to see Ford all by himself, and Chance, who hovered over Lena.

"What's going on?" Molly asked.

"It's about to get kinda wild," Declan answered. He smiled when she moved a little bit closer to him.

"How so?"

"Depends, I guess."

Declan mulled. He didn't like the idea of Molly in a public situation, not even a little bit. He'd joked about it before, maybe even considered it, but now the idea of any of these guys playing with her brought out the Neanderthal in him.

And one of these guys was approaching Molly with a clipboard right fucking now.

"Hi, I'm Jones," he said. "Are you two up for capture the—"

"No," Declan snapped. "Get lost."

Clipboard Man shut his mouth, took one look at Declan's face, nodded his head, and walked away.

"Declan, what was that?" Molly asked. She couldn't hide the amusement in her voice. He didn't care.

"I'm taking you on a damn tour of the club.

C'mon, let's get out of here," he said, guiding her down the hall and away from the main room.

"Declan, you don't *know* this club."

"Doesn't matter."

She was laughing now, trotting after him to keep pace.

"Don't you need sleep before your big concert tomorrow?" she asked.

"Nope."

"Declan," she said, eyes shining, pulling at his hand. "What kind of games?"

He stopped to get a look at her and saw she had a devilish grin on her face.

"You gonna keep walking or you want me to throw you over my shoulder?" he asked.

Molly blushed. "Um…"

He smiled. She'd definitely prefer getting thrown over his shoulder. But they were stopped in front of the private elevator, and Declan saw it went up to the roof. Volare was the entire top floor of this swank hotel and apparently had the roof, as well. He pushed the button, and when the door opened immediately, he pulled Molly into the elevator and jammed the roof button forcefully.

Molly crashed into his chest and he decided to keep her there, his hand plastered to her back. Her breasts pushed into his abs and her hands searched for his rapidly hardening cock.

"I thought you said you were going to spank me in front of all your friends if I misbehaved," she said.

The doors opened. Declan pulled her out onto the roof, under the stars, and spun her around to face him.

"That was before," he said. His voice came thick and low.

"Before what?"

She had been teasing him before, but now she was serious. Nervous. Uncertain. Almost like she was afraid she'd done something wrong—Declan wanted to laugh. Nothing could have been further from the truth.

"Before I realized I can't stand the idea of anyone else even looking at you," he rasped. "Of anyone else getting to see you when you feel the way I'm going to make you feel."

Molly licked her plump bottom lip, and he had to fight the urge to throw her on the ground. Then she smiled only hesitantly, with that uncharacteristic uncertainty, and he wanted to kiss her into delirium all over again.

"So you'd object to my participation downstairs?" she said. "Because back when you had me sign that first contract, you said—"

Declan held himself rigid. "Do you want that?"

"No," she said, startled.

He couldn't help himself. He pulled her close again, not even hearing the sounds of the city below, not paying attention to the lights on the horizon. "We never signed another contract, Molly, so I'm just going to tell you my terms now. No games. No public rooms, no playing with anyone else. Because you are mine now. All mine. Do those terms work?"

For a second she hid her face against his chest. Then he felt her hands grip his shirt and tug.

"Of course they do," she said.

Declan hummed with satisfaction and pushed

her hair out of her face. He was going to have her now.

"But I have a question," she said.

"What?" he bit the word off, trying to be patient. His hand found its way under the neckline of her dress and he'd just discovered that she wasn't wearing a bra.

"Um," she said, her breath coming a little faster, arousal and shyness both vying for supremacy. "What was that capture game?"

Declan squeezed her nipple. Jesus.

"Exactly what it sounds like. Anyone can sign up, and if you get caught by a Dom on your list, you're his. Or hers. But you won't be playing."

She sighed, her hips moving against his, and let that teasing smile come back out to play. "It kinda sounds fun, except for the part where it's not you," she said.

Declan gave her breast one last squeeze, bent down, and whispered: "Run."

Molly's eyes flew open and she let out a small gasp before turning tail and sprinting across the roof deck, towards a rooftop garden, her laughter trailing behind her.

She made it about ten feet.

This time Declan really did throw her over his shoulder, grinning to himself at all the happy noises she made, making a list of things he wanted to do to her before the night was over. First up was making her scream at the top of her lungs over the city of New York. He walked to the high wrought iron fence surrounding the roof, pushing Molly's dress up on the way and letting his free hand wander just because. He put her down just in front of the fence, the lights of the city twinkling through, turned her around to face the city, and said, "Grab on."

Wordlessly she took hold of the fence, her ass straining against that dress. Declan pulled the bottom up and pushed the top down around her waist, leaving her ridiculously exposed in the night air.

"Spread 'em," he said.

He saw her shoulders shudder as she stepped out to the side, giving him what he wanted.

He didn't waste any more time. He sheathed himself, grabbed hold of her perfect, round ass, and plunged into her. She dropped her head and moaned, then arched back into him, meeting him, timing him while he pumped into her. She was always so ready for him, so wet, so damn perfect. Declan let himself fall forward, one hand above hers on the wrought iron, the other searching for her breast.

"Fucking come, Molly," he growled.

She did, like she always did, a freaking miracle convulsing around him with utter abandon. And when she couldn't hold herself up anymore he caught her, turned her around, set her gently on the ground, and then fucked her ever higher, until she had screamed herself hoarse and he had nothing, nothing left.

Nothing except what he had planned for her the next night at Madison Square Garden.

chapter 24

Molly was lost.

Madison Square Garden was *massive*, which wasn't really a surprise, but it was kind of a problem. Even the backstage area was like a small city, if a small city consisted of a warren of hallways and rooms and offices and who knew what the hell was going on.

It was just as well. Figuring out where she was, and where she had to be, gave her something to do rather than think about Declan.

Who was she kidding? She was thinking too hard, anyway. She was thinking about the previous night, another incredible night with Declan, another night that felt like it had changed her life. And yet, in the middle of it, he'd still gone for his phone with that tense expression on his face, the same way he did every night.

Molly knew it was probably Bethany that he talked to every day. She'd figured out that much.

And she knew she shouldn't be jealous, or upset, or whatever she was. Didn't mean squat. Molly still couldn't shake the feeling that there was always something—someone—else intruding on whatever it was that she had with Declan. Which was what, exactly?

Exactly. She had no right to complain.

Except, of course, that it all brought back memories of Robbie the jackass hanging out with his new girlfriend, Janelle, in sight of Molly's trailer within just a few days of dumping Molly for being pregnant. As big of an asshole as Robbie had been—over many, many things, and in many, many ways—nothing he had done had ever made Molly feel so completely worthless as that. As though the whole time they'd been together, she'd been replaceable. Disposable.

And, irrational as it was, that particular wound began to ache whenever Declan left her to go check on his ex, because it reminded her that Declan was not, and probably never would be, all hers.

Which was exactly the situation Molly had told herself to avoid when this whole thing started! Yeah, she had totally failed at the whole protecting her heart, keeping things uninvolved thing. Just an utter facepalm there.

And now she was wandering around the backstage maze at Madison Square Garden, trying to figure out how to deal with it and looking for where she was supposed to be. The guys had a private little huddle going, preparing for their first major comeback show, and Erik in particular needed a bit of a boost. Molly had gone wandering in search of material for the book she still didn't know how to write and had somehow ended up in a dark, twisted little area close enough to the stage to hear the buzz of the crowd.

Along the way she'd observed what amounted to the big leagues of backstage areas. It was like the Olympics for groupies. Like back in L.A., where all the women at that private show had been models or celebrities, or, at the very least, future models or celebrities. Only here the women wore more black, and the sexual exchange going on—sex for access—was a lot more open. More free market, Molly guessed. Something for everyone.

Basically the worst place to be feeling insecure about the man that she had feelings for.

Especially because Molly had just stumbled on a roadie getting a very epic, very loud blowjob.

"Jesus," Molly muttered.

"Jesus!" said the roadie. The woman who was on her knees didn't say anything.

Yeah, that was not something she wanted to be around at the moment. The knot in her stomach that made itself known whenever she thought about Declan tightened a few clicks, and she knew that it was not going to help her make good decisions. Time to get unlost and away from this craziness.

She took the very first turn she saw and barreled forward, only to come upon a dead end and a little room. The only way out was back through the blowjob area. And in here was, oddly enough, a young woman Molly's age and a little boy of maybe eight, engaged in a very intense thumb-wrestling battle.

The boy saw her first.

"Hey, did they go on?" he asked. "Can we come out yet?"

The woman, who was willow-thin and blonde with colored streaks in her hair, like a particularly elegant punk, covered the little boy's ears with her hands and raised an eyebrow at Molly.

"You a fellow blowjob refugee?" she asked.

Molly burst out laughing. "I am."

"I'm Harlow," the woman said, keeping a hold on the little boy's ears. "This is my little brother, Dill."

Dill rolled his eyes.

Harlow went on, "That has got to be the world's longest blowjob at this point. If the dude weren't so damn vocal, I could probably sneak this little guy past."

"He's definitely enthusiastic."

"He's like a male cheerleader."

Dill's patience evidently ran out, and he shook his head free of Harlow's protective earmuff hands. "I am way too old for this, Lo. I know what they were doing. I *saw* them."

Harlow looked horrified. "Oh my God, *lie* to me, Dill."

"Maybe we could say something to security," Molly said, letting her voice trail off as both Harlow and Dill gave her a look like she'd just sprouted a second head. Molly laughed. "Right, never mind."

"Besides," Harlow said, ruffling her little brother's hair. "Dill and I are already on thin ice, because Dill decided to play with some equipment he found lying around."

"They can't kick us out," Dill said with a

mischievous grin, holding up the laminated pass he had around his neck. "We have passes."

"Pfft, they can totally kick us out. Nobody cares about radio contest winners," Harlow said, plopping down on a truly disgusting looking couch in the corner. She changed her tone when she looked at Dill's falling face. The kid suddenly looked younger than eight. "Don't worry, kiddo, you *will* get to meet the band, ok? I will kick all the ass in the world if I have to, I promise."

Molly realized she felt weirdly at home. This was something she understood, a big sister looking out for her brother. It was the first time she felt like she was on solid ground since...well, since meeting Declan.

She felt a sudden pang. Lydia. Molly knew that she'd been a terrible big sister lately. She should be on top of whatever was going on with Lydia; even if Lydia was being a difficult teenager, she shouldn't be letting it all slide just because she was so wrapped up in what was happening between her and Declan.

"You guys going to meet Savage Heart?" Molly asked, trying to get her mind off of it.

Dill's face lit up with a wicked grin. "I'm gonna ask if I can be their new guitarist."

"Wow," Molly said. "That is ambitious."

"It could happen! Come on, I'm a cute little kid, they bring me out on stage..." Dill batted his eyelashes, and Molly made a mental note: *Get this kid on stage.*

"They're his favorite band," Harlow said wryly. "So naturally he's gunning for them."

"Hey," Dill said anxiously, "They're supposed

to go on soon."

He was right. Molly had wandered for far too long. The three of them emerged from the little room, glad to see that the immediate vicinity was now blowjob free—or at least Molly and Harlow were glad; Dill seemed kind of disappointed, which Harlow decided to ignore—and still totally lost. They ran around with increasing anxiety before a harried looking production flak with maybe ten thousand badges slung around his neck grabbed hold of Molly's arm and brought the whole caravan to a halt.

"Are you Molly Ward?" he asked in desperation.

"Yeah," Molly said with relief. "Do you know where Declan is?"

"Declan?" Dill said with awe. "Declan Donovan?"

"Come with me," the flak urged. "He's not going on until you're where you're supposed to be."

Damn. Too late Molly remembered what Declan had said the previous night: he didn't want her in the front row this time, but in the wings. There was something he wanted her to see.

But then Molly looked at Dill. The kid's face—no one with a heart could disappoint him.

"Can my friends come?" Molly asked.

The poor flak stared at her. "Lady, if you can get Savage Heart on stage on time, you can do whatever you want as far as I'm concerned," he said. "But we have to go, *now*."

Which was how they all ended up running through Madison Square Garden, Dill whooping and jumping up to touch the low ceiling at random intervals, Harlow laughing and mouthing a silent "thank you" to Molly, and Molly thinking about Declan.

He wouldn't go on stage without her?

Molly tried to suppress a smile, but it was impossible. Just like it was impossible to tell herself to slow down, to try to proceed with some sense of dignity intact. She was literally running toward him. Of course she was. It felt like she had been this whole time, whether she knew it or not, whether she wanted to or not.

She felt totally out of control, and it was the happiest she'd ever felt.

And when they turned the final corner, spilling into the large area just off the stage, the crowd's chants filling the space, she knew why: Declan.

The rest of the guys were loafing around, ready to go, waiting. Declan was smoldering. Standing there, tall, dark, dominating, and strong, and it was like Molly couldn't see anything else. Nothing but those eyes, burning for her.

But nobody told Dill.

The little boy screamed and ran right for Declan, who broke his gaze with Molly at the last possible second and held out his hand for a high five from a little kid who was literally overflowing with exuberance. Dill hit it as hard as he could and yelled, "You're Declan Donovan!"

Declan laughed. "I know!"

"Sorry," Harlow said. "I mean, oh my God, you are really about to go on stage, and Dill—Dill! Come back here! Seriously, I'm so sorry."

Declan looked at Molly, his eyes shining. "Don't

be. You guys hang out here, and we'll see you after the show."

"'Lo!" screamed Dill, hopping up and down. His sister laughed and hugged him, possibly as a way of keeping him from bouncing off the ceiling, and that left Declan free.

And he came straight for Molly.

"I got lost," she said as he closed in on her.

"I'd have found you," he said.

Molly licked her lips, tried to swallow. Her mouth was dry. How did he do that to her still? Still made her stomach flutter, still made her skin feel too warm, still…

Declan hooked his finger into the waistband of her jeans and pulled her in close in that way that he did. Molly felt weak and strong and wet for him all at once. All the screaming thoughts that told her to freak out, that she was in trouble, that he had a thing with his ex that Molly would never understand—they all shut up the second his lips touched hers.

He kissed her hard, but maybe not as hard as he usually did. When he pulled back, he whispered, "You wouldn't believe what I would have done to you if it wasn't for the kid."

"Show me later?" she asked.

"Thoroughly," he said, and gave her ass a good squeeze.

And then it was time for Savage Heart to take back Madison Square Garden.

***

They were amazing. They were always amazing,

but Declan—Declan was on another level. He stormed out there and owned the crowd, the same way he owned Molly, the same way he owned any room he'd ever walked into. She would never, ever get tired of watching him perform, especially not when she knew what it truly was for him, when she was the only person who knew what that release was.

Or pretended she was the only other person who knew. For right now, she was his sub. Right now had to be good enough, and right now, Molly had trouble taking her eyes off of him.

Which was how she missed the first five calls.

She only figured out her phone was blowing up because of the blue glow that kept reflecting off of Dill's rapt face. Molly looked idly down and saw the one number she hadn't expected to see.

Shauna's.

Shauna, who was housesitting for her, had called her *five times*.

There could be nothing good about that.

Molly backed away, trying to find somewhere quiet enough to take a phone call, her mind racing with the various possibilities. Had something happened to her house? She'd thought she was being paranoid when she'd asked Shauna to stay, but maybe not.

It's just stuff, she told herself. *Stuff can be replaced.*

Molly found another little office, slipped inside, and closed the door behind her. She stared at her phone. The ball of dread that had coalesced in her stomach was not going anywhere, not until she made that phone call and found out what had happened.

She didn't have to. Her phone rang, jangling harshly in the confines of the tiny room. It was Shauna.

"Shauna, what happened?"

"Oh, thank God," her friend said. The reception was terrible and Shauna sounded so far away, and it only increased Molly's anxiety. "Thank God you picked up, Mol. I have *no* idea what to do…"

"What happened?" Molly asked again.

Shauna took a big breath and said, "It's Lydia."

chapter 25

Molly's heart stopped.

She knew it didn't, not really. She didn't actually die. She just lived, for a second that seemed to last an eternity, between the beats, in a moment where she knew the next words she heard could break her heart, and more than anything she didn't want to find out what those words were.

"She's here, Mol," Shauna said.

"Why?" Molly croaked. "What happened? God, Shauna, just tell me."

"She won't stop crying, Molly. She just showed up, hysterical, and she won't tell me anything, and I have no idea what's going on."

"Put her on the phone."

She waited with that iron coil of dread in her belly, twisting, turning, trying not to think of what could have happened to her baby sister while Molly wasn't there to protect her. Molly had been so close, so close to getting Lydia out of there...

"Molly?"

She almost cried to hear her voice, thick with tears. Then Lydia hiccupped, and it sent Molly right into maternal mode. She had someone to take care of.

"Ladybug, what's wrong?"

Lydia started to cry again, then managed to hold herself together long enough to talk. "I'm so sorry, Molly, I am so, so sorry. I didn't want to tell you until we had it all figured out, but then Daddy found out, and I had nowhere else to go, and—"

Gently, Molly said, "It's ok, whatever it is, I promise. Just tell me. What is it?"

There was a pause.

"I'm pregnant," Lydia said, sighing, like it was a relief to just say it out loud. "It was an accident, Molly, I swear I was careful, but now Daddy knows and he is *pissed*, and I just...where are you?"

Molly sat down on some random person's desk with heavy finality. She couldn't believe what she'd just heard. Literally could not believe it. She'd had every safe sex conversation she could have had with her sister. She'd offered to buy her condoms, offered to take her to get the pill, offered to let her keep her things at Molly's place just so their dad wouldn't find anything. Molly had drilled all those lessons home, over and over again, whenever she could, even after their dad had limited communication.

She'd been so confident. So sure she'd done right, so sure that Lydia would be spared the consequences of the mistakes that Molly herself had made, that Lydia wouldn't have to go through any of that pain. And now here she was again, all over again, except this time it was somehow worse. It was worse because Molly *knew*, this time; she knew how much pain might be in store for her sister, and there was not a damn thing she could do about it.

"Molly?" Lydia said softly.

"I'm here, Bug," Molly said, rubbing her eyes. "I'm coming home. Tomorrow morning, ok? Eight hours if I can swing it. Can you hang out with Shauna until tomorrow morning? And you call the police if Daddy shows up, ok?"

"I don't think he will, Mol," Lydia said. She already sounded better, just getting to talk to her sister. "I think he's kind of relieved to have an excuse to get rid of me, to tell the truth. I think I'm safe so long as I'm not there."

"Yeah, well, if he does, you call, ok?"

"I promise."

"Eight hours, depending on the flight and everything, ok? Sit tight."

Molly hung up with a sense of grim determination. Everything had definitely changed, all right. She was going to have to get to the airport, find a flight, get Lydia set up in a new place…

"Everything ok?"

Molly looked up to find Harlow sticking her head in the door. It was only then that Molly realized she was crying.

"Ok, obviously everything is not ok," Harlow said. "But you just made my brother's life, so tell me: Can I help?"

"No?" Molly said. "I don't know. I have to get to the airport. I have to get a flight back to L.A. like, now. My sister is…she's in trouble."

"Oh God." The sibling thing hit Harlow hard.

Molly stood up, running her hand through her hair, trying to remember that she was a badass. She said, "I'm sorry, I have to go. Can you give him a message for me?"

Harlow blinked. "Who? Declan Donovan?"

"Yeah, Declan." It had been a while since he'd been 'Declan Donovan' to her. It made Molly smile wistfully. "Can you tell him...oh God, I don't know. Tell him I had to go, tell him it was an emergency, tell him I'm sorry. I have to get a cab..."

Molly cursed inwardly. She was rambling, disorganized. Panicked. These were not the traits of a badass who was about to go take charge and get things done; this was what she'd been like years ago when confronted with her own ruined life. It had taken a lot of work to get past that. She wasn't going to backslide now.

"I can give him your message, no problem," Harlow said. "But Molly, there is literally zero chance that you will get a cab right now. It's raining, it's late at night, people are getting out of bars, there's the shift change, and there's a livery strike. If you wait an hour—"

Molly shook her head. "No, I'll miss the next flight. I promised her tomorrow morning. I can't..."

Molly didn't even want to finish that sentence. She couldn't bear to break another promise about her sister right now. The only person she knew who could help her was on stage right now, and the idea of throwing this on Declan's lap, of asking him to deal with it... She was not ruining this tour for him. And that wasn't what they were to each other.

No, don't think about him. Do NOT think about him.

She wouldn't be able to hold it together if she did. If she thought about how much she truly needed him right now, about how what she wanted from him was what he'd said he couldn't give, about how she had to leave, knowing...

"Ok, I gotta figure something out," Molly said. "It was nice meeting you, though, Harlow."

"Oh damn it," Harlow said, digging in her pocket. She produced a set of car keys and pushed them toward Molly. "I would be out of my mind if anything ever happened to Dill. You have to go. Just give me your phone number so I don't feel like such a crazy person, and I can't believe I'm saying this, but take my car."

Molly stared at the keys. "What?"

"Seriously, I might snap back to sanity at any moment. Just text me where you leave it at the airport and overnight the keys to the address I send you, ok? And remember I'm broke and this is how I get my brother to and from his weird computer camp where he's on scholarship, and...oh, you don't care about any of that, just freaking take it."

"You're serious?"

"Yes," Harlow sighed. "Look, if someone hadn't done something this insane for me once, I would have..."

Harlow stopped. She almost seemed to blink back tears, but maybe Molly had just imagined that. Maybe Molly just saw something of herself in Harlow.

"Look, if somebody hadn't helped me out, I

don't know where I'd be. I might be dead. I definitely wouldn't have Dill. And I have no idea what would have happened to him," Harlow said, obviously working to keep her voice steady. "I kind of owe the universe. And you are a nice person who went out of your way to make my brother happy. Plus, I can always go after Declan Donovan if I don't get my car back," she said, grinning. "Now, just take the freaking keys and go help your sister before I change my mind."

"Oh my God, you are serious," Molly said, handing over her phone so Harlow could dial her own number while Molly watched in disbelief. She wasn't quite conditioned to accept random, genuine acts of kindness from the world, but screw it—she'd worry about karma and divine plans later. She grabbed the keys and the proffered parking ticket.

"It's in the lot on Thirty-Seventh Street," Harlow called after her. "It's a 1992 Corolla, but it runs. You pay for parking, and just, like…I don't know, go east and then follow the signs? There are maps in the glove box. Please don't kill my car!"

"Deal," Molly said.

She raced out of the labyrinth below Madison Square Garden, taking the first door marked with a big red exit sign, and emerged out into a loading dock, surprising a bunch of smokers who were sheltering from the rain under the overhang.

"Which way is Thirty-Seventh Street?" she shouted.

"You serious?" a guy in a janitor's uniform said. He hooked his thumb to the right. "That way. But it's raining!"

Molly was already running up to the street. She was aware.

~ * ~ * ~

Declan had looked for her. He'd looked for her throughout the whole set. At first he'd thought she was just hanging so far back in the wings he couldn't see her, but there was that feeling in his chest, that emptiness. She wasn't fucking there.

He sang the song he'd written anyway, because he'd said he would. Even if the only person meant to hear it wasn't there.

Declan powered through his set, channeling it all the way he was meant to, thinking about her. But as soon as the lights went out, he was striding into the wings.

He was right. She was gone.

"Where is she?" he demanded.

No one answered. It wasn't the usual congratulatory, hedonistic vibe you got after a show. Maybe his mood had something to do with it. His mood, and the presence of a little kid.

In fact, the blonde woman with the blue and red streaks and her little brother were the only ones who could meet his eye.

"One more time," Declan said slowly. "Where is she?"

He was trying to keep his voice calm, trying to ignore the nausea he felt building in his gut. He knew his physical reaction right now was due to his own issues and had nothing to do with Molly. Declan had known lots of women who'd pulled disappearing acts, chief among them his own mother — which would account for the nausea — but that wasn't Molly.

That didn't mean he wasn't worried. Or pissed off.

The blonde chick raised her hand slightly and cleared her throat. "I, um, gave her my car," she said. "She gave me a message for you."

Declan stared at her.

"She said she was sorry," the blonde woman offered.

Declan closed the distance between them in only a few strides, remembering too late not to bring his full physical presence to bear; the woman and her little brother were both tiny, both nice people. Declan took a deep breath.

"Tell me," he demanded.

"Hi, I'm Harlow," the woman said, one eyebrow all the way up. "You've already met Dill. Molly asked me to tell you that she had to leave, that it was an emergency, and that she was sorry. It was..."

She seemed to hesitate. Declan didn't have the patience.

"I care about this woman," he said through gritted teeth. "And something made her leave in the middle of the show. Tell me what it was."

"Something about her sister," Harlow admitted. "It sounded...I don't know, it sounded important. I can't believe I gave her my car."

"You what?"

"I gave her my car. To get to the airport. I'm just a sap for little siblings in trouble, and she was so upset..." Harlow drifted off. "She's not a nutjob or anything, right?"

"How long ago?"

"Um. A couple of hours. At least."

"Shit," Declan said, then looked down at Dill. "Sorry, little man. Davey!"

Declan was already in motion, his mind racing as the road manager came running up. Declan almost felt bad for the man.

"Get this woman a car," he ordered, pointing at Harlow. "Give that kid the mic from the show. And give me my phone."

"Declan, what are you doing?" Brian called out.

Good question. All Declan could think about was how upset Molly would have to be for a random stranger to lend her a car. That kind of thing didn't happen. It especially didn't happen in New York.

Thinking about Molly in that state, alone, made him feel sick.

"Postpone the next show, Davey," he said grimly. "I have somewhere to be."

"Where the fuck do you think you have to be?" Brian yelled.

"No idea."

But he bet Adra knew.

chapter 26

Molly maxed out one credit card and put a major ding in another one booking a last minute flight to L.A.X., and spent so long explaining why she didn't have any luggage that she had to seriously sprint to her gate. As if the drive to J.F.K. hadn't been stressful enough, in the rain, not knowing where she was going. All in all, Molly didn't have time to sit and think until she got on the plane. And then they sat there for ages, giving her way, way too much time to do all that thinking.

Because all she thought about was Declan.

Which was unexpected. But now that she'd talked to Lydia and knew what the situation was, she'd already formulated the beginnings of a plan. She was upset and stressed and whatever, but all that was expected, and Molly's inner badass knew that she would handle it. It felt like she had it under control, kind of.

Declan was something else entirely.

Molly wrapped herself in the thin airline blanket and shivered. She was soaking wet, cold, and sad. And she had no right to be sad, at least. She'd called Adra from the car—a harrowing experience in its own right—and arranged to have someone leave her miraculously still-functional LeBaron at L.A.X. so she'd have a ride back home, and, rather than demand to know why Molly was leaving the tour or asking about the book, Adra had only wanted to know if Molly was ok. Adra, who was already back in L.A., had even offered to pick Molly up. Molly had said no, because she wasn't sure if Lydia wanted to deal with a bunch of new people at the moment, and it wasn't Molly's call.

But she'd been touched to the point of tears. She couldn't believe how much her life had turned around in such a short time. Didn't realize how lonely she'd been before until she could look back while surrounded by all these wonderful people. She had no idea what she'd done to deserve any of it.

Especially Declan.

Molly hugged herself tightly as the lights in the cabin were turned down and knew she wasn't going to be able to sleep much. She shouldn't have left him. She didn't know what else she could have done, knew she couldn't have sat there *not* doing anything after that phone call, but she still felt like she shouldn't have left him.

Which was crazy, because they weren't... Molly didn't know what they were. She thought Declan didn't, either. Which somehow made it scarier. Because she knew now, sitting alone in an airplane, wishing more than anything that Declan was sitting beside her, that she loved him.

"I am so screwed," she whispered.

No one answered.

Well, no, maybe not screwed. Maybe not entirely. She thought about all the things Declan had given her in such a short time, all the things he'd taught her, even beyond her submissive tastes—how to let go, how to let herself feel, how necessary that safety valve was for her—and she knew all those lessons would stick. They were *hers* now. Part of her. She'd always have them.

But the idea of being without him still felt like a smaller kind of death.

So Molly spent the whole flight trying to reason with her heart. It wasn't something she'd ever had success with before, obviously, but Molly was the type to take on impossible tasks.

She was actually moderately successful.

By the time they started their descent into L.A. and the rest of the passengers were waking up from their incredibly uncomfortable naps, groggy and grumpy and realizing they now had three extra hours in the long day ahead of them, Molly had convinced herself of one immutable fact: Life on a tour bus wasn't real life.

She and Declan had this insane attraction, this whirlwind emotional whatever, and all of it was predicated on the intense intimacy and forced confinement of a tour bus.

Which wasn't real life.

It *wasn't* real.

All of which left Molly completely unprepared to encounter Declan Donovan in her very real home.

***

Molly set her jaw and physically forced herself to make the turn. Pleasant Valley Park. She didn't think it would bother her this much to come home. She'd lived there her whole life, and suddenly every approaching mile felt like pushing against an imposing, malevolent force. Driving the last leg had been like biking uphill, every second a battle against the natural forces of the universe.

Nobody and nothing wanted Molly in Pleasant Valley. The bright sun felt hard and merciless, the heat was oppressive. Molly kept looking around to see faces she knew but that didn't know her—or at least who she was now. And that was the problem. All these people, they all knew her as someone else. Someone they thought had slept around as a teenager and gotten pregnant, someone who'd let herself become a victim of everyone who had decided to hate her for that fairly unremarkable event, just because Robbie had decided it would be so.

She hated coming back here. And like with so many things in the past twenty-four hours, she didn't realize how much she had changed except in contrast to who she'd been in this place, even a few weeks ago. Molly could feel her old self creeping back on her, like an old haunted dress that demanded to be worn. Like some demented form of ghostly peer pressure. There was this weird desire to fall back into old patterns, to accept old truths—that she wasn't a woman people respected, that everybody hated her—and she had to fight to shake it off, hunched over in her car, gripping the steering wheel with white-knuckled hands.

Thinking about Declan helped. Thinking about the things she'd experienced with Declan helped.

Maybe this place wasn't any more real than a tour bus. Maybe the whole point was that Molly should get to choose what would be her reality from now on. She wasn't sure what that would mean, exactly, but she was damn sure it wouldn't involve this place.

And she was just as sure that she wouldn't be that weak, traumatized girl in front of her sister. Lydia needed support, so support was what she was going to get.

Molly pulled the LeBaron up to the curb and stared at the car occupying her packed dirt driveway. It was a sleek silver BMW. It shined so brightly it was nearly blinding. Who belonged to *that* car? And then a moment later, it hit her: how had Lydia gotten here? It must be the father.

The *father*.

Molly threw her head back and laughed from pure joy. She had made so many assumptions, all of them based on her own crappy experience, all of them based, in the end, on what a supreme asshole Robbie had turned out to be. But maybe Lydia, thank God, had better taste in men. Maybe the father of Lydia's baby was a good guy. Maybe he'd decide to actually be there for her, and double plus bonus points if the guy turned out to have the means to support her, too.

Well, assuming he wasn't much older than her. Molly still might have some ass to kick. The BMW certainly raised questions. Molly wasn't ready to relax, and she still had every intention of supporting her sister entirely if necessary, no matter what Lydia chose to do, but the idea that she might not have to do it alone was such a relief that Molly started to cry.

Like, really, really cry. Sobbing. That's what she was doing. Ugly crying, in her car, outside her crappy old trailer, by herself.

Which was exactly how Lydia found her.

"Molly," she said, tapping on the window. "You ok?"

Molly just stared stupidly for a moment. She hadn't seen Lydia in over six months, and here she was, her hair tied back in a lazy ponytail, wearing her favorite Ramones shirt and a pair of jeans that didn't much hide the little bump, if you knew to look for it.

And Molly knew. She couldn't stop looking for it. She got out of her car and wordlessly walked over to Lydia—Lydia, who was looking at her like she'd just escaped from the nuthouse or something—and wrapped her sister up in the fiercest hug she could manage.

"Molly, are you ok?" Lydia asked again, her voice muffled. "What's wrong?"

Molly choked on her little sister's hair, determined to never let go.

"Nothing," she sobbed. "Absolutely nothing is wrong. I am so happy to see you, Bug."

"Then why are you crying?"

"I have no idea," Molly said, finally letting Lydia go from her death grip. "I missed you, Bug."

"Well, don't cry about it," Lydia said, starting to tear up herself. "I missed you, too."

Molly gave Lydia her best serious look and took her little sister's face in both hands. "You know everything's going to be ok, right? We're going to make sure everything's ok. No matter what, we will handle it. I promise."

"Yeah," Lydia said. "That's what your friends said, too."

Molly opened her mouth to speak, but nothing came out. She didn't have any...

"You know, if you'd waited for me," a deep male voice said from the door, "you could have flown private, too."

Declan Donovan. Leaning in the doorway of Molly's house, arms crossed, eyes gentle, looking like everything Molly hadn't allowed herself to dream she could have. Strong, dedicated, and here. Molly started to cry all over again.

~ * ~ * ~

The trip back to L.A. had been tense. Declan's phone began blowing up almost immediately. First the guys had been pissed; postponing tour dates with no notice was a big fucking deal. Declan had explained that it was Molly, and it was a emergency, and Brian had backed off, but the suits back at the label and at Madison Square Garden had been less impressed.

Good thing Savage Heart was such a big act. Declan had never traded much on the power of fame and money, but he was glad to have it at his disposal now, because his mind was well and truly fucked. All he could think about was Molly. Not knowing what was wrong, whether she was ok, what had happened—it was all driving him insane. And he hated the idea of finishing the rest of the tour without her, found himself wondering whether he could do it all. Which was a whole other level of mindfuck when he realized what that implied.

So his phone kept ringing, but it was never the one person he wanted to talk to: Molly. Eventually he'd turned it off, but not before calling the one person he couldn't blow off: Uncle Jim.

And *that* had turned out to be another mindfuck.

"We're not going to make it fishing," Declan had said. He had just landed in L.A. at the ass crack of dawn, Pacific Time, which meant Jim had already been up for a while on the east coast.

"What? I'm not calling about a goddamn fishing trip, though tell that girl of yours I want a rain check. I'm calling because Bethany's done with her program. She's got the all clear, and she wanted you to know, only you don't pick up your phone."

Shit. Declan should have been on top of that. Bethany deserved real congratulations and support, and a whole bunch of other things.

"That's fantastic," he'd said. "But I can't be there right now. I'll call her."

"You got something more important?"

Declan didn't even have to think about it. "Yes."

There was a lengthy, suspiciously satisfied-sounding pause.

"Good," Jim said, and hung up.

It wasn't until later that Declan thought to ask himself how the hell Uncle Jim had known that Bethany was out of the hospital. But by then he'd already pulled into Volare, where Adra was waiting, looking almost as worried as he felt, and the whole thing came rushing back to him.

Right then he decided he'd cancel the tour if he had to. Declan wasn't going to fail Molly if he could help it, not the way he'd failed Bethany, even if risking it was the one thing left on this planet that could scare him. Molly very clearly did not need him, but Declan didn't give a shit. He defined the man he was by the things he did, good and bad, and he was going to be the man who helped Molly Ward if he could.

Because he fucking loved her.

"You find out what happened?" he asked Adra, getting out of his crappy last-minute rental. The air conditioning didn't even work.

"No," Adra said. "You're sure about—"

"Just take me to her place, Adra," Declan said. "If she wants me to leave, I'll leave. But between the two of us I bet there's something we can do for her. Just put it all on me if you have to."

Declan had realized on the plane he didn't even know where Molly lived. His only shot was Adra. He felt like the world's biggest jackass, that he knew so much and so little about Molly, but he was stuck with it for now. He'd fix that later; right now he just needed to get to where she was.

Adra gave him a long, appraising look, and whatever she saw there, she approved of, because she got out the beamer and drove the two of them on out to Pleasant Valley Park, a dry, dusty looking place with little kids playing in the dirt and laundry on the line. Looked like a million other places, with a million other lives. Only this one had

Molly.

"You know much about this situation?" he asked Adra.

"A little, not much," she said. "I know she wants to get out of it."

"She might not even be here," Declan said. "Her sister doesn't live here. It was just the only thing I could think of."

"She picking up her phone?"

Declan frowned. "Not yet."

And then they pulled into the driveway, only to be greeted before they even knocked on the door by a young, pretty woman who looked like Molly, only a little bit rounder in the face — and rounder in the belly. Declan got a good look at that bump and everything suddenly made sense. He said, "You're Lydia."

Lydia was tense, defensive. Arms crossed. "Who the hell are you?"

"She's not a Savage Heart fan," Adra smiled.

"They're ok," Lydia said. "But this is private property, so—"

"Don't be scared," Declan told her. "We're friends of Molly's, not your father's. We're here to help."

Molly's name was the magic word. Lydia's defenses collapsed like a child's sandcastle until she looked like she was about to cry, and then another woman came out of the trailer, all ready to kick some ass, only to join Adra in helping Lydia get a hold of herself. Declan spent the next thirty minutes watching the women work, feeling himself fit into this life of Molly's he'd never known. He was still pissed at her for leaving, for not trusting him to stick around or help out or whatever it was that went through her mind, but now he was grateful for the chance to get to know her in her real life. Here. Like this.

He would help take care of her sister. He would do anything at all to make Molly Ward's life better. That was Declan turned his phone back on and called Ford Colson with very specific, very detailed instructions.

And then he went out to meet Molly.

chapter 27

Molly couldn't quite believe what she was seeing. She hadn't slept much; it was totally possible she was hallucinating.

Declan Donovan, in her house.

And Adra?

"This guy can't be outside too long if you guys want to keep a low profile," Adra said, her head popping out from behind Declan. Then she smiled and waved. "Hi, Molly."

Declan shifted, and put out his hand. "C'mere," he said softly.

Molly didn't need to be told twice.

As soon as she entered his orbit, Declan picked her up by the waist, spinning her into her own home and wrapping her up in those big arms. It was probably the most chaste contact they'd ever had, and yet it set Molly's body tingling and her heart thumping. He was *here*. He was holding her. Like he wasn't going to let her go.

"I needed to know you were ok," he said into her ear.

She shivered.

Then she heard Lydia come in behind her and reluctantly disentangled herself from Declan, surveying her home with all these people in it for the first time. It seemed so much smaller—but warmer. Declan alone dwarfed the place, made it seem miniature. From behind Adra, Shauna waved, looking pretty bewildered. The whole thing was surreal, but she'd never felt as at home in her own home as she did right then, with all of these people crowded into her small living room.

Then Lydia came and took her hand. Lydia, who Molly never got to see. Totally disorienting.

"Don't misunderstand me," Molly said carefully. "I'm so happy to see you guys, but I didn't sleep much, and I'm not fully coherent, so ...what are you all doing here?"

Declan's low rumble filled the trailer. "I'm here to help," he said. "Adra, too. Not complicated."

"Um, he's saying he'll pay for everything, Molly," Lydia said quietly. "Like, everything. No matter what. An apartment, too."

Molly looked sharply at Declan. She should be happy about this, obviously. She should be thrilled. She hadn't been entirely sure how she would support Lydia if need be, only certain that she'd find a way. So why wasn't she doing a happy dance?

"I'll set you up with everything you might need," Declan said. "Whatever happens, you don't have to worry about money. And Lydia, you can call me whenever if anyone gives you any trouble.

Day or night. I'm never more than a few hours away, and I've got people in L.A."

"Thank you," Lydia said, squeezing Molly's hand.

It seemed like only Molly was feeling the least bit ambivalent. Why was that? She worked hard to figure out what she was feeling, because it wasn't all good. It wasn't even mostly good.

She felt weak all over again. Molly realized that she'd actually been looking forward, in some not entirely helpful way, to swooping in and being the one to rescue Lydia, the way she never got to do for herself. The way no one else did for her. And she hated that she felt that, because she knew that this should be about Lydia only, and not Molly seeking closure or whatever for her own issues, but there it was.

Molly felt terrible. Terrible and selfish and…scared. Why was she scared?

"We should talk about where you'll stay tonight, if you don't feel like it's safe here, given your father's feelings," Adra said. "Volare seems like the obvious choice until we get you your own place."

"You said he didn't care enough to come after you," Molly said, somewhat alarmed.

"Well, he didn't, but who knows if he gets drunk," Lydia said. "And you know it's not totally safe here for you, either, with all the stuff Robbie and his boys put you through."

Declan came alive. "What?" he demanded. "What is she talking about?"

"I'm used to it," Molly said, irritated. "I'm getting out on my own, I have a plan."

"You're coming to Volare, too," he said, shaking

his head.

"You don't have to do this," she said bitterly to Declan. "Any of this. I can take care of it."

"Molly..." Lydia said, reading her sister like a book. "Don't."

"But I *can*."

Molly heard herself being irrational and angry and hated it, but for some reason she just couldn't stop. She couldn't look at Declan without wanting him, without wanting to run to him to feel safe and cared for, and that just made it so much worse because it was *terrifying*. She'd worked so hard to be able to become the person who could help her sister, who could take care of anything, who could *handle shit*, and now it felt like Declan was taking that from her, piece by piece. First by making her love him, and then by actually showing up and doing Molly's job for her.

And she couldn't even be angry at him for it, because it made her love him more, when she knew he couldn't love her the way she wanted.

And *that* pissed her off.

Declan didn't get a running commentary, but he saw enough to know she was pissed. He said, "I know you can, Molly."

"Mol, it's my decision," Lydia was saying. "I'd be insane not to take whatever help I can get right now."

The fact that Molly was wrong and knew it was pretty much the last straw. She hated being wrong.

She looked straight at Declan and said, "You had no right."

"Are you fucking serious?" Declan said abruptly. His eyes flashed. "I did this for you. I did this because when I found out something hurt you so badly that you drove to the airport by yourself, in the rain, in the middle of the night, in a stranger's car, and there was nothing I could do about it, *it hurt me, too*. It fucking killed me. So I am going to do whatever the hell I can, cancel whatever tour dates, throw my money around, and move whatever fucking mountain happens to get in the way to keep that thing from hurting you. Right now Ford is setting up a trust in your sister's name with you as a trustee. It'll be yours even if you never want to talk to me again. This is one thing I can do, Molly, and fuck yes, I'm going to do it."

Molly was stunned. She had never seen him like this, never seen him even close to angry. Not at her. She didn't know how to react—until she looked at Lydia.

"Don't say it hurt me, Declan," Molly snapped. Then she turned to Lydia and said, "It didn't hurt me, Bug. I was just scared."

Lydia blinked back tears. "I know that, Mol, you don't have to explain. I'm scared, too. I called you crying, remember?"

"Shit," Declan said, running a big hand through his hair. He looked tired suddenly. "Lydia, I didn't mean it like that. I didn't know what the hell had happened, and Molly was just…gone."

He looked at Molly now, and for the first time she saw naked hurt in his eyes. She hadn't thought about that when she'd left. She'd thought he'd be irritated, but not…

"Ok!" Adra said, clapping her hands. "Lydia, have you ever driven a BMW? Shauna?"

"Nope," Shauna said, clearly relieved.

"Ditto," Lydia whispered.

"Ok, well, let's go cross that item off the bucket list, then. C'mon. We'll be back...later," Adra finished, giving Molly a slightly worried look as she herded Shauna and Lydia out to her car.

In a second, they were alone.

And for the first time, Molly didn't know what to say to Declan. They stood there for what seemed like forever, just looking at each other. Wanting to touch each other, but feeling, for the first time, like there was a wall there.

Until Declan broke through it.

"Fuck," he muttered, sweeping Molly into his arms. He kissed her, one hand holding the side of her face so sweetly, like he was worried she might break, the other crushing her against him like he couldn't get close enough.

This made sense to her. This she could do.

Her body opened to him like it always did, like it knew better than she did, only Molly was grateful for it. Her mind was being an idiot. She let the fire he set inside sweep through her, cleansing her, waking her up. This, right here, was important. This was real.

It was *real*. Happening in her home. In the real world.

She pulled away from him, saying, "I'm going to start crying again."

Declan kept kissing her, her face, her eyes, her forehead, her neck, until she was smiling, almost laughing. So tired, so confused, still kind of...oh God, she didn't even know anymore.

Declan pushed the hair out of her face and fixed

her with a Look. A very Dom look.

He said, "You're the only one who can be there for her when she's scared, Molly. You're the only one who can comfort her. I'm not trying to pretend I can fix everything. But I can do this. I will do this. I will know I've helped you, even a little bit."

"Oh crap, Declan," she said. "Look, I'm…I'm a little emotional, to the point where I'm giving myself whiplash, probably because I didn't sleep much, but that doesn't mean I don't have a point."

"But that's about you, Mol," he said.

Damn him and his X-ray eyes.

"Molly, look at me," he said. "Money wouldn't make you the best big sister she could have. You are already that. You're here. You'd turn your whole life upside down for her. You don't need to prove it a hundred different ways."

"Maybe I need to prove it to myself," she said. "That I could do it this time. Be strong for her, even if back then…"

She shrugged. What was the point? She was never going to get to go back in time. She was never going to get a do-over to be tough and strong, the kind of person who could get through a pregnancy, a miscarriage, a breakup, and a death without letting people make her feel like she deserved all of it.

"You *are* strong," he said, furiously. "You are fucking amazing, Molly Ward. If you don't already know that, paying your sister's way isn't going to do shit."

"Don't yell at me," she said.

Declan's face fell. "I didn't yell. I'm sorry I'm upset, but you shouldn't…" He paused, his face screwed up. "You shouldn't have left like that, Molly. You can't just fucking disappear on people. My mother used to pull that shit all the time, and I'd have no idea if she was dead or drunk or with some guy, so just...don't do that again, all right?"

Oh God.

If Molly had thought she felt bad before, she'd had no idea.

"I didn't know," she said. She sat down on her old couch, feeling exhausted, empty.

"You didn't know what?" he asked gruffly. "That my mother fucked me up, or that you matter?"

"I didn't think..." she stuttered, finding it so difficult to say. This was dangerous territory. "It's just an arrangement," she said, finally. "Isn't it? No obligations."

"I don't know what this should be," Declan said. "And I don't know if I can make any promises, because she did fuck me right up. But I know I care about you."

He walked over to the couch and sat beside her, pulling her into his lap and holding her there, his eyes boring into hers.

"I fucking love you, Molly," he said.

"Oh God," she choked. "I..."

She couldn't say it.

And then she just stared at him in terror. The last remaining bulwark that might have protected her form her own feelings for Declan just came crashing down. She loved this man. She knew if she let it happen that she would come to need this man. To depend on him, the way she promised herself she would never depend on anyone, ever.

To give up control forever.

"Yeah, we're pretty well fucked," Declan said, and kissed her.

She kissed him back as hard as she could, wrapping her arms around his neck, willing her body to melt into his. Molly would just bury all of this in him, in the two of them together, in feeling now, rather than thinking about her future...

"You are not staying here," Declan rasped, pulling away long enough to let her know he wasn't kidding. "Not somewhere you're not safe."

"Declan—"

"No, not an option," he said sternly, and pulled at her shorts. "I will camp the fuck outside your door. Or you can come stay at Volare."

"I have been living here my entire life—"

He growled, and flipped her on her stomach. Suddenly she was over his knees, her ass up in the air. She looked back over her shoulder at him in surprise and couldn't keep herself from smiling at what was coming. Or from squirming. He knew what this did to her—and knew she was arguing now, just because.

"What did I say?" he said, pulling her shorts and underwear down over her hips, down to her knees. Molly buried her face in her arms and lifted her ass ever so slightly in the air, wanting it bad. Wanting him. She looked over her shoulder again.

"You can't make me," she said.

"Worse," he said. "I can make you want to."

Smack.

Smack.

Smack.

Oh God, he was right. She was soaking wet,

wanting nothing more than —

"Oh!" she cried as he pushed his fingers into her, pushing herself off the couch only to have him shove her back down. She clawed at the upholstery while he fucked her with his fingers, helpless to move, to do anything but offer herself up to him. When she was close he stopped and flipped her onto her back, his dark eyes hovering over her, his hand slipping back between her legs.

"I want to watch you come for me," he said, pushing her shirt up over her breasts with one hand, fucking her with the other. "*Come*," he ordered.

She did, fast and hard, mouth open in a mute scream, her muscles fluttering around his fingers like a startled bird. A whole new kind of orgasm for her, surprised and speechless, eyes wide and searching his face for what that just was. It took her a second to remember to breathe.

"Where's your bed?" he asked.

She pointed, her hand shaking.

And then he was lifting her up, effortlessly, half dressed, and carrying her to her own bed. The bed she'd been lonely in for years, the bed where she'd cried herself to sleep for a year after her life had fallen apart, the bed she hadn't been able to see as anything other than the place where everything had been ruined.

Declan was going to make it into something else.

He set her down, took his phone out. "I'm telling Adra to take them for a long lunch," he said. He looked up. "Now take off those clothes."

chapter 28

Molly had never gotten undressed quite that fast before.

She loved being naked in front of him. Molly never thought that would happen, with anyone. Hadn't conceived of being able to stand with her naked body and all its flaws in front of a man and feel...good. But she loved the way he looked at her body, like he needed her more than he needed air, or food, or water. Like nothing on Earth could keep him from her.

A beat.

Then Declan chucked his phone aside, his hand already working his belt. "Get on the bed. Legs spread, eyes closed," he said, pulling his shirt over his head.

A small shiver ran through her, like a preview. A priming current. She did as she was told, laying back with her legs spread, knees bent, knowing he was watching her. She heard his intake of breath and felt herself get even wetter, knowing he could see that, too. Then the rustle of his jeans, the crinkle of a condom wrapper.

His weight on the bed.

His thighs, warm and hard, underneath her own.

She gripped the bedspread with her fingers and licked her lips. She didn't know what he would do, where he would touch her, whether it would be pleasure or pain. She was just his. Whatever he wanted.

She sighed, repeating that to herself.

Then, without warning, he flipped her over, half on her stomach, half on her side. Her eyes flew open while he lifted her leg and plunged into her. She groaned with the intrusion as he leaned over her, heavy and thick and stretching her in entirely new ways, and said, "Mine."

"Yes," she said, and she felt his teeth on her neck as he thrust into her, harder than before, forcing a keening wail out of her.

"Look at me," he said as his hand found her breasts and his dick filled her, again and again. Molly still hadn't caught up with his onslaught, and she was panting, grabbing at the sheets, her body humming, but she obeyed. She looked over her shoulder at him and he kissed her, lifting her leg higher, going deeper.

"Say it," he growled, biting her lip.

"Oh God!" she moaned as he drove into her without stopping. "Yours, Declan! Yours!"

"Come," he ordered, and she did, gratefully, thrashing underneath him while he held her down, his teeth on her shoulder, his cock twitching inside her. When she finally stopped the bed was destroyed, pillows everywhere, her limbs tied up in sheets, covered in sweat.

"What the hell was that?" she murmured.

He didn't answer. Just rolled onto his back, taking her with him so he could hold her close to his chest. Molly felt like a ragdoll, limp and well worn, and was happy just to have a place to rest where she could hear his heart beat out its own rhythm.

She lay there like that until she felt her own heart come down. Until she could hold her hand up above the hair on Declan's chest and keep it from shaking, for the most part.

Maybe it was the sex. Maybe it was the sleep deprivation. Maybe it was just old-fashioned insanity that made her bring it up.

"Declan..." she said, and trailed off. Was she really going to ask?

"What is it?" he asked.

What she wanted to say was, 'I love you, too. I am hopelessly, hopelessly in love with you, and I'm terrified.' But she couldn't. Declan was strong enough to come out and say it, not even needing her to say it back, because he was...Declan. He knew he'd carry on, keep on being the strong, dominant man he always was. Molly wasn't sure of herself like that.

She couldn't say it, but she knew what she wanted. She wanted all of him. She wanted to be as close to him as she could.

"Why did you get a vasectomy?" she asked.

Declan rolled her fully on top of him where she could rest her chin on her hands and put his hands behind his head. He narrowed his eyes, thinking.

"You aren't going to tell me?" she asked.

"I'm going to tell you," he said. "But I think you already know the answer."

Molly tried to hide her smile, but couldn't. She did like being right, even when gloating was completely inappropriate. Even worse, she could feel his cock already getting bigger beneath her, pressing into her belly.

"Maybe," she allowed. "But I shouldn't feel like this while I ask you about it."

"Feel like what?"

She swallowed. "Feel like I want you."

"You always want me," he said, steadily. "Just like I always want you."

This was undeniably true.

"Tell me why you think I did it," he demanded.

Molly suddenly felt tears prick at her eyes. She'd cried more in the weeks she'd known Declan than in the previous four years, and still she wanted to be around this man as much as possible. Most of that had been good tears, anyway. Cathartic tears. This time she was crying for the boy Declan had been. "I think it was because you didn't have a very happy childhood," she said softly.

"Yup," he agreed. "And I'm not going to risk doing that to a kid."

"Not ever?" she asked.

He smiled slowly, his eyes crinkling at the corners. "I never say never. Maybe if I start believing in happy endings," he said.

Molly felt a twinge, deep inside, deeper than she was really willing to look, because, well, maybe she wanted to believe in that, too. Maybe she was already starting to. She quelled the anxiety that came with that thought and focused on the here and now, the thing she thought she was ready for.

"It is reversible," she said. "But that's not really why I was asking."

"I know."

"I want to feel you," she said suddenly, looking into his eyes. "All of you. Inside me."

Declan didn't look surprised, but he didn't say anything, either, not for a long while. Molly hadn't felt this nervous since before the first time they'd had sex. Didn't he want to? Did he—

"Are you sure?" he asked.

"Yes," she said immediately. "Declan, I don't want to be trapped by this anymore. You've already..."

She stopped herself, not wanting to get so emotional again. He knew anyway. He already knew all he'd done for her.

"You've already shown me so much, and I was carrying so much baggage with me, Dec, and I've let a lot of it go," she said. "Because of you, this— whatever. I've let it go. And I want to let this go, too. I know it's not the smartest reasoning, necessarily, but the truth is that I fucking *want* it. I want to know what you feel like inside me, bare, skin to skin," she said, sitting up with him as he rose from the bed, keeping her in his lap. He looked like he was ready to devour her. His cock was rock hard against her vulva as she straddled him, and she sighed.

"I want it so bad, Declan, and the only reason I haven't asked yet is because I'm held hostage by my past. And I don't want to live like that anymore. Please," she said, locking her eyes with his. "Help me with this, too."

"Jesus," he said. He was looking at her with awe. "You have no idea how much I've wanted this."

"Not as much as me," she said, and was thrilled to hear him groan.

She kissed him, letting her hair fall around his face, letting her tongue slowly search out his. He let her take the lead for all of a second before she felt him surge, his body tightening around hers, his mouth devouring her. She moaned into his mouth as he bit her lip again, harder this time, hungrier. Declan pitched forward, holding her in his arms so he could play with her breasts, his mouth hot and urgent on her nipples, pulling, biting, sucking.

Molly moaned again and moved her hips, rubbing her wetness on his bare, hard cock, and the effect was electric. Declan jumped and threw her forward with a grunt, pinning on her back and pushing her legs wide, wide open.

"Look at me," he growled, and moved the head of his cock between her aching folds. As if she could look anywhere else. He held her eyes while plowed into her, slowly, forcefully, dragging out every single inch until beads of sweat broke out on his forehead and Molly's legs trembled around him.

She gasped for air while he lay motionless inside her, heavy and hot, every nerve screaming under his touch.

"You are so beautiful," he said to her, before he thrust them both into oblivion.

chapter 29

Declan lay in the murky dawn light covered in a cold sweat and tried to make sense of his asshole brain.

He'd woken up from the worst dream he'd ever had next to the woman he loved, and now he was replaying the last twenty-four hours, trying to figure out what was real.

Molly leaving. That feeling that he had lost her, the way he lost everyone, because she'd disappeared. Finding her again, in her own home, finding Lydia, knowing he could do something to help, finally, maybe.

Molly's tears. Molly coming with him inside her, skin to skin. Molly's face when he told her he loved her.

Jesus.

And then by the time they drove out of Pleasant Valley, Molly ducking down so no one would see her, Lydia was already asleep at Volare, tuckered out. He'd made Molly dinner and fed it to her in bed, the two of them starving for each other, making love until they were both too exhausted to move.

Then sleep.

Then: nightmares. Or flashbacks, or flashforwards, whatever the fuck they were, rising up to tear him apart from the inside, reminding him of what 'real' was. Finding Bethany, pale and blue at the edges, a thin trail of white vomit on her cheek. Picking her up, so frighteningly light in his arms. It couldn't be right. Looking down as he rushed to his car and for that one moment, that one terrifying moment, he saw his mom, and he was back there, too weak to carry her, and he almost dropped Bethany…

No more memories from that night, not after coming back from the ER and finding Soren. And then everything broke apart.

And this time, in the dream, it was Molly in his arms. And he couldn't hold her, couldn't get her out to a car, couldn't find a phone. Molly, pale blue and dead weight, heavier than he could carry.

Declan couldn't get that image out of his mind. He turned over just to look at Molly's sleeping face, but every time he closed his eyes it came rushing back.

He'd been awake for hours.

This was what happened with people he loved.

"Fuck," he said, sitting up, swinging his legs over the side of the bed. Maybe he had to deal with this shit, but he wasn't going to wake Molly up. He wasn't going to let any of this baggage fall on her head, not like he had with Soren.

Damn.

Declan pulled on his jeans and padded downstairs barefoot, glad that Volare was full of late risers. He'd asked Adra to stay here as long as Lydia was here, make sure Lydia had plenty of support, not have it all fall on Molly, and he knew that was a challenge since Ford was here while he was renovating his new house. So there were people around, but it was still the quiet hour. He needed it. And maybe some food. He'd think clearly with some food in him.

Maybe he could get rid of this sense of impending disaster, too.

That image of Molly. Jesus.

So Declan was half in the kitchen already, rubbing his tired face with his hand, before he realized he wasn't alone. Lydia was munching on cereal, her eyes laughing while she...checked him out?

"Good job, Mol," Lydia said.

Declan frowned. The girl wasn't even eighteen yet.

"I'm kidding!" Lydia said. "Come on, I'm not blind, and you're walking around without a shirt."

"What are you doing up?" he asked. "Don't you need to sleep for two or something?"

Lydia just shrugged. "Yeah, no idea. I've been waking up super early the past few weeks, going to bed early." She took another bite of cereal, which Declan finally got a look at.

He took the bowl.

"You're not eating this sugar crap," he said.

"Hey!"

"Sit down," he ordered. "I'll make you breakfast. Do you have your vitamins?"

"They're upstairs. I'm not supposed to take them on an empty stomach," Lydia said. She was watching Declan critically now. "You are bossy, huh? But Molly seems to like you."

Declan frowned and went hunting for eggs. She liked him, yes. He loved her. And his reaction to that, as he lined up milk, eggs, tomatoes, cheese, and every other delicious thing he could find on the kitchen island before Lydia's great big eyes, was: fuck yes, and thank God.

Thank God she hadn't said it back. How fucked up was that, that he was relieved that the girl he was in love with didn't love him back? But it made sense, in his head. He wouldn't want to have to explain it to anyone else but Soren, who would know, automatically, but that dream? That dream was a reminder. Things didn't turn out too good for the women in his life. He was never there in the end, when they needed them. The idea of failing Molly like that...

Declan felt like a walking time bomb.

"You ok?" Lydia asked. "That's a lot of eggs."

Declan looked down. He'd cracked at least eight in that bowl without even noticing, but he was suddenly ravenous, too. "You think I'm making breakfast just for you?"

Lydia stuck out her tongue and smiled. "No. But you *are* making me breakfast."

Declan smiled, shaking his head. This was Molly's sister, all right. And despite whatever shitshow was going on in his brain, that meant he felt responsible.

"So what about the father, Lydia?" he asked.

She groaned and kind of slumped over the

counter, another reminder that eighteen was so goddamn young. How could Molly only be five years older than that? The answer came to him almost immediately and made him want to punch the world right in the dick: it was because Molly had had to live way too much in those five years.

"Lydia," he said, his tone a warning.

"He's not in the picture," she sighed. "He's younger than me, for one thing. He'll be a senior this year. And I haven't told him."

Declan put down his bowl of eggs.

"Please don't tell Molly," Lydia said.

"Are you fucking serious?" Declan said.

"I know, I know! I just...I remember what happened to Molly, when she told, and I just think it'll all be easier..."

Lydia seemed to physically shrink, all the teenage bravado and near womanhood falling away, leaving her looking like a frightened child. It was astonishing. Declan's Dom sense went into overdrive and he watched her face, watched her recoil from something he couldn't see. Like she was afraid of a memory. Declan couldn't let it stand.

"Lydia," he said, taking her hand, "You are safe here. That's the whole point. I'm not going to let anything happen to you."

"You don't understand," she murmured.

"Molly's told me about some of it," he said gently.

Lydia took that cue and shook her head, getting a little angry. "No, you weren't there. You can't understand what they did to her. But it was worse because it wasn't like... I mean, Robbie wasn't *always* an asshole, you know? Like, Molly had no warning. And I don't know if you know this, but our mom was..."

He watched Lydia close her eyes and take a deep breath, a gesture so like her sister's that Declan could only marvel at it. He could tell she'd needed someone to tell this story to for a long time.

"What about your mom?" he asked.

Lydia exhaled. "She was a shitty mom, ok? It feels so terrible to say that about her, because she's dead and everything, but she really wasn't... I don't know. Molly basically raised me, but I don't think anyone raised her. And Robbie was so sweet when they started going out, you wouldn't believe it. Like, he made her think that he would be there forever, and he'd always, always take care of her, and she believed him. And *I* believed him. I used to *dream* about having a boyfriend like Robbie. I used to dream that one day..."

"What?"

Suddenly Lydia laughed, blushing, looking out the window onto the private garden outside. "It's super embarrassing."

"I think we're tight enough for embarrassing stories."

She rolled her eyes. "Yes, ok, *fine*. I used to fantasize that Robbie would have a little brother. Like a long lost half brother or something, only better looking, and my age? And then we'd both have our boyfriends and go on, like...double dates. Oh God. You're laughing."

"No, I'm not," Declan said, hiding his smile by turning to test the heat. When he turned back, he was serious. "That is pretty cute, though."

"Yeah, I bet you have plenty of dumb fantasies,

too," Lydia smirked.

"Keep talking or no omelet for you," he warned.

"Ok, fine. But you owe me an embarrassing story."

"We'll see. Talk."

"Ok, so, Robbie was amazing," Lydia said. She was animated now, like just getting this out was doing wonders for her. "He was perfect. Until one day he wasn't. I guess he was just playing a part, the way some people do? And now he tries to be big man in the park, just another part. Anyway, it was like a switch was flipped...he was just so mean. Like he wanted to erase her completely, and was so pissed off that he couldn't that he just tried to hurt her as much as he could all of the time. One time I found him and his friends throwing bottles at her. They had cornered her and they were throwing fucking bottles at her."

Declan let the pan crash on the stove and turned around.

Had he heard that right?

"They threw bottles at her?" he asked.

Lydia was silent, staring at him. Declan forced himself to relax and saw it spread to Lydia, who reached for the cereal again. This time he let it go. He didn't want to scare Lydia with the shit he was thinking about doing to the men who had thrown bottles at a pregnant teenage girl.

"Yeah," Lydia said, still looking at him. "Worse than that, too. I think that's why she lost the baby, because of what he put her through. And it all started when she told him she was pregnant and he, like, had to deny it was his, so he told all these lies about her cheating. So anyway. I'm not, like, super excited to tell Zack."

"Jesus Christ," Declan said.

What he'd known about was bad enough. But that level of harassment? What kind of fucking *animal* would do that to someone, let alone someone he had once loved?

This was too much. Declan was already struggling with his own bullshit, his own fears about failing Molly, about how he inevitably would fuck up, and how whenever he fucked up, it was a disaster. It had been maybe manageable when he thought that the stakes weren't so high. So long as she didn't love him. But what if she started to? She'd been failed by everybody before him. Worse than that. Attacked. Hounded. He felt his blood begin to surge, his muscles tense, his asshole brain telling him to go...

Fuck. How much damage was Declan going to do to her when he inevitably fucked up?

"You know, I'm so glad she has you now," Lydia said. "You don't even know. I can see that she's starting to, like...I don't know, thaw? She's always insisting she doesn't need anybody or anybody's help or whatever, but when she looks at you she seems, I don't know, normal. Not like a superwoman or whatever. I don't know how to put it, exactly," she said, throwing some Cocoa Puffs in the air and catching them. She had a pensive look on her face.

Then Lydia went on, oblivious to the loathsome dread snaking through Declan's heart.

"You know what it is? I think she can trust you. Like, I think she wants to trust you. Just be patient with her, ok? It might take her a while, but I promise you, when Molly opens up or whatever, she's all in. Just be patient." Lydia smiled at him. "I mean, I have to try to be a good sister, too, right?"

Declan gripped the edge of the stove, sweat gathering on his brow.

The last person who had trusted him was Bethany.

No. The last person who had trusted him was Soren.

He'd failed them both. He let Bethany slide under. He ruined Soren's life for something that Bethany did just because it made him feel like shit.

And before all of that, his mother.

Declan looked down and saw that his thumb was on the electric burner. Sizzling. He didn't feel it. Felt only cold. Dread. Fear, for Molly.

The truth was, Declan was prepared to love Molly. He wasn't prepared to be loved by her. And he had had no idea that he was this fucked up.

"Declan, you ok?" Lydia asked.

Declan didn't answer as he ran his finger under the tap. Seemed pointless. He wasn't thinking about himself, anyway.

chapter 30

The next day and half moved both too quickly and too slowly at the same time. Molly barely had any time with Declan, when that was, shamefully, all she really wanted. She should have been thinking about Lydia. And she was, it was just that Lydia herself seemed...totally transformed. She seemed happy. Relaxed. She wasn't the mess that Molly had been years before, possibly because Lydia's future looked a whole lot different than Molly's had.

Molly didn't even know if Lydia was going to keep the baby. She wasn't sure Lydia knew. And watching Lydia gleefully walk through apartment showings, planning what kind of furniture they'd get, and how she would decorate her bedroom, concerning herself with, frankly, not the highest of priorities, Molly remembered that Lydia was still a kid, really, and Lydia as a mom kind of frightened her.

And yet Molly had been very different four years ago. Life had a way of making her grow up. Maybe it would for Lydia, too.

But Declan made it easy to forget about Lydia. Because Declan had her worried.

For one, he wasn't all over her. Which was...she didn't even know what to think about that. Molly was used to Declan being the aggressor, except in unusual circumstances, and she could feel that the vibe was all wrong. She could tell he still thought about it—he still looked at her like he wanted to devour her all the time. But he *didn't*. She had no idea why. And Molly didn't realize how much she could miss sex until suddenly she had to go without it for a day or two after having had Declan maul her constantly for weeks.

How the hell was she going to last while he finished the tour?

Because he had to go back. Even Declan Donovan couldn't put off tour dates forever. And now he had to go back while something was very clearly wrong.

It was scaring her, how wrong it felt. How when Declan looked at her, he didn't look happy anymore. He looked wistful. Sad. Worried. He looked the way she felt when she thought about Lydia—*before* Declan had come to the rescue and made them financially secure for life. And it scared her even more that she was too scared to ask him about it. She hadn't the courage to tell him that she loved him, as though she still couldn't risk making her vulnerability real, even though it was real whether she shouted it from the rooftops or not. She hadn't the courage to ask him what was wrong, either.

This from the woman who was supposed to write a fearless tell-all about the breakup and comeback of Savage Heart. This from the woman who'd become brave enough to face her own feelings *because* of Declan.

He'd made her brave, and he'd made her a coward, all at once.

So when they all came back to Volare in Venice Beach, after Molly signed a rush lease, Declan's cash convincing the landlord to make some exceptions about credit checks and whatever, Molly climbed into the bed she and Declan had shared—barely—and waited.

She bit her nails and waited.

And when he came into the room, closing the door gently behind him, she knew.

She didn't want to believe it. But she knew.

"We need to talk," he said.

He looked like he hadn't slept the past two nights. And he hadn't—she'd felt him tossing, turning. Getting up. Now he stood in the warm evening light filtering in from the Venice sunset looking determined—and sad. She'd never seen him like this.

"Declan, what's wrong?" she said. "Something's been wrong, I know it. Ever since…"

"No," he said. "Don't try to pin this on anything."

Molly caught her breath. There was a "this."

"What?" she asked. She could barely force the word out.

Declan drank her in feverishly, his eyes roaming over her body, her face. Her eyes. Like he was saving it up. Like he wouldn't get to look at her again.

"Declan, this is freaking me out a little bit," she said, trying to smile.

"You remember I told you I had those rules?" he said. "About not getting involved. No romantic attachments."

"Yes."

"I had reasons for those rules," he said, still staring at her. "And I broke every single one of them with you from day one."

"Good," she said. "I don't have a problem with that."

"I do," he said fiercely. "Because I love you, Molly. I didn't just say that to say it. I mean I fucking *love* you, like I've never loved anyone else, like I didn't think it was possible for me to love another human being. And terrible things happen when I love people. All the time. Over and over and over again."

Molly was stunned. The force of his words nearly knocked her back on the bed. She couldn't wrap her head around any of it—around him loving her that much, even if she felt it, in her bones, around him saying that terrible things would happen.

"Declan—"

"Don't talk," he said. She shut up. "That's why I have those rules. Had them. Because at some point, when the same shit happens again and again, you have to take a step back and wonder what the common denominator is. And it's me, Molly."

"Declan, you are not making any sense. Like, at all."

Declan walked forward, his jaw set, his face tense. Molly had risen to her knees on the edge of the bed and stayed there, as though in half protest, riveted by what he was saying—by how much he was opening up to her, finally—and frightened by what she was hearing. By what it meant.

He was close to her now. He took her hands in his, looked down, let his thumbs rub the backs of her hands. When he looked up, she'd never seen anything like it.

Such sadness.

"I don't know why I fail the people I love," he said. "But I do, every goddamn time. I knew Bethany was troubled. I knew Soren was, too. I let that shit happen. And then I let Bethany just...drift down. I should have seen those signs, Molly, more than anyone. They were clear as freaking day, looking back. Soren didn't see that every day when he was a kid; there was no reason he could be expected to see it coming, but me? I should have known. And I still blamed him. I still..."

Declan swallowed, rolled his neck. Pushed on.

"I still cut him off for something..."

Molly searched his eyes, looking for anything, a clue. It was like he was watching something terrible unfold before him, and she couldn't see it.

"Declan, what's happening?"

He shook his head and looked at her, his eyes burning. "I don't know if I do it or if I'm just not good enough to prevent it, or what the fuck happens, but I can't do it to you, too. I fucking cannot. I will not fuck up your life. Because I love you, Molly, I can't let you depend on me. I can't become the guy that you need."

Molly wanted to scream. This was all, all wrong. She wanted to yell at him that he was too late, that he was already the man that she needed, that she couldn't imagine her life without him in it, but it wouldn't come out. For the first time, being with Declan meant that she wrapped up her emotions and hid them away. She didn't know why. It felt like drowning, like trying to wake up from a nightmare and finding herself paralyzed.

Why was this happening?

"Declan," she said, and hated, hated to hear her voice quivering, hated that it was the wrong words coming out. "What is this? Seriously, explain this to me like I'm five, because I really want to make sure I understand. Why would you say this about yourself?"

You idiot, just tell him! Tell him you love him!

"Molly, you deserve better. That's what I'm saying. I know better than you do what happens with me, and I love you too much for that."

"So what, you're saying you can't be with me?" Molly said. God, that sounded angry. She *was* angry. She was incredulous. And it was so much easier to be pissed off than to tell him that she loved him. She squeezed his hands and said, "I am calling bullshit on this, Declan. Complete bullshit."

"No, it isn't," he said. "I love you."

"Then what the fuck?" she shouted. She was angrier at herself at this point for not saying she loved him, for regressing at exactly the wrong moment, for hiding back within herself. "Do you know what you've done for me already? Do you know how much happier I am just for having known you? What the hell are you talking about?"

"Molly," he said, his voice stern. "I love you."

Molly ripped her hands free of his and grabbed the back of his head, pulling him down to her. She kissed him and felt him respond, felt his body wanting her the way it always did.

"Then *be* with me," she said.

Gently he took her arms and brought them down to her sides. He was shaking his head, like she simply did not understand.

He said, "You don't get it. I need you to be happy more than I need to fucking breathe. I would rather hurt you a little bit now than break your heart later. I'm in love with you, Molly, and for your own sake...you can't fall in love with me, too. You deserve better."

"No," she whispered.

"I'm sorry," he said. Then he kissed her.

And then he left.

~ * ~ * ~

Declan walked out of the room he'd shared with Molly and went straight to the car he'd rented. He didn't say goodbye to anyone, didn't make any phone calls. Knew he couldn't afford to prolong his exit if he was going to make it out of there. It had taken every ounce of self-control he had to tell Molly he was leaving without her. The only thing that kept him going was that image of a brokenhearted Molly in his brain, the thought of what it would do to her if he screwed up. What Lydia had said: "She goes all in." He never wanted to see that. Not ever.

At least now, at least today, he could leave

knowing she didn't love him.

He would go to the airport and book the first flight back to New York, charter another private flight if he had to.

But first he had a stop to make.

He'd always been good with spatial reasoning. Remembering directions, paths. He found his way back to Pleasant Valley Park in no time, the windows down, the dust covering his sweat-slicked skin by the time he got there.

Just as dry and hot and full of assholes as it had been the last time he was here.

He drove around aimlessly, drawing stares from kids who saw a car they didn't recognize, until he found a group of men about Molly's age. Standing around a grill. Smoking cigarettes. Laughing. Drinking from bottles of beer.

He turned his shitty rental toward them and kept driving. Drove right up onto the lot, right next to the grill, watching their faces to see who got the most outraged. Who wanted to be the big man.

Most of them shut up when he got out of the car and saw his size.

"Which one of you is Robbie?" he said, stretching out his neck.

Silence.

He spoke slower. "Which. One. Of you. Is. Robbie?"

They all looked at each other, each one trying to take a cue from the others. Maybe they were drunk. Maybe they were just that dumb. Declan didn't give a shit.

It was a skinny one in a denim jacket that he'd cut up into a vest who spoke up first, laughing in a high-pitched, nasal tone, his eyes all bloodshot like he'd smoked a joint too many.

"Holy shit, are you really Declan Donovan?"

The rest of them broke. Slapping their legs, putting their hands up to their open mouths, yelling, "Oooh shit!"

He didn't have the patience for this. Not today.

"Robbie," he barked.

"Mr. Donovan," a smooth looking, pretty-boy punk said, stepping out from the group and offering his hand. "Can I just say that I am a huge, huge fan of your music. You have been a serious fucking inspiration to all of us while we've been working on our own demo."

"Are you Robbie?"

"Yeah, man, I'm Robbie. I'm actually the lead singer of our band, Vicious Circle. I don't know if you've heard of us, you know, we're kind of local, but we're getting—"

"You're the Robbie that used to be with Molly Ward?"

The men grew quiet.

Robbie plastered a quick smile on his face. Gave Declan a look, like, *you know what it's like, man, chicks*. Robbie said, "I mean, we had a thing for a while, but she wasn't, you know, serious."

Declan took a deep breath and let it flow to every single part of his body. This was something he could do. This was one small part of the world he could make better for her.

"Robbie, you should run now," he said. "Because I'm going to break your nose."

"What?" Robbie said, and then tried to laugh, looking to his friends. But Declan was already walking. Just two quick strides on his long legs. One easy straight right. One broken nose.

He thought about throwing a bottle. Decided she wouldn't want him to.

Robbie was crying through the blood, clutching his face from where he sat on the ground, his friends keeping their distance, wide-eyed and dumb.

"Why did you do that, man?"

"You know why, you piece of shit. And if I ever hear about any of you bothering her or her sister ever again, I will break every single fucking bone in your body. Twice."

Declan shook out his hand and walked back to his rental. As he opened the door, Robbie was getting to his feet, realizing he'd just been humiliated by his idol in front of all of his friends.

"Take a fucking picture!" he screamed. "You're all witnesses! Fuck you, Donovan, that's going to be the most expensive punch you've ever thrown!"

"Worth it," Declan said.

chapter 31

It was Adra who finally got Molly off her ass, in the end.

Molly tried to get all her old repression skills back, but it seemed like all the things that Declan had taught her had stuck *too* well. The irony: it burned. She couldn't do it. Couldn't just carry on as though nothing was wrong, couldn't lie to herself and pretend she wasn't broken. Only this time, she *had* to; she had Lydia to take care of.

And it was Lydia who brought it all crashing down. Molly actually thought she might be able to soldier on reasonably well until she took a dumb reality TV break with Lydia, just trying to relax while waiting for their new furniture to be delivered, secretly thinking about what she'd get for her sister's belated eighteenth birthday present, when she realized Lydia was furiously texting.

Molly's first thought: *the father*.

Lydia still wouldn't tell her who the damn father was. To the point where Molly had another panic attack, thinking her sister might have been raped or molested or something, and Lydia had to swear up and down it wasn't anything like that. She just didn't want the boy involved. That's what she'd called him—a boy.

Molly knew it had to do with what Lydia had seen four years ago. Molly hadn't been the only one traumatized by the whole thing, and she wasn't going to win that argument right away.

But this? Furious texting? How could this not be a good sign?

"That the father?" Molly asked. Trying to be casual.

Lydia shot her a look. "Smooth, big sister. No, it's not the father. It's Declan."

Lydia misinterpreted Molly's expression for — what? Jealousy? Confusion? Molly would probably never know. She would remember, forever, though, what Lydia said next.

"Don't worry, you bagged a good one, Mol. He's just been texting me to make sure everything's ok with the apartment, the baby, all that stuff," she said, rolling her eyes. "Like big brother stuff, you know? We had a talk the other morning while you were still asleep. We get each other."

At which point Molly proceeded to lose her shit.

Just complete bawling. Crying. Cursing. Like she was possessed or something, just letting it all out in front of her poor, confused little sister.

Molly was still kicking herself for that.

But finding out that Declan was checking up on Lydia had set everything off all over again. How could he be there for Lydia like he was for Bethany and say he couldn't do it for Molly? Molly wasn't even asking anything of him, she wasn't pregnant, she wasn't in a psychiatric hospital! She just fucking *loved* him.

She was consumed with red-hot jealousy.

She was consumed with regret.

Why hadn't she told him she loved him? Why hadn't she been able to do that one thing? Would it have made a difference if she'd been able to say, "Well, too late, buddy, I do need you? Guess I'm already screwed, might as well stay together!"

She didn't understand it at all. If he really wanted her, if he really loved her, wouldn't he be there? She should have told him. She should have found a way, instead of just standing there in stupid, slack-jawed shock.

And then, right on cue, she'd remember that it had been Declan who had taught her not to blame herself. And then it would be back to the crying.

Round in round, in the same circles, digging a worn, raw groove in her shattered heart, never getting anywhere, and always coming back to the same reality: he was gone. Declan had dumped her. Did it matter if she understood why?

He was gone.

And she was helpless. Until Adra finally sat her down.

"Yeah, so, why haven't you been eating, Molly?" Adra said.

"I haven't?"

Molly hadn't really noticed. She just hadn't been hungry.

"No," Adra said.

"Oh. Well, that's pretty dumb. I'll start doing that," she said.

Adra cocked her head to the side and gave Molly a look normally reserved for crazy people. She said, "You know, Lydia is seriously worried about you."

And *that* got Molly's attention. That was unacceptable, no matter what the circumstances.

"Shit," Molly whispered.

And after that it was pretty much impossible not to tell Adra all about it. Adra, who made her feel slightly less crazy just by confirming that the whole thing was nuts. By saying that yeah, she would have called bullshit, too. By being shocked.

And just in the process of actually telling someone about all of it from the beginning, Molly realized that her biggest problem was that she felt weak all over again. Powerless and out of control — and not in the good way. And she needed to take all that back.

Which was when she called Declan.

And a woman answered.

~ * ~ * ~

Bethany had seen the last show. Declan could tell by the look on her face.

"What is wrong with you, Dec?" she asked.

Declan shook his head. Where could he even begin? He hadn't figured on how this would affect him. Hadn't even thought about it honestly; he'd been thinking about Molly. So here he was, trying to make up the dates on a tour, barely fucking functional. He was like a zombie. He didn't have a decent show in him anymore.

The crowd had noticed.

It was almost kind of amazing. Physical. He hadn't understood that being away from her—that knowing he couldn't be with her—would do something like this to him.

"Declan, are you listening to me?" Bethany said. "Brian, what the fuck?"

Declan wanted to laugh. Bethany, sitting here on the tour bus, looking at him like he was the one with problems. It was almost too perfect. And she looked fantastic. She looked *healthy*. He was happy for her, he really was—somewhere underneath all this shit.

She'd met up with them to show Declan how far she'd come, maybe to show him that she was ok, like he was her sponsor or something, which he guessed he sort of was. And she'd found him like this.

Brian and Gage looked worried, too.

"Dude, do you think we can do the tour like this?" Brian finally asked.

The elephant in the fucking room.

Losing Soren was one thing. Losing Soren and Declan was something else. Nobody was under any illusions—Soren and Declan were the heart of Savage Heart. Soren was gone and Declan wasn't himself anymore.

Declan rubbed his hand across his head and tried to locate the giant hole in his heart. He couldn't lie. "I don't know, Brian."

So Bethany had taken him to the back, her face full of a kind of confidence he couldn't remember seeing there before, and demanded to know what had happened.

He told her.

It was easier than not telling her.

He'd dumped the love of his life because he couldn't bear to fail her when she most needed him and then watch the consequences.

And Bethany looked him right in the eye and said, "That is some grade-A bullshit, Declan."

"Christ," he laughed tonelessly. "That's exactly what she said."

"Sounds smart. You were never a coward, Declan, so man up."

"Hey," he said, sitting up. "You think this is easy for me? This has fucking destroyed me. I'm doing it for her."

"Which is the part I don't buy," Bethany said, crossing her legs and arms at once. "You know, I talked about you in group therapy. And they made me see something. You feeling guilty about me or Soren...or anyone else," she added carefully, "is bull, because it means you think you could have done something. Like it was all under your control, like the decision wasn't fully mine. It *was* my decision, Declan; I took those pills for my own reasons that had nothing to do with you. You can't make decisions about what's best for this girl, either."

Declan froze. He stared at her.

Thought.

Then he got up, walked to the front of the bus, and said, "Stop the bus."

"It's the middle of nowhere," the driver said.

"Stop the fucking bus."

The doors swooshed open and Declan burst out into the cool night air, never happier to see absolutely nothing in the distance, and he started walking down the side of the road, into darkness.

Away from the noise.

He'd made the same damn mistake again. He couldn't argue with Bethany because she was right. It would have been like arguing about the color red. His brain knew she was right, that he was an idiot, that his idiocy was almost insulting, but his heart?

Why the *fuck* was he afraid?

He wasn't a coward. He'd never been a damn coward, and he wasn't going to try it on for size now.

He'd been blaming himself, all this time. All these years. Carried it with him so long he'd forgotten it was a burden, and hugged it to himself like a fucking treasure. Like it meant something. Like it was a part of him.

But *she* was a part of him. Molly.

"Declan?" It was Brian. Following him in the dark. Another true friend. "You ok, Declan?"

Declan smiled, relieved just to know.

"I can't live without her, Brian. I mean, look at me. Isn't that crazy? I've known her how long?"

Brian shrugged. Smiled. "I've heard crazier things."

"I can't fucking live without her now. Maybe I needed to try to find out for sure, I don't know. You think I've fucked up beyond all repair this time? I don't know if I even deserve another shot to get it right," he said.

"Man, I'm still trying to figure out how to sleep with a woman more than one night in a row. Beyond that women confuse me. I am not the man to ask."

Declan studied the sky. Letting go of the guilt that kept him from Molly meant letting go of everything, because it *was* everything. And Molly wasn't the only one he'd screwed up with.

"You think the band has a shot?" he asked.

"I fucking hope so," Brian said.

"Yeah."

"Call Soren, man."

"I have," Declan said. Brian looked surprised. "And I will again. I just need him to pick up. In the meantime, Bri, I'm sorry, but we have to cancel the tour. I'll take the hit. There's something I gotta do back in California."

But Brian was smiling, and Declan, Declan felt lighter than he had in months, all the way back to the bus. Right up until Bethany told him his phone had rung and she'd seen the name and picked it up.

"I just wanted to tell her, you know, that you were being an idiot, that you were messed up over it," Bethany said, wringing her hands. "I didn't think she'd hang up. I was just trying to help."

Declan sighed. It wasn't like he could really get any further into the doghouse than he already was.

He had to do something big to fix all the shit he'd broken in the past six months. And he thought he knew what that should be.

chapter 32

For the next five days, Declan called every day, multiple times per day. Molly ignored him.

Molly was *pissed*.

Molly was not in the mood to be fair, or even rational. Not when the memory of Robbie replacing her with another woman, marching her around for everyone to see, kept running through her mind. Not when she knew, just *knew*, that it had been Bethany who answered the phone.

Well, she didn't know, technically. She felt it. But would it be better or worse if it were just some random girl? Did it freaking matter? Was she just that replaceable?

The longer the phone calls went on and the longer Molly spent packing up everything she still cared about in that trailer, the more she realized that it wouldn't be enough if he just said he was sorry. No. She would need to know why he had done everything he'd done in the past few days. She'd need to know that it wouldn't happen again.

Then she'd remember that he wasn't trying to get her back. If he were trying to get her back, he'd do more than call. He'd be there.

And then she'd have to fight off more tears, and *that* would make her angry all over again.

There were a few bright spots. One, being royally pissed off made cleaning a whole lot easier. The place would be freaking spotless for the people who moved in. Two, she had seen Robbie when driving back with a fresh batch of cleaning supplies, and the weasel had two fresh black eyes and giant bandage on his nose and had actually ducked when he saw her.

She didn't know what that was about, exactly, but it was very satisfying to see.

And three?

When her father showed up, self-righteous and hateful and red in the face, just to announce that he was disowning Lydia, too, and that he blamed Molly for turning her sister in a disgraceful, ungrateful, disgusting excuse for a woman, Molly had simply said, "You're no longer my father."

And then she'd slammed the door in his face.

She'd stood there, her back flat against the door, her heart pounding in her chest, not quite able to believe she'd just done that. Molly listened to him sputter and shout outside, hurl insults at that closed door, and she felt strong, and capable, and invincible all over again.

And that got her thinking about Declan.

Again.

The worst part was knowing that she had him to thank for her broken heart, and yet still she *worried* about him. That was the worst, most humiliating feeling. That knowing he was messed up enough to do this, that he hurt that bad—hurt her, too.

Asshole.

And when she was done crying—that time—she started thinking about how she still had a book to write. Because Declan had been right—he might have set Lydia up financially, but Molly had to be everything else. And that meant Molly had to keep going. She had to keep her commitments.

Which now meant writing a book about heartbreak.

So she wrote. She stopped thinking about what it should be, and only wrote what was. What she knew of it. And around day three, she started to see how much she *didn't* know. What big, giant holes there were in her knowledge of what had happened to Declan, and what had happened to the band, and, even, in the way that those unknowns had impacted Declan's life, what had happened to her.

Molly needed Soren. She'd almost called Jim so many times, sure that he knew where Soren was— hell, Molly was pretty sure she had figured it out herself. And talking to Soren might help her understand so many things.

So why was she afraid?

In the end, she got to stay chicken. Jim called her.

"Do you know what I had to go through to get this number?" he demanded. "Like a game of telephone with you people. You couldn't call to cancel our fishing trip?"

Molly was stunned silent.

"I'm kidding," Jim said dryly. "C'mon, laugh a

little. Humor me."

Molly did laugh. Well, more of a laugh-cry. "It's been a rough couple of weeks, Jim."

"Yeah, I heard," Jim said. "Sorry my nephew is an idiot. I promise he's not all dumb, he just gets up his own ass sometimes. That's kind of why I'm calling — where are you?"

"I'm home," she said, confused.

"Jesus, breakups make everybody stupid. Where is home? Gimme an address."

"Why?"

There was a silence.

"I'm betting you know why."

The next day Soren Andersson showed up at her door.

***

"So," Soren said, taking his sunglasses off. The sun reflecting off of his pale blond hair was blinding. Molly almost didn't believe that he was real. "You going to ask me in?"

"Um, yes," Molly said. Every single wheel in her head had tried to turn at once and had apparently jammed. She stepped back. "Come in."

Soren walked into her trailer like he was surveying his territory. The only other person Molly had seen who moved like that was Declan. She had no idea how these two men had ever occupied the same place at the same time without the universe imploding.

Soren looked over the shining, spotless house, then turned that naked gaze on Molly. His eyes went up and down. Up and down.

Her instinct was to cover up, even though she was fully clothed.

"You've been crying," Soren said. It wasn't a question.

"That's none of your business," she said.

"Yes it is."

Infuriating. Completely, totally infuriating. Especially because he was right. And more than that, Molly needed him, and he knew it. She needed to know exactly what had happened between him, Bethany, and Declan six months ago. She needed to know for the book, but more than that, she needed to know for her own sanity.

Molly watched helplessly as Soren moved farther in, taking in the couch, the recliner. He picked the old recliner, what had been her father's chair way back when, and sprawled across it like a king.

"You go around asking questions about my life," Soren said, watching her. "You got involved with my brother. You're my business."

"Your brother?" she said.

"That's what he is."

"Then why haven't you spoken in six months?"

Soren ignored her. He looked for the lever on the side and put the chair back a bit, smiling as he did so.

"Comfy," he said.

Molly caught an impulse to stamp her foot, like a child trying to command attention. Soren had that effect. Instead, she crossed her arms and said, "Why are you here? If you're not going to answer my questions, if you're not going to help me, why are you here?"

He looked directly at her. Ice blue eyes. She was locked in place.

"I'm here because Declan deserves to be happy," he said. "So you need to give him another shot."

Molly stared at him. And then, damn it, the tears came back. Now she really did stamp her foot, cursing, willing her eyes to stay dry. Declan had turned the waterworks on and then thrown away the wrench and now she was just doomed to embarrass herself in every possible situation. She lost every last bit of patience she had left.

"He doesn't *want* another shot!" she shouted. "He hasn't asked for one. He does. Not. Want. Me."

"Trust me," Soren said calmly. "He does."

"I called him," Molly said. "*I* called *him*, after the way he left me, and a woman answered."

"Bethany," he nodded.

"I knew it was fucking Bethany," Molly said. It still pissed her off.

"You don't think a woman should go visit the man who saved her life after she gets out of the hospital?" Soren asked. "Don't be like that. Don't be unreasonable."

"Who the hell do you think you are?"

"Soren Andersson," he smiled. "And you know better than that, Molly Ward. You know Declan better than that. You know he's the kind of guy who would carry a woman who'd taken every damn pill she could find all the way to the emergency room, and then pay for her fucking expensive six-month treatment program at a private psychiatric hospital, all without ever wanting, or getting, anything from her in return, besides knowing that she was better off for it."

Molly felt all of her anger deflate in one sorry breath and walked over to the couch to sit down and cry. That anger had been holding her up. Now all she had left was the loss.

"I'm a moron," she said, crying quietly. "I am a total moron."

"Who isn't?" Soren shrugged.

"Is Declan ok?" she asked, looking up. "Have you talked to him? Are you guys friends again?"

Soren leaned forward suddenly, urgently, showing himself for the first time with a shocking intensity. Molly was transfixed.

"No, he is not fucking ok," he said. "He's a wreck. And no, we are not talking."

"So Jim tells you about him."

"Jim tells me about him. And you."

"You were staying there. When we came to visit."

"I went for a drive. Thought I'd be a fourth wheel."

Molly scooted forward on the old couch. "Can you fix this, Soren? Can you fix this thing between you? Because the thing is, and I don't...I don't know what's wrong with me, or what's wrong with him, but I know he's hurting, too. And I don't know if he can hurt both ways at once. I think he needs something."

Soren blinked. "Are you seriously asking me to be there for Declan after he's broken your heart? Because you're worried about him?"

"Yes," Molly said miserably. "I mean, I go back and forth between that and wanting to kick his ass, but yes. Is that so much weirder than you showing up to help get his girlfriend back after he's kicked you out of his life?"

"You love him," Soren said.

Molly just looked at the floor. "So?"

"Jesus, you're both idiots. Don't get me wrong, Declan is the idiot in chief on this one, but you are definitely pulling your weight. You should have told him you loved him."

"I told you," Molly said, pointing at herself with both thumbs. "Moron."

Soren laughed. "Aren't you angry?"

"Yes."

"So what is it going to take to get you two idiots back together?"

Molly rubbed her eyes and took a good look at the reclusive rock star sitting in her dad's old recliner, playing matchmaker between her and the man she loved. Right. This was happening.

"I don't know," she said truthfully. "I don't understand what's happening. Why he did this. So I don't see a way out of it."

"You know he blames himself for his mother's death, don't you?" Soren asked. "You have any idea what that does to someone?"

"Of course I don't," Molly whispered. "It's unimaginable."

"He was responsible for her his whole life. And then she died. She *chose* to die rather than be his mother. And he found her. You don't have to be a shrink to figure what that would do to a little kid. And then," Soren said, running both hands through his white blond hair, "there's what I did."

This was it. The question. Softly, she said, "What happened, Soren?"

For the first time since he'd shown up at her

house like some previously undiscovered force of nature, Soren looked shaken. Human. Vulnerable.

"I can't fucking believe I'm telling you this," he said. "Fucking Declan gets me to do the stupidest things, even when he's not here. The short answer is: I left Bethany to kill herself. I fucked her for a few months, I was an asshole the whole time, and when I found out she was popping pills..."

He trailed off, then looked directly at Molly. "Look, everyone has their hang-ups, that's mine. I don't deal with that shit. At all. And she lied about it. So I dumped her. And when she told me she was going to kill herself if I left, I told her to fucking do it, because that was some manipulative bullshit right there. And then I left."

"That kind of does sound like manipulative bullshit," Molly said quietly.

"Yeah, but then *she did it*," he said. "Look, bottom line? I fucked a girl I knew to be emotionally unstable, was a dick to her the way I am to every woman I screw, and then left her when she made a threat to harm herself. And Declan found her. Knowing what you know about Declan, do you think he should forgive me?"

"Yes," Molly said. She meant it.

Soren wasn't prepared for that. He sat back and looked at her. Just looked.

After a while, he said, "Listen, if he forgave me, it would mean he'd have to forgive himself, too. He saw himself in what I did, which is fucked up, but which is also totally understandable, and makes my behavior...just a whole new level of wrong. I might not deserve forgiveness, but Declan does, because he never did anything wrong. He doesn't deserve to feel the way he does, and never has. He's not trying to hurt you or pull some commitment-phobe stupidity or anything else. He's trying to protect you from himself, because he loves you so damn much. And because when he loves people, he thinks it means something terrible is going to happen to them."

Molly let the tears run down her cheeks freely, not even caring anymore. She felt like she was listening to a death sentence.

"So that's it?" she asked. "There's no hope? He's just doomed to be miserable and alone forever, and I have to live without him?"

"The fuck if I know," Soren said, launching himself off of the recliner. "I've been working on him, trying to get him to forgive himself, for sixteen fucking years, Molly, and you've gotten closer than I ever have in just a few weeks. You have any beer?"

"Check the fridge."

Soren opened the old fridge, leaning on the open door like he knew the place. He looked back over his shoulder. "This is like a bachelor fridge."

"I'm moving."

"Good," he said, grabbing two PBRs and tossing one to her. "What I'm saying, Molly, is that if Declan has any hope at all, it's in you. Do with that what you will."

Molly wiped her eyes and cracked open her beer. "What about you, Soren?"

"What about me?"

"Don't pull that with me," Molly snapped. "You didn't try to kill her, Soren, you behaved badly in a relationship. People do it every day; it's not a war crime. So maybe you were an asshole. Doesn't mean you deserve to rot in Hell forever or be cut out of his life, especially not when he needs you in it. And when you obviously need him."

Soren gave her a crooked grin, the kind of thing she could see working very effectively on the ladies. "I can see why he digs you," Soren said. "He got lucky that you're so hot."

Molly had just opened her mouth, though she had no idea what she was going to say, when Soren's phone rang. He got up and walked out the door, closing it behind him as he answered his phone. And it was after that that the phone calls from Declan stopped.

chapter 33

Declan was prepared for the phone to ring until it went to voicemail. He was not prepared to hear Soren's voice.

"Hello?"

Speechless. For the first time in his life, Declan was speechless.

"Dude?"

"You picked up," Declan said.

There was the sound of door opening and closing. Soren said, "Well, I've heard some stuff about you screwing up your life pretty badly. I figured you must be pretty desperate."

Declan laughed. "Asshole."

"Yup."

"So we need to talk."

This time it was Soren who took too long to speak. Finally, he said, "Yeah. I guess we do."

"And I need your help with something," Declan said. "You're the only one I can ask, even though… Soren, I know I don't deserve to even call you a friend—"

"Shut up, dumbass. You're my brother. What the fuck do you need?"

Declan smiled broadly, but not because it was funny. Just because he felt *light*, for the first time in months, like the world had just come back into focus.

"There's this girl," Declan said.

"Yeah, Jim told me all about her. I'm here now."

"What?" Declan said, sitting up. "You're there? You're with her right now?"

"Yeah. You ok?"

"Just tell me if she's ok."

"No, she's not ok, dumbass, she has a broken heart."

Declan cursed impressively, stalking around Volare L.A., looking for something to break.

"Dude," Soren said. "Calm down. What did you expect? I came here to explain to her why you're such a dumbass. I don't know, I think it helped. She's crying less, anyway."

Declan started to laugh. He couldn't believe how much more right his life was with Soren in it to call him on his shit, the only person in the world who could do that—besides Molly.

"You ok, bro?" Soren asked. "You're sounding kind of crazy."

"No, I am a dumbass. I don't even know why. I am so fucking sorry, Soren, I never should have kicked you out. I never…"

"I'm sorry, too. What I did…"

They both went silent for a moment. There was too much there. Declan could hear Soren struggling. Finally, Soren said, "I don't even know what to say. I've been thinking for six months about what to fucking say, and I have nothing. That's why I just...I haven't been able to face anyone, man. Except your girl. She just dragged it all out of me."

"She would," Declan said. "I shouldn't have made you do that alone, Soren. You never left me alone."

"So we're both assholes."

"Brother assholes."

Declan could hear Soren smile.

"So," Soren said, "what do you want me to do?"

~ * ~ * ~

Adra insisted that Molly come stay at Volare for the last few days before their brand new lease would go into effect. Molly resisted. Volare meant Declan to her, even if he was halfway across the country. He hadn't called her since Soren had shown up on her doorstep, and Molly was right back to feeling insecure.

Maybe it was dumb. But she was tired. And she just...couldn't.

She'd tried to work on the book instead until she realized she wouldn't have an ending. Then she'd caved and looked Declan up online only to find that the Savage Heart tour had been canceled, and she felt a weird mix of anxiety and elation. And that was about the time she decided she was clearly in the crazy stage of a broken heart and probably needed to be around people.

She showed up at Volare the next day. Adra just hugged her.

"Tell me about it," Adra said.

Molly didn't have the energy to fight herself anymore. "I'm in love with him," she said simply. "I never told him. And he thinks he can't be good for me. So I lost him."

"How do you know you lost him?" Adra said, taking Molly's one dinky suitcase. She was gently leading Molly back to her old room. The one she'd shared with Declan.

Molly hesitated. Then thought, *I can't run forever*.

"Do you see him here?" she asked Adra. "That's how I know."

"Have you called him?"

Molly didn't say anything for a second. She let Adra open the door and sat down carefully on the bed, like she was afraid she might break.

"I'm afraid to, Adra. I know, considering what's at stake, and what Declan has to deal with on his end, that I should. I know that. But I just don't think I can take losing him again. Finding out that he really doesn't want me. I keep telling myself to call him again, but I can't. I'm just not strong enough."

Adra sighed. Then she smiled and walked over to the slim desk in the corner where she picked up a laptop.

"Let me show you something," she said.

The browser was already queued up to a YouTube video. It took Molly a second to recognize Declan on stage—the video title was "Madison Square Garden Comeback — NEW SONG."

"Is this…?"

"Yeah, this is the night you left to come home, so you missed it," Adra said. "The audio quality is crap, but the point is, it's a new song. Look at the comments."

"They all want to know who it's about," Molly said, scrolling through.

"I'll give you three guesses," Adra said dryly.

Molly looked up. "You're kidding. He wrote me a song? And I missed it?"

"Look," Adra said. "I never underestimate the ability of men to act like idiots when they realize they're in love, and whatever he did, I'm sure it was bad. But *this*," she said, pointing at the screen, "is not the song of a man who only kind of cares maybe a little bit. And neither is this."

Adra closed the first tab to reveal a second one. This one was called "Savage Heart back together!!! New song!!" It had been uploaded in the past twenty-four hours and already had one point three million views.

And there were five guys in a studio. Brian, Gage, and Erik. Declan on the mic. And Soren on lead guitar.

And then Adra pressed play.

Declan's voice rang out. He was looking right at the camera.

Looking right at her.

"Oh my God," she whispered.

"...*You're my rhythm*..."

"Is this real?" Molly asked.

"...*You're my heart*..."

"I promise you that it's real," Adra said.

"...*Light...in the dark*..."

"Where are you going?" Adra laughed.

Molly was already up and walking around aimlessly, looking for a phone. "I have to call him," she said, rambling. "I have to... I mean, they're back together, he and Soren..."

She walked straight out of the room and onto the landing before she realized she'd left her bag, with her phone, back in the room. But by then it didn't matter.

Because Declan was there.

Downstairs. Waiting. For her.

Molly couldn't speak. She didn't want to open her mouth and risk it, didn't want this perfect moment to end. Declan looking back at her, a boundless love in his eyes.

"I'm sorry," he said.

Molly put her hand to her mouth. She could feel the tears coming. Dammit.

"I am more sorry about the past week than I have ever been about anything," he said seriously. "The fact that I've hurt you, that I've made you cry, will haunt me until the day I die, Molly."

He didn't need to say anything, was the thing. One look at him, tall and serious in a white shirt and jeans, his dark eyes glowing, she was more in love with him than she'd ever been. And still he kept coming.

"I've been trying to think about how to explain what I did, because you deserve at least that," he said, coming around to the foot of the stairs. He didn't take his eyes off of her. "But I can't. Not entirely."

He began to climb the stairs one by one.

"It was just easier for me to think it was my fault than that there was nothing I could do. And then every nightmare I'd ever had just got eclipsed by one thing. If anything ever happened to you..." He stopped his ascent and took a deep breath. "And I assumed it would, because of all of this crap. Because I had to hold on to that version of the universe where it was my fault."

He shook his head. Resumed climbing the steps.

"But I had to let that go, because otherwise I couldn't have you. And the thing is, I can't live without you, Molly. I know it's fucking insane, but I'm not whole without you, not anymore. So I'm yours," he said.

Declan walked toward her, his eyes steady, his face calm. He took a moment just to trace the curve of her cheek with his finger, to brush her bottom lip with his thumb.

"You showed me how to live, Molly. I love you," he said. His hand slid around her waist to the small of her back, pressing her to his hard body, and her breath hitched. "I love you, and I'm yours. Tell me you're mine."

"Oh my God, Declan," she said, choking back tears.

"Tell me you're mine," he said, and wiped away her tears.

"Of course I'm yours," she said. "Of course I am."

She pawed at his chest, hating his clothing, hating her clothing, wanting to do away forever with anything that came between them. Declan caught her hands in one of his and said, "Look at me. I will never, ever hurt you again. I will spend as long as you'll let me loving you."

"Declan," she said. "I'm so in love with you it's making me stupid. Please just kiss me."

Declan grinned and pulled her head back, her

body trapped against his. "I'm going to do a whole lot more than that," he said.

THE END

A note from the author...

Hi! Thank you so much for reading *Savage Rhythm*. I hope you enjoyed Declan and Molly's story, and that it brought you a bit of happiness. If you liked it, I hope you'll share it with friends you think might like it, too. Declan and Molly will show up in Soren's book this fall—someone has to help him find love, after all!

And I'd love to hear your thoughts on *Savage Rhythm*. You can connect with me on Facebook or email me at chloecoxwrites@gmail.com, or leave a review on Amazon or on Goodreads. I sincerely appreciate every review—I think they help other readers out, and I learn something with every review, too.

'Till the next book!
Chloe

CPSIA information can be obtained at www.ICGtesting.com
Printed in the USA
LVOW06s1928020114

367801LV00001B/82/P